Howl on the Wind

Howl on the Wind

Charmian Hussey

Illustrated by Rose Forshall

ATLANTIC
PRESS

First published in Great Britain in September 2011
by Atlantic Press
55 St Thomas's Street
Penryn
Cornwall TR10 8JW

ISBN 978 0 9557 348 7 8

With the exception of any references to the Royal Family and Nicholas Culpeper, all
characters in this publication are fictitious, and any resemblance to real persons, living or
dead, is purely coincidental. References made to The Times and The London Gazette are
used in a purely fictitious context

A CIP catalogue record for this book is available from The British Library

Book design by Mark Woodhams FISTD

Printed by R Booth, Penryn, Cornwall

Text set in Monotype Garamond

Contents

The Magical Mystery Tour

he trip had started well enough. Tom had checked the oil and the tyres. The old car was running smoothly.

"So where are we going, Mum?" Lizzie asked.

"It's one of those magical mystery tours," her mother answered, smiling broadly.

"But why are we going?" Tom pressed.

"That's a secret for now," she replied, glancing at Tom in the passenger seat. "But don't expect too much," she begged. "We may find that it's all too late."

Whatever could that comment mean? Tom and Lizzie were mystified. From her seat in the back of the car, Lizzie poked Tom's shoulder hard.

"Poor Mum. I hope she's not cracking up," Lizzie whispered into his ear.

"I'm going to pretend that I didn't hear that," their mother said defensively. "Perhaps I should have come on my own … "

After exchanging some puzzled looks, Lizzie and Tom sat quiet for a while: wondering about their Mum. They guessed it must have been a struggle: bringing her children up on her own. They had often heard the story: how their father had sadly died several months before Lizzie was born. They knew she'd had some help from her parents, whom the children never saw because they lived so far away. And so they'd enjoyed a comfortable life: not lavish but with a decent home, regular food and tidy clothing.

Their mother was kind but always firm. Her favourite word was 'moderation'. It was moderation in everything.

Holidays virtually never happened. So when quite suddenly, out of the blue, their mother announced a trip to Cornwall, Tom and Lizzie were very surprised: not just by the fact of the trip, but by their Mum's unusual behaviour. She bore an air of repressed excitement.

"Couldn't you give us some clues?" Lizzie wheedled, a few miles further down the road.

But her mother only smiled. "One thing I can tell you," she said. "You're certainly going to see the sea, because we'll be staying on the coast. I think that's going to be lovely, don't you? You'll be able to run on the beach each morning."

The idea received a rapturous welcome. Brother and sister both loved running: Tom because it kept him fit. He'd soon be off to University, where he'd play football for his college. Strength and co-ordination were crucial. Running, he knew, was the best exercise.

For Lizzie the running itself was special. She just loved running. Running. Running. Powering along on lean, strong legs: enjoying the sense of freedom it gave her, the wind and the weather in her face.

And Lizzie harboured a secret dream. Encouraged by the school games teacher and, of course, egged on by Tom, she believed that if she worked very hard she'd make it to the next Olympics.

It was serious. It was wonderful. It was the focus of Lizzie's life: up at five every morning, out and running with her brother.

Tom was always her greatest supporter. Almost as soon as she was born, although still only a small child himself—a chunky, dark haired three-year-old—he'd taken a special interest in her. He'd been amazed by her arrival: by the extraordinary emergence—and from such an unlikely place—of this tiny but perfect person. He'd sat beside her cot, just staring: intrigued by the teeny, kicking bundle; entranced by her pretty fair hair and blue eyes.

He hadn't seen very much of his father, who often seemed to be away. When he was there, he'd called Tom The Shrimp. Tom sensed it as a loving nickname. And it was fine when he was so small.

But now he was nearly three and a half and often referred to as a big boy, who'd eat up his greens and wouldn't cry. So that when Lizzie arrived on the scene, he passed The Shrimp name on to her. She was the baby now—not him.

"When will The Shrimp eat proper food Mummy? When will she talk? When will she walk?" the little boy had asked his mother. "I could help her with lots of things," he had declared with confidence, much to his mother's delight and amusement.

And that, of course, was exactly what happened. Tom was sitting at the table when Lizzie took her first spoonful of food. "Come on Shrimp. You can do it," he had encouraged from the sidelines, as Lizzie gurgled and slurped on the spoon.

The Shrimp was a reluctant walker. With her beloved, big brother on hand, acting as her constant slave, Lizzie didn't need to walk. She scuttled along in a very strange way, sideways rather like a crab: shuffling speedily on her bottom, swinging herself along with her arms.

Tom found it funny. It made him laugh. He always called it Lizzie's Crabwalk.

But he was there when she took her first steps: enticing her across the lawn by waving her special Crocker at her—a much loved, bright-blue crocodile and his very first gift to her. "Come on Shrimp. You can do it," dangling Crocker just out of reach.

The phrase had echoed on down through the years: her first egg and spoon race, aged five and then the sack race following on; her first sports day at the big school; her first serious tennis match. Her brother was always there for her. His rallying cry echoed in her ears, "Come on Shrimp. You can do it."

As Lizzie dozed in the back of the car, lulled by the voices of those she loved chatting happily in the front, she day-dreamed about the fun that they'd have: paddling in the briny foam; swimming even if it was cold; running on the beach each morning; maybe even building a castle on the golden Cornish sand.

She visualised the lapping ocean; a long, sandy beach; the dawn breaking; and, as the light was filling the sky, the sunshine tipping the edges of waves that crinkled at the water's edge. She could imagine the feelings of pleasure: the fresh, sea breezes whipping her hair; the salty spray on her face, her lips; the wet sand, firm beneath bare feet. She knew they would have a wonderful time.

As the car sped on into Cornwall, drawing ever closer now to their mystery destination, Tom and her Mum were laughing and joking. There was no sense of impending disaster. Lizzie could never, ever have guessed how that journey would change her life.

2

Take Off

I t had been an enjoyable journey. They'd stopped twice for snacks and drinks, but even so it was long and tiring. Skimming past woodland, fields and rivers with sunlight flashing in her eyes, Lizzie had done her best to sleep.

Tom's warning shout "Watch out Mum!" suddenly jolted her wide awake. She sat up sharply in her seat.

A car with blaring horn and loud music was racing along beside their own. Lizzie looked across in alarm. She saw the young man at the wheel, the telephone clamped tight to his ear. She saw the stupid, gaping mouth and the repulsive, lurid wink, as he sped on past with a cheery wave, weaving wildly across the road with both hands off the wheel.

For a moment it seemed as if he would miss them. Their mother's swerve had done the trick. But Lizzie let out a scream of fright as the lurching car crashed into their wing.

The crunching jolt was horrible. All she could do was to watch in horror: her back braced rigid against the seat; her feet thrust forward onto the floor. She saw her mother's frantic attempts at swinging the wheel to control the car. She heard Tom's sudden intake of breath and his groaning gasp, "Oh no!"

Their mother seemed to have lost control. The car was gaining momentum now. Ahead of them the road snaked. Below, to the left, a chasm yawned.

Lizzie had sometimes fantasised—how it would be if one flew off the road, simply taking off from the tarmac? She'd often wondered to herself: if she were a driver, would she be tempted? Sometimes the green and pleasant fields that ran along below a road, looked welcoming, even beckoning: smooth and grassy, a place to land, although they were generally locked away beyond stout fencing that bordered the road.

But this was a very different matter. No barrier stopped the car on the brink. It hurtled over the hard shoulder, ripped across a grassy bank and finally shot off into space.

At first it was almost comfortable. It was like flying and Lizzie was grinning: her eyes wide, staring, disbelieving. In the several seconds that passed between their launch and the final crash, a wild and ridiculous hope clutched her heart. All they had to do was to land …

And then the dreadful reality struck. Surely this couldn't be happening … could it? Not to her and to Mum and to Tom?

"Please. Please. Help us! Save us!" A screaming voice was filling her brain.

3

And Landing

The rocky slope was unforgiving. Jagged fangs of ancient granite lurking in the yellow gorse, jabbed and grabbed at the tumbling car: over and over … rolling … rolling, its occupants like lifeless dolls … dumb and rigid, frozen in terror, strapped securely into their seats.

The forested valley lay there waiting. It sucked them into its hidden depths. Trees and branches and foliage flashed: a smashing and thrashing, a churning and crashing, tearing at the guts of the car.

The sight was blinding. The landing was deafening. It was like some vast, almighty explosion, blasting them into a thousand pieces, spinning them into eternity.

Overwhelming pain struck Lizzie. Pain. Pain. And more pain. And then a sickening blackness took over, like a suffocating blanket, smothering her in its ample folds.

After the terrible noise of the crash, the scene was now surprisingly quiet. There was no sound from the forest of trees that held them firmly in its grasp. No birds sang. Nothing moved. There was only an ominous hissing sound. The engine was snuffed, but not yet dead.

Wracked by pain and barely conscious, a terrifying thought struck Lizzie. Didn't crashed cars burst into flames? She must get out. Yes, she must escape.

But Lizzie was trapped. She couldn't move. The mangled frame of the shattered car was holding her firmly down in her seat. She could move her head, her neck and her arms, but her legs were obviously clamped to the floor, almost as if they were held in a vice. No matter what, she couldn't free them.

And what about her mother and Tom? They must be horribly shaken up, but in the end they'd all be fine. That was obvious, wasn't it?

Lizzie was much too tightly jammed to lean forward towards her Mum. But she could just see the edge of Tom's arm, as he shifted his weight in the passenger seat.

"Shrimp. Are you there?" She heard his voice.

"Yes. I'm here. I'm here," she whimpered.

"Shrimp! Shrimp! Are you OK?"

"Yes … I'm alright … I think … Tom. But I'm jammed. I can't move. And I feel so dizzy … so sick … But what about you … and what about Mum?"

"Please hang on," she heard his voice. "Hang on Shrimp. I won't leave you. No matter what happens, I'll be there for you."

Then Lizzie drifted off again—in and out of consciousness. In one of her more lucid spells, she took a look around the car—or at what was left of the car. Having rolled over several times, it seemed to have ended the right way up. The occupants strapped in their seats hadn't moved.

But luggage and bags had been flung around. Her mother's old leather handbag, which had lain on the seat beside Lizzie, had burst open and cast its contents. It was her mother's everyday bag: navy, very worn and baggy—such a familiar and comforting object.

Despite her dreadful predicament, an overwhelming sadness struck Lizzie, to see her mother's precious belongings spread about in disarray: all her little bits and pieces; all so personal; all so modest. It was Lizzie who always took care of that bag, when her mother was driving the car. She knew it was her responsibility.

"I'm looking after your bag, Mum. I'm taking care of your things," Lizzie whispered.

Although she was finding it hard to focus, she slid her hand across the seat intent on gathering up the items: her mother's wallet; her small squashy purse; the little hairbrush she always carried; and then an unexpected item, a large and strangely decorated key … something she didn't recognise.

Her hand crept out towards the key and, as her fingers clasped the shank, she noticed something else as well. The contents of Mum's make-up bag were strewn out wide across the seat: her favourite compact was split wide open; a cloud of powder hung in the air. Something must have melted her lipstick, which was oozing across the seat. Even Lizzie's mobile phone was lying in a scarlet pool.

"What a shame," Lizzie murmured.

But no. There was something wrong with that. Lizzie's poor, befuddled brain struggled to make some sense of the scene.

The lipstick was the wrong colour. Her mother always wore pale pink. So why was everything, even the key, coated with this shocking, blood-red? Her mother never wore that colour … she would have thought it much too flashy …

Nausea and then more darkness. Lizzie felt as if she were drifting, floating in some murky cloud. Once she thought she heard strange voices and then the horrible noise of a saw: a cruel, grinding, nagging sound. On and on … and on … and on …

And then she was being lifted and swung.

"No! No! … please don't …" she sobbed.

"Leave me. You're hurting me," she wailed, before she finally drifted away.

First the agony … then the bliss of a deep, dark and painless sleep. A sleep that seemed to go on for ever.

4

'Come On Shrimp. Do Wake Up … '

hadows drifted through Lizzie's mind: people moving; talking; laughing; whispering gentle words in her ear. Yet she couldn't focus. She couldn't wake.

Her head was often full of music: a swelling orchestra with strings and the mellow sound of a cello, building and building in her brain. Then soaring high above all else, a plaintive, reedy, haunting song—maybe the voice of some kind of horn. And with it there came an enormous bird, gliding majestically over dark waters, his stark, white feathers glowing brightly.

The swan. Lizzie knew that it must be *the swan*—an old and comforting, much loved friend. She'd met him many times before. And yet she couldn't remember his name …

The long and powerful, sinuous neck held an elegant, bright-eyed head. The golden beak and the emerald eyes were always turning—turning towards her. The swan was watching over her.

Mist hung low on the water's surface: swaying gently in the breeze; swelling with the magical music; then billowing up and engulfing the bird and stealing the vision from her sight.

Rolled and pulled in all directions by kindly nurses attending to her, Lizzie floated on that music. And yet she could never open her eyes. Until one day she became aware of several, dark and looming figures.

"I sometimes get this feeling," one said, "that she can hear us … every word …"

"She simply doesn't want to wake up …" another voice added miserably.

"It's days now … not looking good …"

Lizzie could pick out some of the words.

"… more brain-damaged than we thought …"

" … thought she'd make it … perhaps she won't …"

" … don't want to turn off the ventilator …"

" … perhaps we should simply let her go …"

… let her go … go … go …

Lizzie didn't want to go anywhere. She only wanted her Mum … and Tom. With almost superhuman effort, she did her best to call his name "Tom! Tom! I need you Tom." But she didn't seem able to speak the words; they only rattled around in her head.

Although her eyes wouldn't open and her body wouldn't budge, perhaps, if she tried, she could move her arm. Could she move her hand and reach out towards Tom?

"Come on Shrimp. Do wake up."

She'd heard the familiar words so often, when it was time to get up for their run. If she didn't move pretty quickly, he'd use what he called 'creative measures'. He'd pull up the duvet and tickle her feet.

Lizzie simply hated that. It made her feel almost savagely angry. But somehow Tom always made her laugh, turning her anger into good humour.

"You beast," she always hissed at him, swinging her legs out of bed, preparing to chase him out of her room, but trying to keep the noise down, so as not to wake their Mum.

"Just you wait till I get you," she'd threaten, as beating her to the bathroom door, Tom would close it and push the bolt.

The tickling didn't happen this time. And yet Tom's voice was very close. It was more insistent, more pressing than usual.

"Come on Shrimp. Do wake up!"

She could feel his hand squeezing her arm. Then the room was alive with scurrying figures. The light was painful. The sounds so loud. She wished they'd go away and leave her. All she wanted to do was to sleep.

When at last she could finally focus, she found herself looking into Tom's eyes: brown and smiling, encouraging.

"You beast," she mumbled hoarsely, preparing to swing her legs from the bed and chase him as she always did. But nothing happened. She couldn't move.

Her arms were thrashing in desperation. But she couldn't move her legs. She couldn't get up and chase him away.

Lizzie was gripped by a terrible panic.

And what were all these horrible tubes? Fighting for breath and trying to speak, she sobbed and struggled as best she could. Her hands went up to a tube at her throat.

A stranger had now taken Tom's place. A fair-haired man with troubled, grey eyes was bending over close to her. "It's alright Lizzie. You're quite safe now. But don't upset the tube in your throat. It's very important. It's helping you breathe."

Blue-clad figures surrounded the bed. Kindly voices talked her down. "Steady Lizzie. Take it easy," trying to calm her sobs and her wails.

"Mum! Mum! Where's my Mum?" Gasping, Lizzie mouthed the words.

The figures in their blue scrubs glanced at each other then looked away. It wasn't the time to tell her now. That must keep for another day.

"Tom! Tom! I need you. Where are you?" The words were pounding in her brain.

"I'm here Shrimp," Lizzie heard his voice. "Take it quietly. You'll be alright."

Lizzie was sobbing and clasping his hand.

"Don't leave me Tom. Please don't go … "

"I'm here and you know that I'll always be with you. You know that, because I've told you before."

She jumped when the needle pricked her arm. But soon she was drifting and comfortable: safe in the knowledge that Tom was there. Whatever happened she wouldn't lose him. His whole presence filled her mind. The warmth of his smile filled her heart, before the blackness took over again.

5

My Friend Crocker

Over a period of several days, in and out of consciousness, Lizzie clung on fast to Tom's words. As she gradually came to realise the full extent of her injuries—how badly she had injured her back and how she would need an operation—it was his visits that kept her going: his brown eyes; his smiling mouth and his continuous 'Come on Shrimp …'

When at last she could breathe unaided, she found that she could move more freely, though she wasn't allowed to sit up yet. At least her head seemed clearer now. Although, no matter how hard she tried she couldn't remember the accident. And there were other memory gaps, which she was told would improve with time.

Sudden movement made her feel dizzy. Turning her head with the greatest of care to take her first look around the ward, she found herself looking at Crocker. His beady, blue eyes were smiling at her from where he lay on her bedside locker. From a very early age, his gaping mouth and shining eyes had always made her feel much better.

"Oh Crocker! How lovely to see you," Lizzie whispered in delight. By reaching out she could just pick him up. Tears spilled down her cheeks as she hugged him. He smelt and felt so comforting.

A nurse arrived smiling brightly.

"I'm glad to see that you know that beastie," she said, admiring the bright-blue toy.

"He was a bit of a mystery to us. You'd only been here for a few hours when he appeared—quite out of the blue." She giggled at the silly pun. "Somebody must have brought him in."

Lizzie lay there hugging the beastie.

"He's my friend Crocker," she said defensively.

To her it was perfectly obvious. Tom would have known that she'd need her Crocker. He'd have made sure that she had him beside her, ready for

5

5

when she finally woke—in case he couldn't be there himself. Wasn't she lucky to have such a brother?

"Oh, and there's something else as well," the nurse scurried around the bed, opening up the bedside unit. "Now where is it? I know it's here somewhere." She fumbled amongst the things in the drawer.

Lizzie waited expectantly.

"There's something I'd like to ask," she said shyly. "Was somebody playing music to me? When I was lying here unconscious?"

The nurse looked up in surprise.

"Music?" she asked. "What do you mean?"

"A CD player or tape recorder? Maybe some kind of classical music—I don't know what. I can't remember." Lizzie knew it sounded silly.

"Not that I know of," the nurse assured her, continuing her search in the drawer.

"Ah yes. Here it is," she said, holding up a big key.

"You were clasping this tightly in your hand, when you first arrived in Emergency. I felt that it must be important to you, so I cleaned it up and put it away."

Lizzie, intrigued, held out her hand: taking the object gingerly; turning it over on her palm; peering closely and trying to focus.

The key was several inches long, made of dark metal—probably iron. A third of its length was taken up by an unusually fancy handle, in which there was set a round brass plate, about the size of an old-fashioned penny—nearly an inch and half across. This bore a simple, incised design—some kind of primitive shield perhaps. Something you'd find on a coat of arms.

The object stirred a distant memory. But try as she might, Lizzie couldn't remember. Where on earth had she seen it before?

6

The Challenge

In the hospital's spinal unit, Lizzie struggled day after day. There was so much that she had to learn: how to look after her body, her skin; how to be endlessly shifting her weight, to avoid developing pressure sores.

And then there were other special techniques that would help her to cope with her bladder and bowels. Lizzie was horrified at first. She'd never considered such things before. But, as she whispered one day to Tom, "It's just amazing what you can do, if you're told that your life depends upon it."

When she finally got to the point of being allowed to try a wheelchair, Lizzie felt quite jubilant. She'd been waiting a long time for this. She remembered an ad on the television: a group of young men dancing and rapping—whirling like dervishes in their wheelchairs. They'd made it all look easy … and fun.

"If they can do it, so can I," Lizzie had confided to Tom, with a confident grin on her face.

"Now I can go and do what I want," she mumbled defiantly at the nurses, as they settled her into a wheelchair.

But it wasn't to prove that easy. Lizzie found it very hard work: the daily exercise and the physio—building up her shoulders and arms and the muscles in her trunk, so that she could power her chair. And the thing seemed to have a will of its own. She lurched from collapse to determination.

When at last she had mastered wheel-tipping—a technique to help her cope with stairs—she let out a most unladylike whoop and spun her chair in celebration. Then she whizzed up and down the ward, boasting loudly, proclaiming success. The next day found her resting in bed—having completely exhausted herself.

The gash on Lizzie's head had healed well; and despite the early fears that she might have sustained brain damage—she was virtually back to normal, although her memory was patchy. And she had the occasional lapses: drifting into a dream-like state, when all she could hear was that music again; when all she could see was the fabulous swan. These episodes were usually brief. Lizzie accepted and welcomed them. The swan, after all, had become a friend—although the music was puzzling.

Everybody kept telling her what a lucky thing she was: that because her spine had been injured low down, she could do most things for herself … that *if* she would accept The Challenge, she could be fully independent.

Lizzie hated being told. And she certainly didn't feel lucky. She felt extremely unfortunate.

"Oh why, oh why did it happen to me?" she asked herself over and over again.

A young man taught her wheelchair skills. Peter had lost the use of his legs in a motorcycle accident. He was a dedicated trainer: an inspiration to everyone. But he was strict. A hard taskmaster.

"Come on Lizzie. Face The Challenge." His words pounded in her brain. And when she wavered at her task, "Go on! Go on! Go on! Go on!"

Peter quickly became her mentor. She tried so hard not to let him down. But she was often dogged by failure.

Frustration was her greatest enemy. And yet it wasn't all doom and gloom. She had real moments of euphoria—having learnt to manage simple tasks, which had seemed impossible since she'd lost the use of her legs—such as putting on her shoes.

The staff said nothing was truly impossible. 'Difficult things take time,' they said. 'The impossible takes a little bit longer.'

There were hilarious moments too. Some of the patients got up to such pranks—usually the boys, of course. And there were lots of silly jokes, all aimed at wheelchair users. And even a book of funny cartoons. 'Laughter,' so the nurses said, 'was the best way of coping with disaster.'

So Lizzie had learnt to laugh again, though the laughter often ended in tears. The release of emotion was overwhelming. It could quickly become uncontrollable.

However, she soon came to realise that there was always somebody else, who was in a worse condition. So she tried hard to get away from focusing only on her own problems. It wasn't easy.

There was plenty of time to make friends; they did what they could to support each other. But, despite the sense of camaraderie, most of Lizzie's friends were frail. Like her, they teetered on the brink of finding that they could not cope—or sometimes deciding they would not cope. And each one's failure affected the rest.

It was like an emotional roller coaster. If it hadn't been for Tom's visits, Lizzie didn't think she'd have managed to get to a state where, within a few months, she was able to leave and go home—though not to her much loved, family home.

7

A New Beginning

The solicitor dealing with their dead mother's affairs had made it absolutely clear that the family home would have to be sold in order to provide for Lizzie. A decision had been made to purchase a single storey apartment on a small development especially designed for paraplegics—for people who've lost the use of their legs—and for other disabled people.

It was a great relief to know that at least they would have their own place. But nevertheless the sale of the house, which had always been their home, was bound to be a terrible wrench. Lizzie was all for hanging on there. Guided by Tom's wise words, she reluctantly came to realise that they'd have to let it go.

When she moved into the new home, Lizzie was delighted to find that there was access to a garden—a large, well kempt communal garden. But she knew she would miss their old garden, especially the ancient apple tree and the colourful cottage style borders. And then there had been the veg patch that she and Tom had always tended.

Life would be very different now. Sitting in the small apartment and staring out through the French window into the pleasant garden beyond, this message was pushed relentlessly home. There'd be no scampering on the grass. No lolling on the old garden blanket. No wandering amongst the shrubs, weeding as you went along.

Each unit in the development, which was a bit like a small village, had been designed for wheelchair users. Lizzie's apartment provided a light and airy bed-sitting room with plenty of room for two single beds. There was an adjoining kitchen and next to that a shower and a loo.

Lizzie wheeled herself around, amazed by the custom-built design and by all the special gadgets. The kitchen sink was the most intriguing. At the simple press of a button, it could be raised or lowered at will—like the sink in the spinal injuries unit. Tom, she knew, would enjoy this device. Lizzie pressed the button with glee, adjusting the sink to a level to suit her.

She was pleased with the big bed-sitting room. One corner had been allotted to Tom. His clothing hung clean in his wardrobe. His slippers stuck out from beneath his bed, ready for when he needed them.

All his old and much loved posters—some of them rather tatty now—were arranged on the wall behind his bed, together with scarves and football jerseys: emblems of the team he supported. His books had been arranged in his bookcase together with several cups and shields that he'd won for various sports. She'd have to keep those brightly polished.

All Tom's bits and pieces provided a colourful, pleasing aspect. Lizzie knew it would cheer her up, when she found herself on her own. Tom would have his college course. He couldn't be with her all the time. Lizzie knew and accepted that.

To both Lizzie and Tom's delight, all the furniture in their apartment had come from their original home. It looked familiar and comforting. They were thrilled to see the chest of drawers—the one that had stood in their mother's bedroom and which had been moved with its contents intact.

One small drawer at the top of the chest was full of their Mum's very personal items, including some of her toiletries: a tub of Old English Lavender powder; a bottle of her favourite perfume. Tom and Lizzie had clubbed together and bought her Chanel No. 5 every Christmas, knowing full well it would give her pleasure.

From time to time Lizzie opened the drawer, withdrew the stopper from the bottle and took a good, long sniff at the perfume … closing her eyes … remembering. One day, when she could find the courage, she knew she should sort through all the drawers … but for now they could keep their secrets.

There were plenty of other things to sort. A stack of large cardboard boxes still stood in a corner close to the window. These, she'd been told, contained the bulk of her mother's personal effects: all her clothing and her shoes; and other items like bags and hats. Lizzie knew it was going to be painful, sorting out and throwing away any of their Mum's belongings. But Tom had insisted: they couldn't keep everything; they simply didn't have the room.

The boxes were taking up so much space. And they were blocking the French window. She knew that she, together with Tom, would have to face up to the sorting … soon.

A small collection of family photos, stood on the top of the chest of drawers. It included a picture that Lizzie loved: all three of them in the garden, having a picnic on the lawn. A blanket had been spread on the grass in the shade of the old apple tree. Their Mum was looking very summery, wearing her favourite, flowery dress. Tom, who must have been aged about six, was sporting a very colourful T-shirt, which boasted 'I'm The Boss Here'. His arm, protective, encircled Lizzie, who was snuggled up beside him with her Crocker tucked under one arm. Her rapturous smile said it all.

Lizzie spent ages staring at the photo, feeding off the happy faces. Underneath, a caption read, scribbled in Tom's then childish hand: 'Mummy, Tom, The Shrimp and Crocker'. It always made Lizzie smile, but it also made her cry.

Glancing at the rest of the photos through a haze of spilling tears, Lizzie had a sudden thought. She pulled herself forward, wiping her eyes: staring puzzled at the photos. There were no pictures of her father. She'd never seen a photo of him. And, what's more, now she came to think of it, she and Tom scarcely spoke of him. He had played no role in their lives. It was as if he had never existed.

He'd seldom been mentioned by her mother—except to say that sadly he'd died. He'd disappeared in the mists of time. He'd vanished from their consciousness.

This fact had never struck Lizzie before. But surely it was strange, wasn't it? For the first time in her life, Lizzie started to wonder … why?

8

The Key

Lizzie's life slipped into a pattern. The community had a resident warden. The woman, named Betty, was kind enough, dropping in casually morning and evening—just to keep an eye on her.

Lizzie didn't enjoy the visits. She looked upon them as an intrusion: struggling daily with resentment; trying hard to be pleasant to Betty. Then, later, feeling ashamed by her rudeness and knowing she ought to apologise. Yet never quite getting around to it.

She'd been well trained in the spinal unit, even down to some sound advice on how to respond to offers of help without upsetting the would-be helpers. So that when she felt like snapping at Betty and telling her in a grumpy voice 'Go away and leave me alone,' she did her best to smile and say 'I'm fine, thank you. I can manage.'

And, indeed, she could manage. The doctors and nurses were proved right. She could be fully independent. Though she'd learnt that she had to be organised: that she had to plan her manoeuvres with care. As long as she focussed and tried hard, concentrating on what she was doing, she could transfer with ease from her bed to her wheelchair—a technique she'd learnt in the spinal unit.

She could cope with the shower and loo unaided—what Tom always called her ablutions. And she could dress and undress herself. Of course, the shoes were difficult—but, as she well knew, not impossible.

"Nothing is impossible," Lizzie mumbled to herself as she struggled with her trainers.

Even if she fell on the floor, it certainly didn't spell disaster. She'd been taught how to climb back into her chair, although the knowledge that she could do it didn't always prevent the misery of lying in a heap on the floor, feeling sorry for herself, swamped by tears of choking frustration. By the time that Tom appeared, she'd dried her tears and composed herself. The sight of him always filled her with joy: his brown eyes and smiling face; the tousled hair; the scruffy jeans. She'd ordered a new T-shirt for him, suitably large for his chunky frame, proclaiming 'I Am Still The Boss Here'. The sight of that was encouraging.

His usual 'Come on Shrimp. You can do it,' brought a smile back to her face. And then, of course, she found that she could.

"It's a matter of perseverance," Tom was always telling her.

With Tom away at college most days, Lizzie spent lots of time on her own. And that was how she preferred to be: enjoying the privacy of her home after the months in the hospital; loving the peace of her own space. Her swan still came to visit her and when he did she was pleased to see him. Occasionally he seemed quite restless and, as the music swelled in her brain, she visualised him taking off: rising from the glassy water; whipping up waves beneath his feet. When he had faded, she sat for ages puzzling over the bird and the music; trying so very hard to remember.

Lizzie was learning about her rights; refusing all offers of education. Now she was sixteen, she couldn't be made to return to school against her will. But there was something else she'd discovered of which she might well take advantage: that if you had a spinal cord injury, you could learn to drive at sixteen. You could even have your own car.

"Why don't you let me fix it up for you?" Betty had asked in a kindly voice.

"No thank you," Lizzie had answered firmly, doing her best to smile at Betty. " I can manage on my own—when I feel like doing it."

The idea might tempt her—in due course. For now, she didn't want to try. She didn't feel confident enough—yet.

No more school was a great relief and, despite all Betty's suggestions, she didn't want to see old friends. One of them had come to see her, but the visit was not a success and it wouldn't be repeated. Lizzie who'd always been so active and whose friends continued to be so, couldn't see any point in seeing them. It only served to rub more salt into the wound of her lost pride.

Crocker still played an important role. During the daytime he lay on Tom's bed, in a special place of honour. At night he lay beside her pillow. When Lizzie found herself on her own, she chatted to him regularly. He was always a source of comfort.

Of course she knew Tom had always loved her. But she knew something else as well: that he'd want her to accept The Challenge, to find the courage to battle on, to find new meaning in her life. Tough love was the order of the day.

So although Tom's heart would be full of sorrow—not only for her and her broken body, but also for the loss of their mother—she knew he wouldn't be patronising. Since they had always been so close, he would know how best to help her, even if he found it difficult: standing back and watching her struggle, without trying to help too much; without trying to take her over. Encouraging her independence. Not aggravating her more than necessary by helping when she didn't want help, like some might do with a disabled person.

And Lizzie did her best for him: doing all she could for herself and trying not to ask for much. And yet there were days when the future looked bleak: days when all she wanted to do was to cling on tight to her lovely big brother … to sob her heart out on his shoulder.

Every day she couldn't help asking, "Why oh why did this have to happen? Why did it have to happen to me? How will I live if I can't run again?"

And every day she heard Tom's answer. "Lizzie, it's easy for me to talk. But you're alive and that's what matters. Where there is life there is always hope. Do you remember Mum quoting that? I think it was one of her grandmother's sayings. And it's right, I know it is," Tom insisted vigorously. "Besides, I'll always be there for you. Together we shall battle through."

On her very blackest days, Lizzie wasn't sure about that. For there were days when she despaired: days when she didn't want to go on. What was the point of being alive?

Her wheelchair and its stupid behaviour often made her very angry. Why wouldn't it do what she wanted? She sometimes struggled with tipping back and trying to balance on her wheels. The chair could seem so wretchedly heavy. Her arms and shoulders would ache so much. She'd end up fighting down the tears.

Some mornings it was touch and go. Sometimes she couldn't get out of her mind the picture of that wicked man: the idiot driver who'd wrecked her life … his stupid mouth … his lurid wink. How he'd just gone rocketing on, horn blaring, arms flailing, oblivious of their dreadful plight.

Then she would speed round her room in anger, consumed by memories of the man. If she could make it through to lunchtime … if she could hang on to thoughts of her brother, his smiling eyes, his loving presence, she knew that she could hang on to life. On several, certainly shameful occasions, it was only the thought of Tom that stopped her from doing something silly.

She had, some little while ago, attended the funeral of a friend: a girl who'd committed suicide. She'd been prepared for the family's grief and maybe even their sense of guilt, but she hadn't expected to see such anger targeted at the suicide victim: the red hot fury of family and friends, to think that the person they'd loved and valued could, through a seemingly selfish act—a gruesome exit from life itself—inflict such cruelty and such pain. A punishment directed at them?

Lizzie knew that Tom would be heartbroken, if she ever took that exit. But he'd be something else as well. He would be overcome by anger—and the anger would be directed at her. She couldn't bear the thought of that.

If she found the days hard going, the nights could often be much worse. When she awoke yet again from a nightmare, a flashback to the terrible crash—the flashing, the smashing, the explosion of noise—she would lie trembling in her bed. She was only able to calm herself by looking across to Tom's shadowy corner: seeing his tousled head on the pillow; seeing the strong, firm, line of his jaw. By clinging on to that comforting vision, Lizzie could lull herself back to sleep.

And Lizzie's dreams weren't always bad. There were, occasionally, heavenly dreams that swept her along in an ecstasy: running … running … running fast. She could feel the beat of her feet on the track. She could feel the muscles in her legs.

And then she was winning … winning … winning. The medal was hanging around her neck. She could feel the gold against her skin. It was wonderful. Fantastic.

Waking up was terrible. It took her a little while to remember. And then the sense of bereavement was stunning. The feelings of loss were overwhelming.

In an effort to keep herself busy and to take her mind from such things, Lizzie was often on the move: wheeling her chair backwards and forwards; in and out of the kitchen and bathroom; clearing and cleaning where she could; cooking food on her special stove; washing dishes at the sink. Then she'd wander around the big room: looking at Tom's books in his bookcase; considering his cups and medals.

And then, of course, there was the key. It lay on the shelf amongst his trophies. No matter how hard she focussed upon it, Lizzie simply couldn't remember if or where she'd seen it before.

On her trips around the room, she would often stop and pick up the key: polishing it on her sleeve; inspecting the unusual handle with its fancy decoration—what looked like a shield from a coat of arms. And there were traces of some kind of writing. But Lizzie couldn't decipher that. It was worn with age—unreadable.

"What secrets are you holding, Key?" Lizzie would mutter quietly, frowning.

A strange idea returned to haunt her. The key was a very special treasure. One day, that key would unlock her future.

9

Visitors

One evening, when Lizzie was on her own, there came a knocking at her door: three loud raps and then silence. Knowing that Betty was due very soon and assuming that she'd forgotten her key, Lizzie thought nothing of shouting out "Hang on Betty. I'm on my way."

She got a shock when she opened the door. Two men, complete strangers, were standing in the gloom on the step. They stood very close, quite filling the doorway.

One was an enormous man. The light from the hall lit up his face: the misshapen nose, the cruel mouth. Lizzie had never felt so vulnerable. Once she could outrun most people. Captive now in her chair, she felt helpless.

She ought to be wearing her panic button. But she hated the wretched thing. And she'd never expected to need it.

The hulk wore an ugly, grey-black suit. The jacket looked too small for the man. The single button that closed the front was straining across his bulky frame. But it was clear that the bulk wasn't fat. The upper arms of the jacket sleeves were wrinkled and creased over bulging muscles. Pale stains ringed the shiny cloth: spreading out across the jacket, down the sleeves and across the breast from the region of his armpits.

His head was huge and domed and shaven. Enormous, ugly, cauliflower ears stuck out wide on either side. The rims of the ears were red and crusty.

Massive hands hung low by his sides, the nails bitten and blackened with grime. A ludicrous question came to Lizzie. Whatever must they taste like, those fingers? Her stomach churned at the very thought.

The other man was completely different. He was slightly built and neat in appearance; upright, wearing a stylish grey suit and underneath it a fresh white shirt. Lizzie noticed the dazzling collar and the very smart silk tie: elegant silver stripes on navy, held in place by a diamond pin.

There was a matching stud in his ear. His thin, fair hair lay smooth and sleek. His clean-shaven face looked almost waxy. The eyes were light—an unusual colour.

The smile crinkles around his eyes and the turned up corners of a generous mouth made him look both kind and friendly. When he smiled and showed his teeth, they reminded Lizzie of rows of fine pearls. When he spoke and gesticulated, diamonds flashed from rings on the fingers of his perfectly manicured hands.

"Are you Miss Tregarrow?" the man asked. His voice was gentle. His smile was warm.

Lizzie looked mystified.

"No," she answered truthfully. "You must have got the wrong address."

But as she moved to close the door, the big man made a step towards her, slipping a huge, booted foot in the doorway and forcing the door wide open again.

"What about Robert Tregarrow then? I expect you must know him, don't you?" the kind man said, still smiling sweetly.

"I've never heard of him," Lizzie insisted. "What's all this about?" she asked, edging her chair back from the door, suddenly overcome by the smell that seemed to be coming from the men: expensive aftershave from one, but much too strong and overpowering; stale sweat and other foul odours from the big man who loomed above her. The combination was disgusting.

"We're only making our enquiries," the friendly man said, flashing his teeth. "Most people are happy to help us, but others sometimes need persuasion … don't they Sid?" he prompted quietly.

"Oh yes!" The big man agreed. "We have our ways and means, you see. Just a little friendly persuasion." He gave a horrible, leering laugh and started moving into the room, towering over Lizzie's chair, pushing her backwards as he went, leaning down too close to her face.

Lizzie shrank away from the man. The stench of his body was overwhelming. She tried to turn her head to the side to avoid the sight of his horrible face.

A sweat broke out on his greasy, lined brow. Blackheads clustered on either side of broad, hair filled, gummed up nostrils. Numerous yellow-headed spots lurked in the stubble on his face. When he opened his mouth in a grimace, the blackened teeth looked quite revolting: a row of rotting, broken stumps. Their terrible odour enveloped her.

Lizzie was starting to feel quite faint when a wonderfully welcome voice rang out:

"What are you doing?" the voice was angry. "It's much too late for visitors. Do I have to call the police?" Betty was standing well clear of the men, waving her mobile phone in one hand.

"Sid! Do come along, dear boy," the man with the smiles was quiet but firm. "We wouldn't want to outstay our welcome."

Sid, who was clearly enjoying himself and psyching himself up ready for action, stamped reluctantly out of the room. He glared at Lizzie, snarling angrily.

"I'm sure we'll meet again," he hissed, showing her his stinking fangs.

"I hope we'll meet again, Miss Tregarrow," the smooth man said in his quiet voice. "I have enjoyed our little visit." He smiled and nodded politely to Betty.

"I *don't* like the look of them," Betty said, slamming the door behind her. "And what's all that about 'Miss Tregarrow'?"

"I've no idea," Lizzie whispered, feeling very weak and wobbly. "Could you please make me a cup of tea, Betty?"

"Yes, of course. We'll have one together." She screwed up her face as she sniffed at the air. "But first I'll switch on all the fans. The smell in here is terrible. Though … I don't think I'll open the doors … or the windows."

Lizzie breathed a sigh of relief. Betty was watching her, looking concerned.

"If those men ever come here again or if you see any sign of them, Lizzie, you must push your emergency button," the woman begged, her voice distraught.

She gave the girl a good looking over, noticing that the emergency device that should be hanging round Lizzie's neck was certainly not where it ought to be. She could see it lying beside the girl's bed.

"I'm only a short distance away," Betty continued firmly. "You know that I'd always come if you called me—at any time of the night or day. But you must call me," she added more gently, seeing that Lizzie was close to tears.

"If you won't use your emergency button, at least we must get you a new mobile phone. Why won't you let me do that for you?" Betty had asked this several times since she had started helping Lizzie. "Surely," she continued hopefully, "surely a phone is good idea?"

"No!" snapped Lizzie. "I don't want a phone." And then more gently, on the verge of tears, seeing Betty's unhappy face, "I am so sorry." She started sobbing. "I can't explain. But I don't want a phone."

The truth was Lizzie had horrible flashbacks and in those ghastly nightmare flashes she saw her phone in a pool of blood … she couldn't bear to think whose blood … She would wake and lie sweating in her bed, unable to rid herself of the image. And when she awoke the following morning, she would find herself saying over and over "I'll never have another phone."

Lizzie spent a miserable evening: angry because she'd lost her cool and knowing that she'd upset Betty. It was all the fault of those hateful men. She had to admit it … they'd terrified her.

"Oh Tom! It was horrible," Lizzie said later, "I was so frightened. I wish you'd been here."

10

The Wooden Box

As the weeks had drifted by, Lizzie had started to feel more at home. Her spirits had been gradually building. She'd even been getting to the point where she'd wondered about a car. Perhaps she would ask Betty to help—in setting up some driving lessons

But the horrible experience with the visitors had completely unnerved Lizzie. It had destroyed her growing confidence. Although she didn't say much to Tom, it left her feeling increasingly anxious.

Her kitchen window looked out on the road. Goodness knows how often each day she made her way across to her kitchen and found herself gazing out through that window: endlessly watching out for those men.

Each of the individual dwellings had a private parking space set within its tiny front garden. But visitors left their cars on the road. There were always a few parked along either side.

From a position in her kitchen, peeping out from behind the curtain, Lizzie surveyed the cars in the road, watching out for new arrivals. But, because of the bend in the road, she found it continually frustrating. She couldn't see more than a hundred yards. Anyone parked just around the corner … could be keeping her under surveillance … and she would probably never know.

Lizzie tried to forget that idea, telling herself it was fanciful. And yet the horrible thought persisted. So she pulled her curtains early each evening. She listened for footsteps on her path and, if anyone knocked on her door, she sat frozen in her chair, waiting for them to go away, her hand poised holding her alarm, which she now always carried with her.

As if this wasn't bad enough, with the passing of each day, Lizzie became increasingly anxious about the job she was dreading the most: sorting out her mother's belongings. Every night she lay in her bed, looking across at the stack of boxes: struggling to make the decision that she and Tom would do it tomorrow. But when she got up on the following morning, she could always find some excuse for putting it off for another day.

Concentrating on her brother, without whom she knew she couldn't live, Lizzie had managed to stave off thinking about the terrible loss of her Mum. It was too painful; too devastating. Focussed on her beloved Tom, she could avoid the pain and the tears, which thoughts of her mother were bound to bring. Somehow she had to remain strong; she couldn't afford to keep breaking down.

Finally one night Tom said, "We can't put this off any longer, Lizzie. If you get Betty to unpack the boxes, to lay everything out on the floor, we'll go through it all tomorrow evening."

The Boss had spoken. Lizzie knew it was right. She would ask Betty to unpack the boxes.

And so it was that the following evening Lizzie was sitting on the floor staring at her mother's possessions, laid out neatly in lines on the carpet. Her clothing, shoes and her bags. And a host of other items.

Torn between wanting to handle everything and then not wanting to touch a thing, Lizzie didn't know where to start.

Finally, Tom's voice broke through. "We can't avoid it. It's got to be done."

Lizzie shuffled along on her bottom, lifting her legs along as she went, hauling herself slowly backwards, along from one heap to the next.

"Thank goodness for your brilliant Crabwalk," Tom laughed. "I always knew it would come in useful."

The words brought a welcome smile to Lizzie. She hadn't heard that expression for years. Crabwalk. She remembered it well. She could even hear Tom's childish voice. 'Mummy come and look at The Shrimp. She's doing her funny Crabwalk again. But, Mummy, when is she going to walk?'

Now she would never walk again. She knew that she mustn't think like that. All those happy memories should be used to lighten her mood. They could make her feel much better. She giggled merrily at Tom.

"My Crabwalk is crucial now," she said. "Although it's needed some adaptation."

Lizzie, governed by Tom's wise words, knew that there wouldn't be any point in keeping all their mother's clothing. Besides, they didn't have room for it. But throwing it out was a different matter. That was going to be very hard.

"We'll send it to the charity shop," Tom insisted with authority. "Then we won't be throwing it out. It will be more like giving gifts. I'm sure that Mum would be happy with that."

But despite these charitable thoughts, Lizzie clung on to some of the items, although she knew that she'd never wear them: her mother's favourite high-heeled shoes, black and shiny and kept for best; and a dress that her mother had had for years. It certainly wasn't fashionable now. But Lizzie had always loved that dress. It was made from a fine, glossy cotton-lawn; summery with pretty blue flowers and with emerald-green piping on bodice and cuffs—the dress her Mum wore in the photo. She simply couldn't let that go.

Lizzie sat looking across at the photo: stroking the dress … choking back sobs.

"Sorry Tom," she said at last.

"We have to get on and finish," he said. "Betty will put it all into bags and take it away to the shop tomorrow … but we must do the sorting for her. Come on Shrimp. I know you can do it."

Lizzie was feeling exhausted now, but she smiled at his rallying words, trying to pull herself together.

"Have you seen that curious box?" Tom asked. "I'm looking forward to opening that."

Lizzie looked across the room to where there lay a stout wooden box. It was beautifully polished, with brass-bound corners: eighteen to twenty inches in length, sixteen wide and maybe twelve deep.

"I wonder where Mum kept that?" she said, dragging herself towards the box. "I've never seen it before, have you?"

"Probably in her wardrobe," Tom laughed. "That wardrobe was always sacrosanct. I remember when I was ten years old getting into a lot trouble, ferreting about in there. But I only did it once. She gave me such a tremendous lecture."

"I do remember," Lizzie laughed. "The bottom section of that wardrobe was stacked up high with what Mum always called her stuff. I suppose the box was lurking there. But why the secrecy, I wonder?"

She and Tom had never considered that their Mum might have any secrets. She'd always seemed such an open person. Though Tom was right about sacrosanct: the wardrobe had always been out of bounds.

There had been a few occasions when, after a lot of pushing and pleading and for a very special treat, their Mum had opened some of the boxes that cluttered up the floor of her wardrobe, exposing some of her special treasures:

things like Tom's first pair of bootees; and a pretty baby's hairbrush, together with tiny ballet shoes, which Lizzie had worn as a very small child.

"Oh dear! Oh dear! Oh dear! It's locked," Lizzie exclaimed now in dismay, struggling to open the box. Pushing a small metal plate aside, she found a tidy brass rimmed keyhole. And then she noticed something else.

"Just look, Tom!" she gasped in delight, her finger pointing to the lid. A polished brass plate was set into the wood. It bore a decorative coat of arms. And there was something familiar about it.

"The key," she said excitedly.

Heaving herself across to the bookshelf, she reached up and grasped the key. Then turning it over in her hand, she gazed open-mouthed at the shield on the handle.

"I bet this key will open that box."

I I

A Pandora Moment

Slipping easily into the slot, the key turned smoothly to open the lock. Uncertain now, Lizzie paused. For some inexplicable reason, she was reluctant to lift the lid.

"Come on Lizzie," Tom implored. "I don't expect there's a jack-in-the-box. And if there is I can handle him."

"Yes," Lizzie laughed. "I'm sure you can. But it's not Jack that's worrying me. This is an ancient box of secrets. I can feel it in my bones."

She ran her fingers across the lid, tracing the lines of the coat of arms.

"This," she announced, her voice full of drama, "this is a Pandora moment."

"But I've always fancied Pandora," Tom chuckled in her ear. "I've always liked the sound of her."

"Yes, I'm sure you have," Lizzie giggled. "But you know the story of

Pandora's Box—once you've opened the lid of the box and let all the contents out, no matter whether they're good or evil, you can never put them back. You have to live with the consequences of your possibly unwise action—in opening up the box in the first place."

"Yes," Tom said. "Who knows what we'll find? It's exciting, isn't it? Come on Lizzie. Do get on with it."

Lizzie's hands were shaking slightly. As she slowly raised the lid, she and Tom both held their breath.

"Poof!" said Tom disparagingly. "It's only half full, after all. There's not much here, just a tatty box and a load of crummy old papers."

"It's not just a tatty box, Tom. I think it's Mum's old jewellery case." Lizzie opened the lid of the case. "I recognise this string of pearls. And look, those are her bracelets and brooches."

In one corner of the case there was a small, blue, leather-bound box marked with the name and address of the jeweller.

"Old Bond Street, London," Lizzie read.

"That sounds very posh," said Tom.

"Yes it does," said Lizzie thoughtfully, prising open the lid of the box. As she did so a card fell out. She read the handwritten message aloud.

"A Special Gift for a Special Girl on our First Wedding Anniversary—with all my love always, Bob xxx"

"How extraordinary!" Lizzie exclaimed.

"Who on earth was Bob?" Tom asked.

"I've no idea," Lizzie answered. "Oh, but look at this," she continued.

Something excitingly shiny and yellow was nestled in the silk lined box. She lifted out a long, fine chain on which there hung a glowing pendant.

"Isn't this beautiful?" she gasped.

"Oh yes. Lush!" said Tom. "But I don't remember seeing Mum wearing it."

"It's gold," Lizzie said, "with emerald eyes."

"It's brilliant workmanship," Tom said. "Made by a master craftsman, no doubt."

"Yes, I'm sure you're right," said Lizzie, peering closely at the pendant swinging on its golden chain … a tiny but perfectly formed swan.

12

The Scrapbook

With the special treasure replaced in its box, Lizzie inspected the rest of the trinkets. After handling each in turn, her hand crept up to her neck, where her mother's rings hung on a ribbon. She carried those everywhere with her now: a wide gold band, her wedding ring; and her diamond engagement ring, an unusual setting with tiny emeralds.

Struggling to hold back tears, Lizzie placed the case aside and dipped back into the wooden box.

"Oh look," she murmured in surprise, lifting out a bulging scrapbook. It seemed to be stuffed with masses of cuttings. And there were lots of photos too.

With Tom close beside her, Lizzie opened up the book. The first page bore a large wedding photo: the bride in a flowing, white gown walked hand in hand with the groom who was dressed in a military uniform. Other photos followed on. And then there was a newspaper cutting: a feature all about the wedding together with a splendid photo, which showed the happy couple emerging through an archway of raised swords, held aloft by rows of smart soldiers.

"How cool is that!" Tom exclaimed.

"It must be Mum … and our Dad?" Lizzie said hesitantly. "But if it is, I don't understand … " Her voice faltered. Her finger pointed.

"Bob and Allison Tregarrow leaving the church after their wedding," Lizzie read the caption out loud.

"But that can't be right, Tom … can it?" Lizzie was looking mystified. "It's obviously Mum in the photograph—but her name is Jennifer. So why does it say 'Allison' here?" She stabbed the cutting with her finger.

"That's not her second name is it?" asked Tom.

"Not that I've ever heard," said Lizzie. "And look, there's another problem too. Who on earth is Bob Tregarrow?"

"If it's our Dad it should say 'John'. And, of course, 'Stevenson'," Tom added.

"Mum didn't marry twice … did she?" Lizzie asked uncertainly. "Do you suppose this is somebody else? Some other man that she had in her life?"

"I don't think that's too likely," said Tom. "Though it's true that she never talked about Dad."

"But Tom, when he died you were nearly three. Surely you must remember him? Surely you must have known his name?"

"I always thought his name was John," Tom said in a doubtful voice. "But it's odd when I come to think of it, because I hardly ever saw him. He must have been away a lot. I'd always thought that he was a soldier, but later on when I asked Mum about him, she told me that I'd got it wrong. She said that he'd been a travelling salesman."

"That is really weird," said Lizzie. She was peering at the photograph. "You do look very like this man. You have the same dark, curly hair. Your eyes and your mouth are similar. I'm sure this has to be our Dad."

"You don't look anything like him," Tom said.

"No. But that doesn't surprise me," said Lizzie. "Mum always said I took after her. That sometimes happens in families … doesn't it?"

Lizzie turned the next page warily. Facing them was a large colour picture: not a paper cutting this time, but a proper photographic print and, beneath it, a handwritten caption: 'On our honeymoon in Cornwall, visiting Bob's family home'.

The young couple in the photo were standing in front of an old, oak door—gnarled and knobbed with big, black rivets. Above the arch at the top of the doorway, Lizzie could see the lower part of a handsome, chiselled relief, deeply cut in the granite blocks from which the wall of the house was built. She recognised it immediately.

"Now we're getting somewhere," she said, closing the lid of the big box and comparing the two designs. "That's the shield from this coat of arms."

"Yes," said Tom, "I think you're right. The prancing animals are missing. But it certainly looks like the shield."

"Oh Tom. Something dreadful just struck me. Did you see the name … Tregarrow?"

The words of the smiling man came back to her: 'I hope we'll meet again, Miss Tregarrow.'

Lizzie shuddered at the memory. Feeling suddenly chilled and afraid, she glanced quickly over her shoulder, terrified lest she see those men standing at her door again.

13

A Brave Hero

Shaking herself back to the present, Lizzie continued turning the pages. There were more photos of their Mum posing together with the man. And there were some of the man himself, smartly dressed in a military uniform and looking, as Lizzie exclaimed, "Very handsome!"

She stared at all the photos closely: gazing into the man's eyes. It was like looking into Tom's eyes. But the man in the photos was much older. And even though his eyes were smiling, the line of the jaw was lean and tight. This was a strong man. Maybe a hard man.

Turning the pages over slowly and commenting on each new photo, Lizzie and Tom were stopped by a headline: a cutting from one of the national newspapers.

Victoria Cross for Brave Hero

Her Majesty the Queen has awarded the Victoria Cross to Lieutenant Robert Tregarrow in a ceremony at Buckingham Palace. Tregarrow is known as a modest man, but a brave and fearless Royal Marine, with more than his fair share of courage and perseverance. He's a man of whom we can all be proud.

Despite his own wounds, Tregarrow not only rescued two of his men whilst subject to incessant enemy fire, but rallied his troop to renew their successful assault, leading from the front and showing personal gallantry of the highest order.

Because of Tregarrow's selfless action in rescuing two members of his troop—both of whom were severely injured—his men have nicknamed him 'The Angel'. Although it is only fair to say that the name is a joke amongst his men, especially since, until his recent engagement to be married, Tregarrow has always enjoyed a very lively reputation.

"Isn't that amazing Tom?"

She peered at the accompanying photo. She read the caption—several times. 'The hero together with his fiancée, photographed outside The Palace after the award ceremony'.

"Doesn't Mum look young and pretty?" She whispered in amazement to Tom.

"She looks wonderful," he answered.

Lizzie delved back into the box, determined to find the Victoria Cross. Although she had never seen one before, she guessed it would have its own smart case—probably something rather impressive. Finally she found the case sealed in a padded envelope.

Sliding it out of the envelope, she sat with it gently cupped in her hands: a slim, leather covered box—around about five inches long by a couple of inches wide—surprisingly small and unimpressive.

"Oh!" said Tom. "Just look at that. I thought it would have a really posh case."

"It's simple and understated," said Lizzie. "It's not ornate … but I think it's classy. I love the chocolate brown of the leather and this delicate pattern of leaves, embossed as a border around the lid."

Her hands shook, her heart beat fast, as Lizzie held the special case. As she turned it in her hand, the gold of the gilt caught the light from her window. Her fingers caressed the soft, smooth leather. Her mind struggled with the thought: 'My father must have held this case …'

She closed her eyes and concentrated. Even though he was long since dead, could she find some sense of him here? A trace of his touch … his being … his spirit?

She shivered, troubled and uncertain. Then trying to pull herself together, she pressed the little brass knob on the case, clicking and opening up the lid.

"Oh Tom! Just look at this … " she gasped.

They sat admiring the white silk satin that lined the inside of the lid on which there was printed a royal warrant.

"By Appointment," Lizzie read. "But the writing's so small I can't read the rest."

"Obviously to Queen Victoria," Tom's voice chipped in.

"Hancocks and Co." Lizzie continued. "They must be makers of the cross. And, I suppose, they commissioned the box … or maybe they even made it themselves …"

And there it was … the Victoria Cross … sitting on a bed of cream velvet.

Lizzie's fingers crept to the medal and lifted it reverently out of its nest. It dangled on its scarlet ribbon. Tom whistled. She held her breath.

At first they admired the front of the medal: the handsome lion, the words 'For Valour'. Then turning it round, they examined the back. A date was engraved in the central circle.

"June 1982," Lizzie read the date aloud.

The cross itself was attached to the ribbon by a narrow suspender bar on which a name had been engraved.

"Ltn. Robert Thomas Tregarrow, Royal Marines," Lizzie read out.

She sat quietly, looking bewildered.

" I think it's very odd," she said, slipping the medal back in its case. "There seem to be several mysteries here … including the fact that Mum never told us that you'd been named after your father. I find that amazing, Tom … don't you?"

Jammed inside the padded envelope, Lizzie found a piece of paper. It looked like a page from a magazine. She teased it out as flat as she could.

Surmounted by the royal arms, the text proclaimed:

SUPPLEMENT TO
The London Gazette
of Friday, 8th October 1982
Published by Authority

Written across the top of the paper there was a note in her mother's handwriting.

"Bob's citation," Lizzie read.

"That will explain why he got the VC," Tom said excitedly. "Go on. Read it out now Lizzie."

Lizzie read the citation aloud:

"Monday, 11th October 1982
Ministry of Defence
Honours and Awards
Navy Department
Whitehall, London, S.W.1

The QUEEN has been graciously pleased to approve the award of the VICTORIA CROSS to the undermentioned in recognition of valour during the operations in the South Atlantic:

Lieutenant Robert Thomas TREGARROW, Royal Marines

On the night of 11th/12th June, 1982, 45 Commando, Royal Marines launched a silent night attack against strongly held enemy positions on the craggy hill feature of Two Sisters, ten kilometres to the West of Port Stanley in the Falkland Islands. Lieutenant

Tregarrow was a troop commander in X Company, which had as its objective the feature's southern peak.

X Company's approach to Two Sisters was particularly arduous and the attack started late. The first troop led the way up the slope, but shortly after a second troop moved forward into the lead, the enemy became aware of the advance. From strong, well entrenched positions, heavy and intensive fire immediately broke out. Machine-gun, mortar and artillery rounds began to fall across the exposed positions held by the Royal Marines. Undeterred, Lieutenant Tregarrow led his men towards the right flank of the enemy's position on the summit. During the advance, he was wounded in the hand. Inspired by his lead, his troop broke into the enemy trenches but could not maintain their position. To the left, other Royal Marines also advanced towards the crestline. But enemy resistance proved too strong and X Company were forced to pull back to re-group.

During the withdrawal, two of Lieutenant Tregarrow's men were severely wounded close to the enemy's lines. As soon as his troop was secure in its new position, and ignoring his wound, Second Lieutenant Tregarrow charged back over 200 metres to rescue the first of his men. Lifting him onto his back, he carried him in full view of the enemy to a position of safety. As he returned with the Royal Marine, he was again wounded. However, in spite of this, Lieutenant Tregarrow immediately went out for a second time to rescue the remaining survivor of his troop. In retracing his steps, he again crossed exposed ground in order to pick up and extract the casualty. Throughout this time he was subject to incessant enemy fire.

Despite his exhaustion and the discomfort of his wounds, when X Company renewed their assault on the still strongly held crestline, Lieutenant Tregarrow was once again at the forefront of the charge. His troop again secured the vital right flank of the attack, driving the enemy out of its well established positions and beating off all attempts to recapture them. Lieutenant Tregarrow's cool and determined command of the right flank during both assaults was a vital part of X Company's success in taking the southern peak of Two Sisters.

Throughout the long advance from San Carlos Water to Port Stanley, Lieutenant Tregarrow repeatedly showed personal gallantry of the highest order. His courage and leadership galvanised all those around him. His behaviour epitomises the finest traditions of the Service."

"That's awesome!" Tom exclaimed, when Lizzie finally finished reading.

"There's more to all this than meets the eye, Tom. This is a mega mystery," she said.

"We're going to have to read all these cuttings," Tom agreed, "and carefully."

Lizzie was turning the pages steadily, when a headline caught her eye.

"Oh no!" she suddenly said in dismay. "I don't like the sound of this, do you?"

Captain Angel Fallen from Grace

14

The Fallen Angel

Lizzie flicked through the pages of the scrapbook, surprised by the many nasty headlines. It looked as if every national newspaper had taken pleasure at the time in running the sensational story.

British Officer Fallen From Grace

The Mystery of the Vanished Traitor

The Times had written:

The Fallen Angel

Lizzie read the text out loud:

"Her Majesty the Queen's state visit to Africa has been marred by a most unpleasant incident. The so-called hero, Captain Bob (The Angel) Tregarrow has proved himself to

be more of a devil and, what's more, a foul traitor.

Corporal Johnny Finn was a member of the Captain's special operations team, which was guarding the Queen and her jewels. On the morning following their theft, Corporal Finn declared himself to be surprised by the Captain's behaviour.

He said: 'I wouldn't have thought it of the Captain. But there you go. These things happen. I knew him to be a brave man and he always seemed honest to me. But I must have been mistaken.'

A worldwide hunt is on for Captain Tregarrow. But as it is universally accepted, both by the authorities and by his peers, that the Captain committed this treacherous crime, his reputation is now in ruins. He can never return to his unit, nor return to his wife and child. When caught, he will face certain arrest and, no doubt, a lengthy trial."

And there was a photo too, together with a brief caption:

A family photo of Captain Tregarrow, together with his wife and son, taken in happier days.

Lizzie and Tom stared at the picture. The man who was holding Tom in his arms was standing together with their Mum on some beach beside the sea.

"I wonder where this photo was taken," Lizzie said thoughtfully.

"And when?" Tom wondered. "He's obviously been promoted to Captain."

"You look about two years old," Lizzie said.

"Yes", said Tom, "I think you're right. But what's that in the background?" he asked.

"It's a small island," Lizzie mused.

"I wouldn't mind betting," Tom said, "that whoever took this photo, included the island as part of the picture."

"Linking the people with the island? I think you might be right Tom. Perhaps there's a beautiful house on the island … an old and stately family home? We saw them standing in front of that door. It looked like a very grand doorway to me." Lizzie was excited now.

"Don't get too excited," warned Tom. "We may never be able to trace it."

Lizzie looked closely at the old box. She ran her fingers across the wood and then across the coat of arms, emblazoned in brass on the lid of the box. She traced the line of what must be a motto.

"I can't read a word of this, can you? It isn't Latin, is it?" she asked.

"No," Tom answered. "It isn't Latin."

He spelt the strange words out … one by one.

"P R E S T   C O L O N N E K   H A   D Y W Y S Y K … It must be some weird foreign language. I haven't got a clue what it is."

Lizzie sat staring at the photo.

"An island, Tom. Wouldn't that be great? I've always wanted to live on an island."

15

The Shameful Ending

ome on," she said impatiently. "We'll have to read everything in this book."

Most of the other newspaper cuttings appeared to deal with the same story. Some were carefully worded and brief, whilst others had obviously grasped the sensational. Lizzie kept on turning the pages until a new headline caught her eye:

Traitor's Wife Disappears

Allison Tregarrow, the wife of the traitor, Captain Bob (The Angel?) Tregarrow, has disappeared. Shame has driven her into exile, probably in some foreign land. It would appear that she's changed her name and so we've been unable to trace her. Friends and relatives, when questioned, refused to comment.

The brief text said it all.

"Poor Mum," Lizzie said sadly.

"Yes. Poor Mum," Tom sighed.

Lizzie was feeling exhausted and upset. But they mustn't give up yet—not 'til they'd looked at all the cuttings.

Another immediately caught their attention.

Special Branch Storms Traitor's Home

Although it is now some considerable time since Captain Bob Tregarrow disappeared, the worldwide hunt for him continues. To that end, the family home of the traitorous Captain was recently stormed and searched by members of the Special Branch, intent not only on tracking down the Captain himself, but also hopeful of finding clues to the whereabouts of the Queen's lost jewels together with her famous tiara, stolen in a daring raid by Captain Tregarrow some years ago.

No evidence whatsoever was found at the old family home. Local people displayed a sense of disgust regarding the Captain, who had, until his shocking downfall, been heralded as a much loved local hero.

Our correspondent reports that customers in the village pub, all childhood friends of Tregarrow, now only wish to heap scorn upon him. Some suggested that the Captain had always been no more than a coward and one man declared 'We hopes to never see the likes of that foul man here no more,' a clear indication of the disgust in which the memory of the Captain is now held by Cornish people.

Towards the very end of the scrapbook, Lizzie found the final cutting: a short, single width column:

Shameful Ending

Our regular readers will remember our sensational coverage of the disgraceful story of Captain Bob (The Angel) Tregarrow. It was our African correspondent who first brought you the story of a man of supposed courage and goodness, decorated for his bravery, who proved to be a greedy traitor.

Seven years after his disappearance, with little chance of his survival in the deserts of Africa and with no trace of him ever having been found, despite rigorous searches by the authorities, the man, more suited to the name of Devil than Angel, is now assumed dead.

This piece of news may or may not please his widow, who, despite all efforts cannot be traced. With any luck, the legal acceptance of the man as dead will allow us to close the final chapter of this shameful story. The stolen goods may never be found. The secret of their whereabouts will have gone with the Captain to his grave, together with his tarnished reputation.

Lizzie and Tom sighed heavily, feeling tired now and depressed.

"What a horrible end," Tom said.

"It's very late," Lizzie said. "I think we should pack this lot away. It isn't going to help us much. It all happened so long ago."

Tom agreed. As Lizzie lowered the scrapbook back into the box, something else caught her eye—the corner of a brown envelope. She hadn't noticed it before. It was pressed against the front wall of the box: something perhaps slipped in there in haste. She slid it out and took a quick look, preparing to put it back again.

"It's just an old letter addressed to Mum," she said, too tired to take much interest.

But then she suddenly noticed the postmark.

"Oh, look Tom. How extraordinary. It's postmarked April 10th last year. That was only a few days before our trip ... "

Lizzie was frowning and looking perplexed.

"It might be the last letter Mum ever got," she said. "But it's a bit odd, isn't it? She kept all her letters in her desk. So why is this one locked away?"

16

The Letter

The envelope held two sheets of paper: one was a piece of A4, clean and white and neatly typed; the other much older, ragged, discoloured, bearing what looked like a primitive map.

Lizzie, propped up with Tom close by, read the letter slowly out loud, starting with the letter heading:

" *St Luke's Hospice for Victims of Cancer. London.*
April 1st 2010

To Captain Bob Tregarrow ... wherever he may be ...

Bob,
This will be my last letter and it will be my final confession. The chaplain here's a good guy. I'm dictating this letter to him. I'm too weak now to write it myself. He'll type it out for me to sign and then he'll send it off to your wife. I think I've finally managed to trace

her. It wasn't easy. She's changed her name.

Sorry mate. I let you down. I was the one who took the Queen's jewels—together with some so-called friends. Don't ask me how I was led astray. Of course we had the baby then—a child with serious disabilities and needing a lot of special care. We were desperate for money. Smith and Reilly promised just that—wealth beyond our wildest dreams. They had a buyer for the tiara—some potty multimillionaire. The rest of the stuff would be broken up and fed out through the usual channels.

Very soon after we'd taken the jewels, brought them back to the UK and got them safely hidden away, my poor little girl sickened and died. And then I lost my wife and all. I wanted out. What more can I say to you? I never thought you'd come off so badly.

Smith and Reilly 'bought it' somewhere—probably at the hands of the henchmen.

The rumour was that Mr Big wanted the crown for his darling daughter—his beloved 'Little Princess'. Nothing was too good for her—she was more than equal to the Queen.

As a small child he had stood in the rain, watching the coronation procession. He'd seen the wonderful golden coach. He'd seen the Queen with a crown on her head. He dreamed that one day he'd have that crown. Years of abuse and deprivation only made him more determined to have what he wanted and prove his worth.

When you look back, it seems mad now. But with money no object and frightened villains who would do his every wish, he made his plans to get the crown. I doubt if he even realised that it would not be a big state crown, but some kind of fancy tiara—the one that the Queen often took on her journeys, leaving the state crowns in The Tower.

When he learnt that we'd disappeared and he found that he'd lost his crown, Mr Big was not amused, so he sent his evil henchmen out after us. But they never caught up with me. They never knew where we'd stashed the loot. Only Smith and I knew that. Of course they have their ways and means and over the past few years I've been hounded, taking refuge where I could.

Although this happened years ago and the girl must be a woman now, he paid a lot of money up front—he's bound to want his pound of flesh. So just be warned. They are out there somewhere—serious villains without any scruples.

According to the quacks around me, I only have a few days left. I need and want you to get this confession and to have the enclosed map, which shows you where the stuff is hidden.

By the time you get this letter I'll be gone—to a better place. I can't take any more of this. Sometimes I lie in pain and dread, wondering if this serves me right. Maybe it's a judgement on me. But I only know one thing—that I mustn't and will not go to my grave carrying the secret that's wrecked your life.

Everybody is saying you're dead. But even if it's too late for you, I want your wife to clear your name. The chaplain has promised to post this to her.

I'm sorry I can't tell you more. I know I'm fading fast now. It's taken me several goes already—just to dictate this little lot.

Sorry mate and all the best,"

Lizzie came to the end of the letter. It finished with a squiggly signature.

Underneath was printed neatly *'Dictated by Johnny Finn to Michael, Chaplain at St Luke's Hospice'*. It was dated and followed by Michael's signature.

Lizzie read the letter again. They sat together in stunned silence.

"Johnny Finn," Lizzie said at last, remembering the paper cuttings. And then she thought of something else.

"Oh Tom," she said, in a shaky whisper. "Those two men that I told you about … "

17

Symbols

Lizzie had bumbled along for weeks: intent on getting through each day; facing endless little problems and, depending how well she coped, overcome by hopeless frustration or maybe bursting with joy and success. But with the discovery of the scrapbook and the reading of the letter, the focus of her life had changed.

With the new found knowledge about her father, her situation seemed suddenly dangerous. The more she thought about those men—the smiler and the stinking man—the more she thought that they must be the henchmen who were mentioned by Johnny Finn—'villains', he'd said, 'without any scruples'.

Tom wouldn't want her left on her own, but he couldn't always be there to protect her. Last time, she'd been fortunate. Betty had arrived in the nick of time.

Lizzie now carried her alarm at all times. She threaded the vital key for the box onto the ribbon she wore round her neck. It wasn't exactly comfortable. But she dared not let it out of her sight.

With Betty's help, she made a trip to the local library to photocopy Johnny Finn's letter. She wouldn't photocopy the map. Having the original lying around would be dangerous enough. A second copy would double the risk of it falling into the wrong hands.

She tried not to think about whose wrong hands; tried not to think about the two men. She was still haunted by those hands: the one set pale and immaculate, flashing golden rings and gems; the other set so big and filthy, with stained nails and calloused palms—hands of strength and evil intent.

It was obvious, wasn't it? Those men had visited her for a purpose. They were bound to follow up their visit. Whenever she was away from home, they might get in and ransack the place. She had to prepare herself for that.

And so, with more of Betty's help, Lizzie made another trip, this time to the local bank. In the privacy of her home she'd sealed the map and the original letter inside a strong, brown envelope. Labelled by a clerk in the bank, the envelope was whisked from her sight to be stored in a safety box in the vault.

Lizzie sighed a sigh of relief. It didn't mean that she was safe. But at least it meant that the documents were—until the time came when they might be needed.

She and Tom had lengthy talks about the best way to go ahead. Whilst it was clear that their father was dead, there was a mystery about his background. They couldn't simply leave it there. They'd have to go and search for his roots … and in doing so hopefully find their own. The first step on the searching road must be to trace the coat of arms.

On her frequent tours round her room, Lizzie would stop and stare at the box, peering at the coat of arms. On one of her trips into town with Betty, she visited the library again. A helpful librarian explained to her all about The College of Arms—the proper authority on such matters.

Armed with the relevant information, Lizzie set about contacting them, managing quickly, to her delight, to strike up an e-mail friendship with a young man at The College—an assistant to one of the Heralds. William was helpful and very kind. His sister was in a wheelchair, he said, and so he understood her problems.

William explained the heraldic devices which made up what were called the arms that Lizzie had described to him. The shield, central to the design, bore a single, sloping band. It was not unusual, so Lizzie learnt, for very early versions of arms to be represented by only the shield—just as it was in that photograph, where she could see it carved in the granite over the doorway to the house … and also on the key.

In the full form of the arms, as seen on the brass plate on the box, animals pranced, supporting the shield … a stag on one side, a boar on the other … well known Celtic symbols for lordliness, courage and perseverance. The correct term, so Lizzie learnt, for the prancing animals was 'rampant'.

The large bird that stood at the top of the arms was undoubtedly the chough—a very important symbol of Cornwall—extinct in the wild now, William thought, but being bred in captivity with hopes of releasing it in due course.

William needed still more time to trace the origins of the arms and to translate the family motto. Lizzie waited impatiently. She was longing to see the final report.

"Try to be patient," Tom advised. But Lizzie found it difficult. She checked her e-mail over and over, mumbling loudly to herself:

"Come on William. I need that report."

18

The Decision

illiam's e-mail arrived at last. Lizzie read it hungrily. Then she read it over again, to make quite sure that she'd got it right.

'The arms in question,' Lizzie read, 'belong to a very old Cornish family. Their ancient home is Tregarrow House.'

Lizzie gasped when she saw the name. There it was again. Tregarrow.

But William had only had partial success. The family motto was proving a problem—even for someone with his experience. It was, he suspected, ancient Cornish. But he'd have to find an expert. And, as he warned, it could take time. Such experts were very thin on the ground.

Piecing the family history together was like building a jigsaw puzzle. But most of the pieces were fitting now. Lizzie and Tom were making real progress. They spent ages discussing the subject and they pored over maps together. According to the Ordnance Survey, the house stood on an offshore island, very close to the North Cornish coast.

They ought to go and find the place. Lizzie knew it wouldn't be easy. But they had to make a decision.

Even deciding to make the decision—that this was her quest, her focus in life—was proving difficult for Lizzie. She was very tempted to drop the idea. It would be so much easier to go on just the way she was: pottering along from one day to the next; maybe joining the organisation that Betty said helped wheelchair users and was focused largely on sport: wheelchair basketball and tennis and host of other activities, some of which sounded … almost fun …

Yet, no matter what she did, Lizzie couldn't forget her visitors, especially now that she had to accept a connection with the name Tregarrow. Cars drawing up outside made her tremble. She was always dreading the knock on the door. Sometimes at the dead of night, when she was jolted wide awake, she fancied that she heard that knock: the three loud raps on the door. She even fancied she smelt the smell.

Lizzie simply couldn't resist opening up the big wooden box: handling the medal again; taking another look at the scrapbook. And every time she opened the pages and gazed into her mother's eyes and then across to the eyes of the man who, she supposed, must be her father, she knew she would have to follow it through. She simply couldn't let them down ... although she continually found herself wavering.

And Tom was adamant. They must go.

"Come on Shrimp. You can do it." His words, as always, gave her strength. And, of course, he'd be there with her. Together they would follow the quest. Together they would manage ... wouldn't they?

If Lizzie needed a final push, the family motto delivered that. William had found the expert he needed. His e-mail sounded jubilant.

'Wonderful news,' he had written to Lizzie. 'My expert certainly knows his stuff. He was immediately able to tell me that the motto is written in Middle Cornish—that particular form of the language in use from the thirteenth century, through and into the sixteenth century. And I have a translation for you.'

"Oh my days!" Lizzie gasped. "It's ancient. I bet you can't pronounce that Tom."

Tom did his best to pronounce the Cornish. "Prest colonnek ha dywysyk."

Lizzie searched hungrily for the translation.

Then she mouthed the motto over quietly ... over ... and over ... and over again.

"Ever Courageous and Persevering".

There was no way out for her now. This would have to become *her* motto. Now she knew what she had to do.

19

Plans

Rather against her better judgement, because she had so resented the woman, Lizzie was now very fond of Betty. She had become a stalwart friend. So having spoken first to Tom, Lizzie entrusted the box to her care. She took it home and locked it away.

"Somewhere very safe," Betty told her the following day.

However, despite Betty's kindness, Lizzie guessed it would not be wise to give her new friend all the details of their plans for the trip to Cornwall. The woman would worry. She might try to stop them.

"It'll be a lovely holiday," Lizzie had said lightly enough. "I won't need any extra help. The place is designed for wheelchair users. And, I gather, it's all brand new."

Nevertheless, Betty gave her a lecture.

"I know it's not my place to tell you, but I do get worried for you. You know how vital it is," she continued, "for you to take proper care of yourself—to exercise and look after your skin. And don't forget your pressure relief routines—shifting about as much as you can."

"Yes. Yes, Betty. I will. I'll wriggle myself about all day, if that's going to keep you happy," Lizzie added with a giggle.

Betty eyed the girl doubtfully. "And don't forget the nights," she continued.

"Oh dear! Oh dear!" Lizzie groaned. "Any moment now, Betty, you'll give me the lecture on bodily functions. I am a big girl and I can manage."

"And there is something else," Betty warned. "Whatever you do, don't swim in the sea."

"I swam a lot in the rehab unit," Lizzie insisted, pouting at Betty.

"Yes, I know you did," said Betty. "But the water in that pool was warm."

"In fact, my swimming was pretty good," Lizzie boasted, grinning at Betty. "I could beat most of the other patients."

"I don't care who you could beat," said Betty. "You might not beat hypothermia. In your case, that might well be fatal. You know that, surely?" Betty sighed.

"I know. I know," Lizzie snapped. Then hastily following with an apology. "I am sorry," she added gently, seeing the woman's worried face. "I promise I won't swim in the sea.

"I'm only going for a week. Everything's packed. I've even got Crocker. I really won't need your help at all."

"That's as maybe," Betty said. "But I shall come to the bus station with you, to help to settle you onto the coach. You can't stop me doing that.

"I know you told me," she carried on quickly, seeing Lizzie's stubborn face, "that the bus is 'wheelchair friendly'. But I've seen it all before. Just because they've made the claim, it doesn't mean to say that it will be."

Unfortunately, when they arrived at the bus station, Betty's suspicions were proved to be right. The one and only bus in the fleet, which was designed for wheelchair users, had been taken out of service—that very morning, so it seemed.

"The impossible takes a little bit longer," Lizzie muttered, gritting her teeth, as she heaved herself up the steps on her bottom.

"Come on Shrimp. You can do it," Tom, as always, was egging her on.

"Not elegant, but expedient," Lizzie giggled to her brother. Thank heavens that when she found her place, it was one of those modern seats where the arm could be raised up out of her way, so that she could haul herself up and settle into the seat unaided.

"I shall expect at least one postcard. I shall miss you," Betty called out.

As the coach drew away from the station, they didn't notice the big, black car, parked in the road beside the station, its occupants hidden by darkened glass. Nor did they notice the same vehicle following behind the coach … out of the town and onto the motorway … on and on towards the South West.

20

A Welcome

Lizzie had made the arrangements herself. She'd booked their accommodation online: a cabin on the edge of a village. It looked as if it was close to the sea: almost opposite the island and, of course, Tregarrow House. Someone who ran a taxi service would pick them up from the nearest town.

"You'll not be staying long, I s'pose?" The taxi driver was short on smiles. He was a small and wiry man, wearing clean, blue overalls. An old cloth cap was fixed to his head.

The man was clearly disabled himself. His body was twisted out of line. Every step was clearly an effort. His brown face was lined with pain. He struggled with Lizzie's chair in silence: trying to fit it into the boot, but refusing any assistance.

"I bet he sleeps in that cap," Tom whispered.

"Shssh! Tom," Lizzie giggled.

"I'm not sure," she answered the man. "I've booked for a week. But it could be two. It just depends how long it takes. We're on a mission, do you see. Perhaps you might be able to help?"

"Mebbe," the man said grudgingly, as he started up the engine and drove slowly out of the station. "But we're not much used to visitors here."

It was anything but a welcome.

"You don't belong to that twitching band, do ee? They'm a daft lot." The man's voice was grumpy.

"Twitching band? What do you mean?" Lizzie asked, nonplussed by the question.

"You know. They bird watching people. Emmets causing nothing but trouble." The man's voice was sulky now.

"I think you must mean twitchers, don't you?" she said.

"Something like that," the man mumbled crossly. "Always rambling on about choughs."

"Choughs," said Lizzie. "Aren't they extinct?"

"Course they are," the man growled back.

"Well, I'm certainly not a twitcher." The driver was irritating Lizzie. "Investigator would be closer," she said in a very positive voice, determined not to give in to the man.

Lizzie, watching the man's lined face reflected in the driving mirror beneath the rim of the old cloth cap, saw his fleeting look of dismay, tinged with what she could only call fury. His eyes hardened. He drove in silence.

Once out of the town and into the country, the landscape opened up before them: a stunning patchwork of fields and woodland and in the distance the rugged moor. As they drove steadily on, Lizzie pushed the man from her thoughts. She sat back beaming with delight, thrilled by the colourful panorama.

Tomorrow would be the last day of April. The roadside banks were full of colour. It was nearly bluebell time. The purple buds of the bells to come, jostled with glowing buttercups, caught in the light of the evening sun—a flash of gold in the lush vegetation that rippled in the wake of the car.

21

A Warning

It was late in the evening when Lizzie and Tom arrived at their final destination: a fishing village beside the sea. It was approached down a steep, narrow lane: little more than a rough track. Lizzie could see the line of a quay; the lights of boats tied up in the harbour.

Their taxi drove slowly into the village, passing a string of small cottages.

Nothing moved on the cobbled street. Curtained squares glowed warm in the dark. As the car cruised quietly by, lights were extinguished in some of the windows. Curtains twitched. Pale faces gazed.

The car drove steadily through the village and out along the coastal road. Lizzie lowered the window beside her, her eyes searching for the island. She knew it must be out there somewhere.

She could see and hear the waves on the shore. She could smell the salty, seaweed tang. But heavy clouds obscured the moon. Though she fancied she caught a fleeting glimpse—a shapeless mass across the water.

"Look, it's the island," she whispered to Tom.

An angry voice barked out at her:

"Shut that window. You'll let in the cold."

Lizzie closed the window quickly, taken aback by the man's sharp tone.

"And, besides, we're nearly there," the driver added hastily, putting a smile back into his voice, although it sounded like an effort.

The brand new wooden cabin, which Lizzie had booked for their week's stay, stood on the outskirts of the village. The owner was outside ready to meet them when the car drew up at her gate, almost as if she had had prior warning of their imminent arrival. In the dusky gloom of the lane, Lizzie got a general impression of a short and shapeless figure with long hair piled on top of her head.

"I'm Hester Rowe," the woman said pleasantly, but without offering Lizzie her hand. "I'm glad to see that my brother found you."

As soon as they entered the short drive, security floodlights lit the area: one lighting the owner's cottage which stood on the right, end on to the lane; another illuminating the cabin, which stood in the garden opposite and towards which they were making their way, when Mrs Rowe suddenly stopped.

"You just hold on here a minute. I need to have a quick word with Wes." She trotted hastily back to the car. Lizzie could see the pair of them, huddled, deep in conversation. But she was very soon back again.

"I do hope Wesley's looked after you? I know he can be cantankerous.

Those old wounds do trouble him some. But he's a very good man at heart."

She bustled ahead into the cabin, holding the door wide open for Lizzie.

"Let me show you around the place. I'm sure you must be tired and hungry. I've left a tray with some supper for you." The woman's tone seemed friendly enough. "I hope you're going to enjoy my cabin," she said, eyeing Lizzie uncertainly. "It's brand, spanking new," she added with pride.

Lizzie liked the look of the place. It was a single storey building with a light and airy aspect and, as she said later to Tom, it smelt delicious—of fresh pinewood. There was a good sized bed-sitting room with a couple of single beds, one on either side of the room, a small kitchen and a bathroom.

"This is perfect," Lizzie said, reassuring Mrs Rowe.

"Breakfast will be served in the cottage," the woman said. "At nine o'clock sharp."

"Is there a ramp to your door?" Lizzie asked.

"Oh yes," Mrs Rowe bristled. "You'll find that our brochure's as good as its word."

"That's a relief," Lizzie said with a smile. She could manage a single step with ease, but she still had problems if there were several.

" 'Twas the only way we could get our permission and our grant to build the cabin," Mrs Rowe was quick to explain. "The planners are all PC these days." She curled her lips in disapproval.

"All new places meant for visitors must have proper wheelchair access," she continued. "It's all a bit much, if you ask me. Although," she changed her tone quickly, suddenly aware of what she was saying, "I s'pose it's quite a good idea … for somebody like you, I mean, " she added as an afterthought, sighing and smiling down at Lizzie.

Lizzie was used to patronising comments. She usually did her best to ignore them. But she was always irritated by that silly term PC.

"Politically correct! Ugh!" She gritted her teeth and mumbled crossly. She felt Tom's hand tighten on her shoulder. She could almost hear his disdainful chuckle. It helped her to smile back at Mrs Rowe—sweetly.

"I gather you're an investigator?" the woman said with a sly look.

"Goodness," Lizzie murmured to Tom. "News travels fast here. I wish I hadn't said that now."

"And what might you want to investigate here?" Mrs Rowe asked suspiciously.

"We're looking for a man called Bob Tregarrow. Perhaps you know him?" Lizzie suggested.

The woman turned abruptly to Lizzie. The name appeared to have caught her off-guard. Her eyes narrowed thoughtfully.

"We've not seen him for a brave few years," she said. "You'd do better to try elsewhere. Though, of course, they do say that he's dead. Died in Africa, I believe. Roasted alive in one of they deserts, I shouldn't wonder," she cackled with glee. "And I'd have to say that I'm glad. Good riddance to bad rubbish!"

Hester Rowe was on a roll now. "A regular rogue, he was," she muttered, her face twisted in disgust. "It was shameful what he did. He don't deserve the name of Tregarrow. We'd never want him here again."

Lizzie was stunned by the woman's performance. She remembered the cuttings in the scrapbook: the very harsh comments made at the time by the local Cornish people about the man that they'd once called a hero. But she hadn't expected such a violent response—not now—after all these years.

"Is there someone else we could ask?" Lizzie asked innocently. "Perhaps they'd help us in the pub—you do have one of those, don't you?"

"Yes, we do," Mrs Rowe bristled. "But nobody will help you there. You'd do best to keep away." The woman was glaring down at Lizzie.

"We're respectable God-fearing folk. Only the men go into the pub. It's not a suitable place for a maid," Hester Rowe added, looking shocked.

"Why don't you just have a nice few days' holiday?" The woman's voice had softened now. "I'm well-known in these parts for my cooking," she smirked. "I'll make you some of my famous dishes—my pies, my pasties and the like. You could have apple crumble and cream. And then there's old Jago down by the quay. He makes a lovely fish and chips. The fish comes fresh off the boat each morning.

"Enjoy a holiday while you're here," she continued. "Then go back home and forget this place. That would be my advice to you.

"But," she added with a glare, pursing her mouth in an unpleasant grimace, "if you meddle where you're not wanted, you could be making a big mistake. I'd hate to see you come to harm … especially in your circumstances," she added as an afterthought, glancing down at Lizzie's chair.

"Goodness!" Lizzie said with a frown, when the woman had gone away. "What was all that about Tom, do you think?"

22

A Disappointment

izzie was up at dawn next morning, longing to get her first look at the island.

"Oh Tom. Just look," she cried out in surprise, sitting in the open doorway and looking out across the bay.

Her mouth dropped open in dismay. They'd talked about the island so much. They'd gazed at maps and a photograph, which showed their parents in a doorway. They'd visualised a friendly island, on which there stood a splendid house—more or less a stately home. Tregarrow House—it sounded grand.

Lizzie had thought about it a lot: imagining how she would first see the island across a blue and beautiful ocean, tipped by dancing, crested waves. How she would see the elegant house, snuggled in green vegetation, facing south with the sun on its walls. How that sight would fill her with joy.

The reality was very different. The sea was dark and smooth and glassy. A long way out across the bay, further than she had expected, the island almost seemed to be floating, wreathed in bands of pale grey mist. A craggy hill of dark boulders rose up out of a lifeless sea, topped by a rugged outcrop of rock. And from the living rock there grew the ruins of an ancient castle.

Lizzie was stunned. She just sat staring: trying to curb her disappointment;

stifling a rising shiver.

"Oh Tom," she moaned, shaking her head. "What a bleak, unfriendly place. It's not at all what we expected."

"No," Tom agreed. "It certainly isn't."

Food To Die For

Mrs Rowe's kitchen was a colourful room. Blue gingham curtains hung at the windows. The floor was constructed of big, grey slates, their straight edges, tightly butted. It almost shone with cleanliness.

The room was also a living room. Two ancient and sagging armchairs stood one on either side of the Rayburn—the old-fashioned, solid fuel cooker. There was a stack of ready cut wood. Lizzie noticed a rack of old pipes on the wall beside one of the chairs. A work basket stood by the other chair, its lid forced up by its bulging contents: knitting needles, wool and the like.

Worktops ran along the walls and, above them, wooden shelves. They were wide and deep on one side of the cooker and packed with a big assortment of books. Some, Lizzie thought, must be antiques: the big, leather-bound, baggy tomes were mixed with modern paperbacks.

On the other side of the cooker, narrow shelving reached to the ceiling. It was chock-a-block with small glass jars, each containing some mystery substance, ranging from dried, discoloured leaves to fine powders in many colours. Each jar with its tight glass stopper bore a dusty, handwritten label.

Bundles of herbs hung down from the rafters, together with strings of bead-like berries, a bright orange-red in colour. A pale-green glass globe, like those that are used as floats by fishermen, hung in a net amongst the herbs. It swung in the warm air from the cooker, together

with other unusual items that Lizzie didn't recognise.

Two large mortars stood on the dresser—those special bowls that are used for grinding—together with substantial pestles—the club shaped instruments used for pounding. Cooks used them, Lizzie remembered. She'd seen them on the television.

A long, pine table ran down the room, its surface scrubbed to a light honey buff. Several old-fashioned, wooden chairs were ranged neatly around the table, each with a bright, floral-patterned seat-cushion. One of the chairs had been moved away, leaving a gap for Lizzie's wheelchair.

Hester Rowe was very busy. A kettle sang on the Rayburn cooker. Bacon frizzled in a pan, filling the room with a lovely aroma.

The breakfast table looked inviting. A large bowl of fresh herbs sat at one end of the table. It contained a wide variety of leaves of many shapes and colours and textures and, in one case, even flowers—tiny and mauve on a bushy stem. Lizzie thought she could smell the thyme mingling with the frying bacon.

The cutlery on the table shone. All the china cups and plates were cream in colour with broad blue stripes, matching the ones displayed on the dresser. The gingham napkins matched the curtains. Woven rush place mats provided the happy expectation of the delicious, cooked breakfast, which was soon to follow on—after the cereals, fruit and yoghurt.

A burning hot plate was placed before Lizzie. There were eggs from the hens she could see through the window, pecking in the field next door; eggs fried just the way she liked them. And there was plenty of crispy bacon: from local pigs, so their landlady said; and tomatoes roasted in the Rayburn. Caramelised with blackened skins, they were one of Tom's favourite foods.

"Awesome!" Lizzie heard him mutter.

"Oh boy! What a sumptuous meal." Lizzie tucked in with pleasure. She wasn't used to a cooked breakfast, although she knew that her brother would love it.

The sight of Tom tucking into his food had always given their Mum great pleasure. She and Lizzie had laughed together about his amazing appetite. "Where on earth does he put it all?" their mother had often exclaimed with delight, admiring her son's slim, athletic figure.

Lizzie sat remembering, smiling, as Mrs Rowe cleared the table.

"Goodness! Is there more?" she asked, noticing a small loaf, which stood on a rack beside the cooker—bread, still obviously warm from the oven.

The loaf was lifted tenderly, placed on a spotless wooden board and carried proudly to the table, where, with all due ceremony, Mrs Rowe took up a knife and chopped it into steaming chunks.

"See what you think of this, m'dear," she passed the board across to Lizzie. "This is my prize-winning bread," she beamed. "I won the cup again last year. The Best Baker in the County."

She scuttled hastily out of the room, only to return seconds later clutching a very large silver trophy.

"We keep it in our front room," she said. "I think it's safer there," she added, standing it carefully on the table, close enough for Lizzie to admire, but not quite close enough to handle.

"And look! You have another treat there." Hester pointed to the butter reposing in a blue striped bowl: a large pat, several inches square—a wonderful golden yellow in colour.

"That's freshly churned butter," she said. "It was made by my sister Dority. She and Hedley farm close by. They have the finest beasts in the county. They win all the prizes for cream and butter. 'Naughty but Nice' as they used to say," she added with a coy giggle, slapping her all too generous rump, before lifting the silver cup and carrying it carefully back to its sanctuary.

With a chunk of fresh bread on her plate, Lizzie was placed in a dilemma. A group of obviously home-made conserves stood in the middle of the table, all of them looking so enticing. There was marmalade, thick with fruit and, so she learnt, sweetened with honey. There was blackberry jelly and raspberry jam; dark-red strawberry and purple plum. Their jewel-like colours glowed through the glass. Lizzie didn't know which to try first.

While Mrs Rowe was out of the room, she had a bit of a giggle with Tom. "I bet you, Tom, whichever I choose, it will turn out to be a prize-winning jam. The front room's probably stuffed with trophies."

A large tub of honeycomb trimmings stood beside the pots of jam. Lizzie had always loved honey, but never eaten it on the comb. Closely watched by Mrs Rowe, who was proud of her hives of bees and of the quality of her honey, Lizzie spread a crust from the loaf: first with lashings of golden butter that melted quickly into the bread; and then with a spoon of the honeycomb, which she mounded on the top.

"Scrumptious," she murmured happily. She had simply never known that honey could be so deliciously crunchy. Washed down with a cup of tea, it was a perfect end to the meal.

As Tom would say privately later on, "That was food to die for, Shrimp."

24

A Touch of the Raven

Having eaten more than was wise, Lizzie sat at the table resting: quietly watching Hester Rowe, as she bustled about the kitchen, cleaning the cooker and washing dishes. She looked as if she were in her late forties: a short and somewhat dumpy figure. Although her arms and legs were slim, she had a large and rounded bottom. Lizzie tried to avert her gaze. Her Mum would have commented 'broad in the beam'.

"Doubtless from all that Cornish cream and the occasional succulent pasty," she heard Tom whisper with a chuckle.

Mrs Rowe wore narrow bottomed, baggy trousers, a dull denim blue in colour. Her open-necked shirt was a faded, pink check. An old fawn coloured cardigan, which had clearly seen better days, hung loosely about her hips.

This simple combination of clothing, all rather plain and worn, should have produced a most ordinary sight. And yet, as Lizzie puzzled later, mulling the whole thing over with Tom, she seemed an unusually colourful character with a strangely flamboyant air. It was not precisely what you'd expect in a Cornish fisherman's wife.

There were other unusual things about Mrs Rowe. Her hair was thick, a lustrous black, but with a very slight edge of red. A touch of the raven. A hint of rowan. Lizzie spotted silver strands.

The hair was obviously very long. Drawn tightly back from her face, it was rolled up into a big, fat bun and piled up high on top of her head. The bun was encased in a coarse, silver net, itself held vigorously in check by a host of metal hairpins. A large, carved, wooden, hair comb, stood up proud at the back of the bun, holding it firmly in its place. The comb kept catching Lizzie's attention, decorated as it was with a most peculiar design: a complex, curvilinear pattern, the lines carved deeply into the wood.

"Isn't that strange," Lizzie murmured to Tom, unable to hold back a shiver.

Mrs Rowe's complexion was clear: her cheeks plump and rather pink. Her eyes, under their hooded lids, were unusually dark and piercing, although the host of laughter lines must, as Lizzie knew perfectly well, be testimony to a sense of humour.

"And what are your plans for today?" Mrs Rowe asked, turning unexpectedly and catching Lizzie's blatant gaze.

"Exploration," Lizzie said hurriedly, aware that she'd been staring rudely. "This seems like such an interesting place. And the weather is picking up. The sky's clear now. The sun is shining. It's going to be a beautiful day."

Hester Rowe was looking doubtful.

"It might look almost like summer today, but we get some nasty weather in May," she warned. "It can be a tricky month. I think tomorrow's going to be bad. Rough with gales, I shouldn't wonder. Even today, you ought to take care. Don't go far. That's my advice."

"I'm going to explore along the road. I can take a better look at that island from somewhere closer—down on the shore. Is there a causeway across to the island? We thought we could see one on the map."

"There *was* an ancient causeway … once. But it's long since been destroyed," Mrs Rowe insisted firmly. "No one's travelled that path for years. Don't go near it, whatever you do." The piercing eyes were turned on Lizzie. "Too many people have drowned on this coast. You wouldn't stand a chance out there."

"I don't intend to try it today," Lizzie said. "I think I'll go and explore the lanes."

"You won't find that easy in your wheelchair," Mrs Rowe returned, looking flustered.

"Wouldn't you like to sit in the garden? I could bring you some coffee and cakes, or some of my famous buns," she wheedled.

"Thank you, no," Lizzie laughed. "After that fantastic breakfast, I'll never eat again," she joked.

Back in the cabin, Lizzie prepared herself for her trip.

"Tom, it's such a glorious day. Perhaps you should go for a run," she suggested. She knew he'd be longing for exercise.

"I'll be fine," she reassured him. "I'm going out for a run myself. I'm going to exercise my wheels." They laughed together at the joke.

25

The Cottage

It pleased Lizzie to think about Tom—out there enjoying himself. She visualised the tall, strong figure, jogging along towards the village wearing his favourite pair of trainers, his navy shorts and a clean white T-shirt. An old sweatshirt would be tied round his waist. His dark, shoulder-length, curly hair would be held back by that scarlet band—the one that she'd given him for his birthday.

Tom would want to explore the village and the harbour and the boats. He'd be stopping to chat-up the local girls. Lizzie had never ceased to wonder at the effect that her big brother had. His broad grin and brown, smiling eyes had always stood him in good stead. He'd soon be surrounded by girls of all ages. Even grannies found him charming.

And he'd be talking to old boys too: gleaning information where possible; doing his best detective act, whilst finding a welcome sense of freedom that he could never hope to find, if he were tied to her apron strings. They'd still have their lovely chats in the evenings, when they'd discuss the days' adventures. For now she banished him from her thoughts, as she set out in the opposite direction, wheeling briskly in the sunshine along the road beside the sea that rippled and glittered to her left.

To Lizzie's considerable irritation, Hester Rowe was being proved right: for although the road was fairly level, the surface was extremely poor with ruts and cracks and lumps and bumps. The wheelchair ground its way along. She was finding it hard going.

After a few hundred yards she stopped. A concrete ramp led onto the beach. The tide, so it seemed, was going out. As the water sucked back down the shore, Lizzie fancied that she could see the beginnings of a pathway of boulders—packed tight—the start of the causeway that linked the island with the mainland.

When sorting through her mother's belongings, Lizzie had been pleased to find an old pair of binoculars.

"I bet they'll be useful on our trip," she'd said to Tom, when packing their cases. Wriggling awkwardly in her seat, she fumbled now for them in the bag that hung across the back of her chair.

"How maddening," she mumbled. She must have left them in the cabin. That was so frustrating because, away from the prying eyes of the village, this was an ideal opportunity to examine the island more closely. It was a perfect vantage point. She mustn't forget to bring them next time.

Lizzie sat at the top of the ramp, looking out towards the island, enjoying the sun and breeze on her face. Set now in a turquoise ocean and framed by the bluebell-blue of the sky, the island didn't look so grim. The sun-kissed boulders looked almost friendly.

She sat with her eyes fixed on the island: watching out for any movement; wishing she had the binoculars. But there was little to be seen: only a few, winged, listless shapes, cruising over the battlements. She could hear occasional distant cries: the haunting calls of circling birds, carried towards her on the wind; mingling with the voices of waves breaking gently on the shore.

"Ummm. Wonderful," Lizzie sighed, breathing deeply with enjoyment: the fresh, salty tang of the ocean; the wafting pong of rotting seaweed banked towards the back of the beach.

With the tide retreating fast, Lizzie could now see the causeway clearly. It looked surprisingly sound and smooth, the waves glinting on rounded pebbles. Lizzie frowned as she watched it emerging, remembering Mrs Rowe's words of warning.

"Why did she tell me all that rubbish?" Lizzie asked herself out loud. "Saying the causeway had been destroyed? It looks pretty good to me."

Despite the brightness of the sun, the onshore breeze was crisp and cold. Lizzie soon felt stiff and chilled. She set off briskly in her chair.

Further on along the road, she came to a halt by a small wooden gate. Set well back, away from the road, a building was almost hidden from view behind a screen of evergreen trees that formed a dense, dark, windswept barrier, through which the narrow gate gave access. An old board attached to the gate might have once proclaimed a name. Now the letters were worn away. By man or the weather? Or possibly both.

A path led up to a cottage door. The grass on either side of the path had obviously been recently cut, but it wouldn't count as a lawn. The garden itself was plain but tidy.

"Well, I wonder …" Lizzie mused, leaning forward as far as she dared and peering through the overgrown foliage that hemmed the gate on either side. Was there something about the cottage—something that she recognised? Perhaps the peculiar form of the porch, flanked as it was on either side by very tall, flat slabs of stone and topped with a matching grey slate hat.

Had she seen it in a picture? Or maybe even a photograph? Or had she seen it in her dreams?

"What a sad and lonely place," Lizzie whispered to herself. With curtains closed at all the windows, the cottage had a lifeless look, as if its eyes were shut and sightless; as if it had been long deserted.

A movement caught her unawares.

"Uhhh!" Alarmed, she held her breath, as the fingers of a hand appeared at one of the upstairs windows. They drew the curtain slowly aside, revealing the form of a shadowy figure standing back inside the room. A face stared briefly out at Lizzie, before the curtain fell back into place.

The brief glimpse was more than enough. The apparition wasn't friendly.

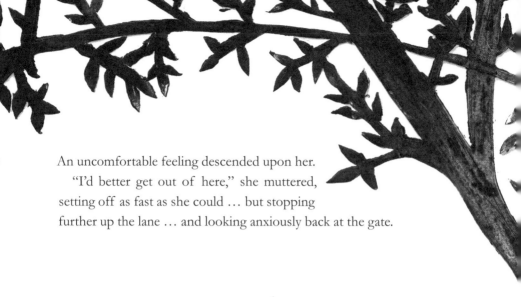

An uncomfortable feeling descended upon her.

"I'd better get out of here," she muttered, setting off as fast as she could … but stopping further up the lane … and looking anxiously back at the gate.

26

A Shocking Sight

A few hundred yards further on, a narrow lane joined the road. It sloped up gently away from the shore. In the hope of finding shelter away from the chill of the cutting sea breeze and away from the hostile cottage, Lizzie swung herself into the lane.

It was not much more than a rough track, twisting and turning ahead of her. Grass and weeds grew down the middle. But she pressed on hopefully: finding tarmac where she could; confident that it was leading her somewhere. Perhaps to a farmhouse? To friendly people?

The steep banks on either side towered up high above her head. They were thick with lush, green, spear-like leaves from which there thrust a host of stalks, many bearing purple buds. Other stalks bore full blooms, their heads of dainty, bell-like flowers nodding blue on slender necks. The bluebells would soon be at their best.

Lizzie had never seen such hedgerows. They positively glowed with colour: the shocking-pink of campion, standing proud above the blues; the stunning gold of buttercups. Lacy sprays of tiny white flowers wove their way

through everything.

And ferns were sprouting everywhere: their brown-green fronds unfurling and pushing through the riot of vegetation. Lizzie smiled with delight at those. Her Mum had had a passion for ferns.

When she had been ten years old, she and Tom had schemed together. They'd saved their pocket money for months in order to buy a length of material, which they knew their Mum would love, because of the pretty pattern of ferns.

The birthday present was a great success. Their mother was obviously delighted. She made the material into curtains, which she hung in the family bathroom.

When Lizzie had moved away from the house, she couldn't bear to leave the curtains. She'd had them carefully taken down, tenderly folded and packed for the move. Taken apart and remade—with a lot of help from Betty—the curtains now hung in her new home, brightening up her tiny bathroom.

Lizzie sat remembering. Enjoying the ferny-feathered banks. Hedgerow shrubs made the tall banks higher: blackthorn, buckthorn, elder and may. The may was garlanded with blossom, creamy white and buzzing with bees.

Rounding another bend in the lane, Lizzie found an enormous tree: a huge ash growing out of the bank. Coppiced over centuries, it spread its ancient, gnarled arms wide. She peered up into the lofty branches.

The breeze ruffled the infant leaves so recently spouted on its twigs. And yet the tree seemed strangely still. It crouched along the top of the bank, like some wizened, grey-skinned crone … inviting her into a cold embrace.

The armpits harboured mysterious holes—perhaps the homes of owls or squirrels. They were rimmed around with feathering plants: miniature ferns and draping lichen. Plush, green, velveteen moss-creep clothed the tops of the spreading arms, as if the old girl were dressed for a party.

"Perhaps she's sleeping," Lizzie whispered. "Maybe I can slip past quietly."

She wheeled herself hurriedly on up the lane. Her mind was alive with thoughts of the crone. She didn't dare to look over her shoulder, afraid lest she see the ash tree spirit … slipping silently down from the bank …

following stealthily behind.

"Sanctuary at last. Thank heavens," Lizzie murmured to herself, as finding a convenient gateway she turned in towards the gate and settled herself to enjoy the sunshine. Nestled in a sheltered corner, with her back to a granite post and with foliage tapping her shoulder, Lizzie wrinkled her nose with delight, sniffing the earthy smell of the bank.

Although it was covered in greenery, it wasn't simply a grassy bank; it must have been built a long time ago from large blocks of rough-hewn stone. Massing grasses and wild flowers sprouted out of every crack, spreading across the rocky face, masking the structure of the bank. Here and there big stones protruded, providing useful platforms for creatures. Only inches from her head, a tiny lizard basked in the sun.

Lizzie closed her eyes and dozed. She could smell the scent of the blossoming may in the hedgerow above her head. She could hear the contented humming of bees.

This was such a heavenly place. Nobody passed to destroy the peace. As she sat enjoying the sun and feasting on the delicious smells, the lines of a poem came into her mind.

The verse, so Lizzie had been told, was the work of a little known woman poet—way back in the twentieth century. Granny had passed it on to her Mum, soon after Lizzie's Dad had died. And although she had learnt the verse as a child, Lizzie had never thought much about it. Now, as she spoke the simple words, they suddenly seemed important to her.

"Let us seek out simple beauty,
Whether made by Man or Nature,
Let us feast upon the sight
To feed our minds and strengthen hearts,
To manage the dark days in our lives
And drive our purpose towards the light."

This lane, these flowers were simple beauty. Lizzie feasted and felt happy— better than she'd felt for months.

Fully awake now and feeling refreshed, she set off up the lane again,

determined to go just that little bit further. The lane twisted and turned on its way, rising slowly but not too steeply. Lizzie hoped that she wouldn't meet traffic. With a vehicle in the lane, there'd scarcely be enough room for a walker, let alone a bulky wheelchair.

Nothing came. She felt quite safe: pressing on as fast as she could; wanting to know where the lane would lead her. Rounding yet another bend, she came to a sudden grinding halt.

"Whatever is that?" she gasped out loud, confronted by a shocking sight.

Only a few feet ahead of her, an obstacle was blocking her way. A cord was stretched across the lane, some two or three feet above the ground. It wasn't so much the sight of the cord that had stopped Lizzie in her tracks, but rather the objects that hung from the cord. Were they tiny, dangling bodies?

Her mouth had gone dry. She licked her lips. Then she started slowly forward to take a better, closer look.

"Oh dear! Oh dear! Oh dear!" she mumbled.

Several bodies hung from the cord. Lizzie knew they must be moles. Their once beautiful, black velvet jackets were bruised and marked by a violent death.

Her eyes were slowly filling with tears. "Who could have done such a horrible thing?" she whispered out aloud to herself.

Wiping her eyes with the back of her hand, she tried to focus on the bodies. The sight of them made her feel quite sick. Some appeared to be freshly killed, with gaping mouths and bloody chins. Others might have been dead for days: stiff and swollen, almost putrid, with rigid limbs stuck out either side.

One of the bodies was heaving with maggots. A swarm of bluebottles rose to greet her. They circled excitedly round her head.

"Yuk! Gross!" Lizzie muttered. She tore a bracken stem from the bank and used it to swot at the beastly things: backing quickly away from the line, as the flies zoomed back to the stinking bodies.

She sat staring from a distance. It wasn't just a nasty sight. Lizzie found it frightening too. The line was clearly meant as a barrier: a cruel attempt to drive people away?

Aware of a noise in the lane behind her, Lizzie quickly swung her chair. Was it the crunch of feet on tarmac? Footfalls, muffled by grass on the track?

27

A Long, Grey, Scrawny Arm …

hen Lizzie turned there was nobody there. Nothing stirred in the lane itself. She sat still, listening carefully.

Bees droned busily in the hedgerow. Swallows swooped and chattered above. Lizzie could hear the song of a lark, though she couldn't spot the little bird that was hovering somewhere high in the sky. Bluebottles buzzed—but that was all.

With a last, unhappy look over her shoulder, she made her way back down the lane. The place had suddenly lost its charm. All she wanted now was escape.

The downhill slope aided her progress. It was surprising how fast she could travel, when she got herself properly going. Relieved to be leaving the horrible scene, she free wheeled boldly around the corners, singing at the top of her voice: "Wheeeeeeee !"

Suddenly there was another obstruction. She only just managed to stop in time … lurching to a grinding halt … very nearly thrown from her chair.

"Oh no! Not again!" The colour drained from Lizzie's face.

Another line just like the first was spanning the lane and blocking her way. It was stretched beneath the ancient ash. Small dead bodies swung on the line—some slimy, swollen and dripping.

The sight of this second sickening barrier made her feel even worse than the first. It wasn't just nasty. It was spooky … as if some evil force were at work. Perhaps the old grey crone in the tree?

Lizzie had never believed in magic. Thoughts of witchcraft had left her cold. But now she couldn't help wondering…

She grunted angrily to herself: "Must pull myself together." She glanced warily up at the ash tree, crouching on the bank above.

'There's always a rational explanation'. That was one of Tom's favourite sayings.

Holding on to those calming words, Lizzie tried to assess the scene. A sudden thought came to her. There were several moles on each of the lines. If somebody wanted so many moles, catching them would take time and effort. They wouldn't be sitting there ready, would they? Simply waiting to be caught?

When she inspected the creatures more closely, she thought that some looked strangely bedraggled—almost as if they'd been packed and stored. Had they perhaps been kept in a freezer?

Finding a way past the gruesome obstacle wasn't easy. 'Come on Shrimp. You can do it.' She could hear the familiar words in her head as she struggled to position her chair below the mighty, groping ash. She had to get tight into the bank—close enough to untie the line.

The cord was securely tied to the tree, knotted around a slender root that curved across the face of the bank. The root then disappeared back in the bank, thrusting through the mossy matting, as if it were holding the tree in place.

"It's like a long, thin, bony toe." Lizzie's imagination was spinning.

"Oh! Oh!" She puffed and panted: struggling desperately with the knots … looking up anxiously into the branches. It wouldn't be wise to upset the old crone.

"I'm sorry. I'm doing my best," she muttered, trying to reassure the tree … alarmed by the very unpleasant thought of a long, grey, scrawny arm descending on her from above.

At last the line came free in her hand. But even then it wasn't easy: lifting and holding the line well clear without getting it caught in her wheels or wrapping itself around her legs. As she swung the cord away, the grizzly bodies jiggled and danced. They even threatened to bounce in her face.

Hardly daring to look at the tree, Lizzie made a run for it. Powering her wheels along with her hands and muttering miserably under her breath, she jolted clumsily down the track. In danger of spilling out of her chair, she only just managed some of the corners. But she didn't dare to stop... or look back.

By the time she arrived at Mrs Rowe's gate, Lizzie was sobbing and gasping for breath. Her hair, which had escaped its band, hung loose and wild about her shoulders; it clung to her sweating brow and cheeks.

Hester Rowe stood by the gate.

"Why m'dear!" the woman exclaimed, her face a contorted mask of concern. "You look as if you've seen a ghost."

As Lizzie shot in through the gate, Mrs Rowe called after her: "I've left the fish and chips on your table. I hope you'll feel well enough to eat."

Lizzie was undoubtedly shaken. It took her a little while to recover. But over their lunch of fish and chips, which also included some mushy peas, Lizzie told Tom about the moles.

"I don't like the sound of that," he said. "I think it's some kind of primitive warning. I think we need to be very careful."

28

Wise Women

"Have you by any chance seen my binoculars?" Lizzie asked Hester Rowe over breakfast the following morning.

"No m'dear. That I haven't." The woman's voice was positive, although her face was out of sight, as she worked at the stove with her back turned to Lizzie.

"I seem to have lost them," Lizzie said. "It's very strange. I know I had them."

"P'rhaps you dropped them yesterday." Mrs Rowe suggested brightly, heaping bacon on Lizzie's plate.

"No. I didn't take them," Lizzie said. "I know, 'cos I wanted them while I was out—to take a closer look at that island."

Hester Rowe looked up sharply.

"I thought I had them in my bag," Lizzie continued. "But I must have left them in the cabin. Now they seem to have disappeared."

"Most likely you dropped them in your excitement. You did come back in a terrible rush. Looking flustered and quite upset. As if you had had a nasty experience?"

The question hung in the air, unanswered.

"Strange things happen round these parts." The woman's voice had dropped to a whisper. Her eyes, like slits, watched Lizzie closely.

"There are Wise Women here about." She nodded knowingly at Lizzie.

"Wise women?" Lizzie queried.

"Some of them use powerful spells. It doesn't do to upset them, you know." She smiled at the girl's frozen face.

"You meet them sometimes, in these lanes." She waved her arms dramatically, as if embracing the surrounding countryside.

"P'rhaps you met one yesterday?"

"I don't believe in all that stuff," Lizzie insisted with a grimace.

"Do you not?" Mrs Rowe said, surprised. "Most of them live out on the moor. Although not all," she added quietly.

" 'Tis said they inhabit the circles of stones that have stood on the moor since time began." The woman gave a dramatic shudder.

Lizzie couldn't restrain a shiver. She stopped chomping on her bacon. "It's alright, Shrimp," she heard Tom's whisper.

Hester Rowe sat down at the table, opposite Lizzie and leaning towards her.

"Once, when I was only a child and staying with my Auntie Maud in her cottage at Bolventor, I strayed up onto the high moor," Mrs Rowe continued quietly, her eyes alight with the memory.

"It was foggy and I was lost. My mother had always said to me, 'Whatever you do, keep away from they stones. Never, never go into the circle, unless the sun is shining bright, unless the sky is clear and blue.' But what with the mist and my eyes full of tears—because I was lost and frightened and lonely—I'd crossed the threshold before I knew it."

Mrs Rowe's gasp was full of drama. "Ahhhh! Ahhhh!" the woman moaned.

The gasp took Lizzie by surprise. She sat rigid at the table, her food abandoned on her plate. Her heart beat fast. Her eyes stared wide.

"I have never been so afeared in my life," Hester continued in a stage whisper.

"For, suddenly, when the cloud lifted, I found myself in the very middle, surrounded by a circle of stones. They were tall and grey. They towered around me. And, do you know what? They were coming towards me. Closing in on me … bit by bit …

"I could hear their ghostly voices—almost like a choir they were—chanting mysterious incantations. They edged ever closer, surrounding me … as if they were drawing me into their fold … as if they would never let me go … "

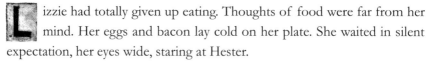

29

Manifestations

Lizzie had totally given up eating. Thoughts of food were far from her mind. Her eggs and bacon lay cold on her plate. She waited in silent expectation, her eyes wide, staring at Hester.

After a long and dramatic pause, the woman sighed deeply and shook her head. "I probably shouldn't be telling you this. I don't want to frighten you, after all," she added with a weak smile.

"But tell me how you escaped," begged Lizzie, much affected by the tale and longing for Tom's comforting hand.

"That I don't know, to this very day," Mrs Rowe continued thoughtfully. "I think I must have fainted away. I felt as if I was being carried … floating through the swirling mist. When I came to, I was outside the circle. And then I remember running fast, not stopping till I got back to Auntie and never daring to look behind me."

"Whatever did your Auntie say?"

"Not a lot. She weren't pleased. But she could see I was terrified. It took me several days to recover. Come to think of it," Hester added, "I never felt quite the same again."

"And are you honestly telling me that even in these modern times, people still believe in these spirits?" Lizzie asked uncertainly, doing her best to steady her voice.

"Indeed they do," Mrs Rowe said. "And they believe in Wise Women too. And have you heard about the Charmers? There's one in almost every village—sometimes a woman, sometimes a man. They're often referred to as Cunning-folk. They use their healing skills and their knowledge—getting rid of warts and lumps, clearing ringworm and stopping bleeding, both in animals and people. They can do a power of good."

"My Mum would have called that mumbo jumbo," Lizzie said disparagingly. But, even as she spoke the words, she knew she'd made a foolish mistake.

Mrs Rowe's expression hardened. She glared at Lizzie through narrowed eyes.

"Never mock what you don't understand. You might find that you come to regret it.

"And never doubt the Wise Women." She emphasised the word never. "They use herbs and ancient spells—recipes that have been handed down from one generation to the next—often from father to daughter to son."

Lizzie sat fixed and still in her chair, as Hester's voice sank down to a whisper.

"They use their wisdom and their spells to summon up powerful manifestations." The word was rasped from the woman's throat.

"Manifestations?" Lizzie asked. "Whatever do you mean by that?"

"Visitors from the spirit world." Mrs Rowe nodded wisely. "They're invoked by the wise ones as a warning. And mark my words," she glared at Lizzie, "it doesn't pay to ignore their warnings."

Lizzie couldn't restrain a shudder. "I see," she said nervously, looking away—trying to avoid those glinting eyes.

The woman slid quickly around the table.

"The wise ones are a power for good. However," she hissed close to Lizzie's ear, "some have been taken over by evil. It is they who practice the black arts.

"They are dangerous. So … Beware!"

Lizzie sat clasping her hot mug of tea, grateful for the warmth of the liquid to counteract the chilling story. Hester Rowe moved away from the table. She stood with her back to the old Rayburn, propping her bottom against the rail and observing Lizzie closely. A faint smile curved her generous lips.

"The moor is a wild and mysterious place. You'd do best to keep away."

Those piercing eyes bored into Lizzie.

"And if you're beset by manifestations—whatever shape or form they may take—you should remember what I've said. You would ignore them at your peril."

Nicholas Culpeper

"Well! What did you think of all that, Tom?" Lizzie asked later back in the cabin. "Visitors from the spirit world? Whatever did she mean by that?

"It's very spooky, don't you think? I didn't like the sound of it," she continued. "I couldn't even finish my breakfast. I missed out on that wonderful honey," she added with a note of regret.

"I don't know what to think," Tom replied. "But you mustn't let her frighten you."

"No," Lizzie affirmed with vigour. "We mustn't let her drive us away."

"After yesterday's excitement, I think you should take it easy this morning," Tom advised his sister firmly. "We still have a long way to go with our quest. And you're going to need all your strength."

"Yes," Lizzie said. "I know you're right. What do you think we ought to do next?"

"I think we should visit the pub," Tom responded.

"You haven't forgotten Mrs Rowe's warning?" Lizzie asked. "She seemed to think that would be a mistake."

"No. I haven't forgotten," Tom said. "But we're not going to take any notice of her. Whatever she says, we'll go this evening."

When Lizzie had sent Tom off for a run, she pottered about outside in the garden, enjoying the old-fashioned cottage borders. Given another week or two, those borders would be a riot of colour. Pale mauve stocks were already in bloom. Delphiniums were growing strongly; later they'd add some fabulous blues. And hollyhocks were growing up on either side of each of the windows. They'd been one of her Mum's favourites plants—those with the wine-dark, almost black flowers that had grown in the garden of their home.

She paused in front of the door of the cottage. Picture book roses grew round the porch. It was too early for the blooms. But deep pink slits in clustering buds promised a fine show for the summer.

The old and crooked door to the cottage was painted a very jolly yellow. Intent on coping with the ramp and getting in for breakfast each morning, Lizzie had never studied the door. Now she noticed something unusual. A bundle of twigs was attached to the doorjamb. They were bound together with bright red thread.

As she sat staring at the twigs and wondering about their purpose, the door was suddenly flung wide open. Startled, Lizzie shrank back in her chair.

"I'm sorry if I made you jump." Mrs Rowe smiled warmly at Lizzie. "I noticed you enjoying my borders. Perhaps you'd like to see my garden?"

"Oh yes," Lizzie agreed hastily. "Yes please. I'd like to do that. But I thought that this was your garden?"

"Ah … well now … that's where you're wrong. It don't do to assume, you know." She beckoned Lizzie into the hall. "It's easier this way. Come on through."

With one last puzzled glance at the twigs, Lizzie followed Hester Rowe along the hallway towards the kitchen. The door to the front room was ajar. With her landlady walking in front, Lizzie felt free to pause for a second to crane her neck and peer into the room without the woman noticing.

A swirly carpet covered the floor in red and blue and green and gold. The modern fireplace was tiled in cream. High backed chairs on curving legs stood one on either side of the hearth. Their spotless velvet upholstery, in an elegant maroon, was protected by equally spotless covers: cream linen, edged with crochet; one on either arm of each chair; and there were other matching covers protecting the backs of each of the chairs from dirty heads or greasy hair. Lizzie remembered her mother using the old-fashioned term antimacassar.

A long row of silver cups was ranged along the mantelpiece: doubtless more of Mrs Rowe's trophies. Perhaps for her cakes and her honey and jams? The cups were reflected to great advantage in the fancy, gold framed mirror, which hung behind them on the wall.

"Looks good, my front room, don't it," Hester stated pointedly, facing Lizzie in the kitchen.

'She must have eyes in the back her head,' Tom would have said if he'd been there.

"Oh yes, beautiful," Lizzie mumbled, trying not to look too guilty at having been obviously caught out snooping.

"It looks like a lovely room," she said, "but I only caught a glimpse."

"Quite so. A glimpse," said Hester Rowe. "But a glimpse is often enough, don't you think?"

Lizzie didn't know how to answer. "What are you cooking?" she asked instead, noticing the pot on the stove and doing her best to change the subject.

"It's one of my special recipes," Hester Rowe said guardedly, giving Lizzie a sideways look.

"And is that your recipe book?" Lizzie asked, indicating an ancient tome that lay on the worktop beside the stove, its pages ragged and discoloured.

"That is my Culpeper," Hester replied, smiling lovingly at the book. "One of my oldest friends he be. Nicholas Culpeper that is," she said, by way of explanation.

On seeing Lizzie's blank face, she added with a hint of impatience, "Surely you must have heard of him? Our most famous herbalist? He was born four hundred years ago and yet he produced this wondrous book. It's often referred to as Culpeper's Herbal. I can't believe you don't know his name. What do they teach the children these days!" Hester's voice was full of disgust.

"No, I've never heard of him," Lizzie could only answer lamely.

"Every known herb is within those pages," Hester Rowe continued with passion, "and their associations and uses."

"Associations? How do you mean?" Lizzie asked, intrigued now. She wheeled herself slowly forward, closer to the ancient book, which lay open on the counter.

"We judge plants by their associations," Hester Rowe explained to Lizzie. "All the important medicinal plants are known to be under the dominion of one or other of the planets or maybe the signs of the zodiac too. You may take a careful a look if you like."

"Thank you," Lizzie answered her, surprised by Hester's kindly voice, but still not entirely understanding.

The old-fashioned text on the pages looked tempting. And there were illustrations too. But even though she craned her neck, from the position of her wheelchair she was too low to see them properly. She would have liked to take hold of the book, but she simply didn't dare and so she kept her hands in her lap.

Hester Rowe was watching Lizzie out of the corner of one eye. "You may slide 'im towards you and tilt 'im up, as long as you're very careful with 'im."

So Lizzie did exactly that and started reading one of the headings.

'HEMLOCK (CONIUM MAKULATUM)'

She read the heading to herself, struggling to cope with the Latin.

'Saturn claims dominion over this herb. Hemlock is exceedingly cold, and very dangerous, especially to be taken inwardly.'

Lizzie thought it sounded dicey. Suddenly she couldn't help wondering why Mrs Rowe had the book opened there. Of course there were other plants on that page. It was just that this one had caught her eye.

'It may safely be applied to inflammations, tumults, and swellings in any part of the body, as also to St. Anthony's fire, wheals, pushes, and creeping ulcers that arise out of hot sharp humours, by cooling and repelling the heat.'

Yuk and gross! It all sounded horrible.

Sliding the precious book carefully back, Lizzie's eyes strayed up to the shelves that ran on the wall behind the counter.

"You have a fantastic collection," she said, in a voice that showed her surprise. "It's almost like a small library. What's that handsome book up there?" She pointed to a large volume with a bright red leather spine.

"'Tis another ancient book of my Gran's," Hester answered cautiously.

"The Key of Solomon the King", Lizzie read slowly out loud, struggling with the worn lettering. "May I look at it please?" she asked.

"Not just now," the woman said tersely. "I might show you another time," she added hastily and more gently, emphasising the word might.

"I need to stir my brew," she said, taking up a big wooden spoon.

Lizzie sat watching the woman stirring. Something was simmering in the pot. She could hear the fluid bubbling. A strange odour filled the air. What could she possibly have in there?

She'd never seen such a big pot before. It looked as if it were made of iron. The word cauldron came to mind.

Lizzie had noticed another book—much smaller than the Culpeper, but lying on the worktop beside it.

"What's that little book?" she pointed.

"That one?" the woman asked sharply. "That's my old Gran's Book of Shadows."

"May I …?" Lizzie started to ask, reaching her hand towards the book.

Before she could even finish the question or her hand could touch the book, Mrs Rowe had grabbed her chair and was wheeling her firmly out of the kitchen: bustling through the utility room and out of the back door of the cottage—well out of sight and reach of the book.

3 I

The Garden of Heaven

Lizzie loathed being taken over.

"Oh no!" she grunted angrily. But all she could do was to hold on tightly as she was bumped down several steps and brought to a halt on the paving below.

"Well now. What do you think of that?" Hester asked with pride in her voice. Her arms waved in a dramatic gesture.

Lizzie could only gasp, "Oh!" Her scowl had faded. Her eyes stared wide.

Together with Tom and their Mum, who'd always been a keen gardener, Lizzie had visited many gardens. But she'd never seen one like this before. It was like stepping—or in her case wheeling—into another magical world—like stumbling on an exotic oasis.

The large garden behind the cottage was completely enclosed on all four sides: behind her by the wall of the cottage together with a row of outbuildings and on the other three sides by high walls. In the wall at the far end, Lizzie could see a substantial doorway. The heavy, wooden door was closed.

Even so early in the season, the garden was a profusion of plants. The central area was taken over by a block of small square beds, each one raised above the path and restrained by old railway sleepers. Some were clearly freshly dug, the fine, dark tilth awaiting planting. Others sported rows of seedlings.

The remains of last year's vegetables still flourished in some of the beds: tall crinkly-edged, green kale; and broccoli, thick with purple heads; the tail end of spinach beet with its large and fleshy leaves, some dark green and others orange. And there were promising signs for the new season: potatoes sprouting and already banked. Even some little lettuce plants looked as if they'd soon be ready.

The high walls that enclosed the garden supported a mass of greenery. There were climbers and ramblers and honeysuckle and, along the south facing wall, various cordoned fruit trees. Lizzie even spotted a vine.

"I am astounded," she told Mrs Rowe, her voice full of admiration, "that you can grow all this stuff here, when you live so close to the ocean. I wouldn't have thought it possible."

"That's all down to my Gran and my Granfer—on my father's side," Hester said. "Granfer it was who built they walls—every stone with his own bare hands. He built them high and he built them strong to protect Gran's plants from the salt and the gales. In doing so, he created a sun trap—a secret haven for all Gran's treasures."

She bent down close to Lizzie's ear.

"Some say my Gran had special powers." The whispered words made Lizzie gasp.

"Green fingers, of course, I mean," the woman added hastily. "A magical way with plants and flowers."

Standing up, she continued with passion, "She was a wise and wonderful woman."

And then without the slightest warning, she sprang away along the path. The sudden movement made Lizzie start. Turning back towards the house, Hester stared up into the sky. Then stretching wide her arms with a flourish, she flung them high above her head.

"God rest our Gran in the Garden of Heaven," she cried aloud at the top of her voice, gazing excitedly into the blue. "In the name of the Father … Son … Holy Ghost."

Lizzie leant back as far as she could and, twisting her neck, she gazed into the sky, fully expecting to see the old Gran—and maybe even the Granfer too—smiling down at their wonderful garden. Just a glimpse would have been enough.

She loved the thought of the Garden of Heaven—a place where gardeners' spirits might roam—eternally happy and peacefully free.

"Maybe that's where Mum is now," Lizzie murmured to herself. "Up there with the Gran and the Granfer."

In future she'd try to imagine her there: tending the heavenly roses and veg; supplying Saint Peter with his spuds; waging organic wars on pests. The idea brought a big smile to her face.

"Gran and Granfer worked hard together," Hester's voice interrupted her thoughts. She seemed quite calm now—back to normal, as if the outburst had never occurred.

"They were forever tending the soil. Always weeding and manuring. What people now call organic gardening—but long before that term was created." The woman beamed with satisfaction.

"They never used no chemicals here. No sprays. No powders. No poisons. It was all down to love and hard work."

Lizzie moved on down the garden. On three sides, below the walls, long, narrow beds were packed with plants. So close was the planting, so lush the growth that she could scarcely see the soil. The range of colours and forms was amazing.

"These are my herbs," the woman said modestly. "Most were planted by my Gran, or they're descended from her stock. She worked on here well into her nineties," she added by way of explanation.

Each variety grew in a clump, producing an overall patchwork effect. There were bushy plants like fat cushions with tiny leaves, pale grey or yellow; tall purple stalks with budded spikes. Low, spreading mats of silvery leaves were creeping out across the path. Lizzie did her best to avoid them.

Hester walked along in front: tweaking off leaves and even small shoots, crushing them between her fingers, then handing them over for Lizzie to smell. She pointed out each species with pride. Many had local Cornish names, but she knew their Latin names as well.

Lizzie was completely amazed. She simply hadn't assessed the woman as being well educated or smart. Yet the breadth of her knowledge was astounding. She not only knew the Latin name for every one of her precious plants, but she knew its history too: which plants had originated in Britain; which had been brought from foreign parts—and even when they'd been brought—and by whom.

"What do you do with all these plants?" The sudden question came to Lizzie.

Mrs Rowe looked back sharply.

"I use them for all sorts of things," she said guardedly, turning away. "Yes, I assure you ... they all have their uses."

It wasn't a satisfactory answer. But Hester Rowe had made it sound final.

The garden had a strange atmosphere. The air was heavy. And no bird sang. There was only the endless buzzing of bees.

Lizzie wheeled her wheelchair slowly along the narrow central path: listening to Hester's voice droning on; crushing leaves and sniffing their odours. Some smelt odd or even unpleasant; others were sweet and deliciously fragrant. Lizzie was enjoying herself. She hadn't felt so relaxed for ages.

Her lap filled up with a heap of crushed herbs. From time to time she gathered them and, cupping them tenderly in her hands, she held them up to her nose and breathed deeply. Heady perfumes filled her brain. They seemed to be taking over her senses—lulling her into a curious state.

The sun shone brighter than ever before. Colours and light were intensified. The hum of the bees was unnaturally loud, drowning out Hester's voice and filling her head with a pulsing buzz.

Lizzie was starting to feel quite woozy. It was exciting. She loved the feeling. She felt as if she was drifting … drifting … into some secret, enchanted land.

When she arrived at the end of the path, she came to a sudden, startled halt. Hester Rowe was blocking the way—with her back to the doorway in the wall. Behind her the big wooden door stood closed.

32

The Best Informed Bees

Lizzie, struggling to focus, gazed up into Hester's face. Her glinting eyes were more piercing than ever. Her arms, spread wide, protected the door. Lizzie could see two serious bolts: one near the top and one at the bottom.

She noticed something else as well: a seemingly endless stream of bees was flying in and out of the garden through a barred but unglazed window. The window, Lizzie could only suppose, had been cut in the door for this special purpose—a very convenient entrance and exit for the bees that produced the prize-winning honey.

Lizzie sat rigid in her wheelchair, hardly daring to move or speak and wondering what would happen next. Finally she found her voice, though it seemed to come from a long way away.

"What is behind the door?" she asked.

"It's a secret," Mrs Rowe hissed, glaring fiercely down at Lizzie. "How do I know if I can trust you?"

"I've always been good at keeping secrets," Lizzie ventured, hopefully. "My mother always said I was. And come to think," she added wistfully, "my Mum was right about most things … although I couldn't always see it." Lizzie's voice was full of regret.

Hester Rowe's expression softened.

"Do please show me, I won't tell a soul," Lizzie promised, crossing her fingers under the pile of herbs in her lap. She could tell that the woman was tempted to show her.

"I'll let you have a quick look, as long as you behave yourself. As long as you show proper respect," Hester Rowe agreed at last. "I don't show many, mind," she added. "You should count yourself as very privileged."

'What can it be?' Lizzie wondered. 'And how is she going to open that door? Being so very short and dumpy, she'll never be able to reach the top bolt. And I can't help her, stuck in this chair.'

Almost as if she'd guessed Lizzie's thoughts, the woman turned and said sternly, "You needn't wonder how I shall do it. I always have my ways and means. You would do well to remember that."

With yet another threatening glare, she turned quickly away from Lizzie. Then sweeping aside some vegetation she exposed a large, square chunk of stone, which stood by the wall to one side of the doorway. Scrambling on to the big stone block and balanced precariously on her toes, she managed to slide the top bolt back; then, slithering down, slid the bottom bolt too.

Lizzie waited expectantly as Hester grasped the old iron latch and pushed the big door slowly open, stepping aside to let Lizzie see through.

"Oh!" gasped Lizzie in surprise.

It wasn't at all what she'd expected. She'd guessed that she'd see the hives for the bees, probably set in the pasture beyond, but she hadn't expected this weird little yard. It was not much more than twenty feet square, completely enclosed by high, stone walls, exactly like the rest of the garden.

Four, large, old-fashioned beehives stood in the small slate paved enclosure: one hive set squarely in each of the corners. Lizzie could see there were masses of bees: crawling in and out of the hives and taking off in all directions. Their droning buzzing filled the air. She ducked as some zoomed over her head, making the best of the open doorway.

"You may come in slowly … but not too far." Mrs Rowe's voice held a note of warning, as Lizzie slipped over the granite step. "I need to be sure that my bees will accept you. Bees are sensitive, knowing creatures. I won't have you upsetting them.

"They're not used to visitors, though I come to see them, myself, everyday, to give them the very latest news. Bees always like to hear the news—births and deaths and other such things. When friends call in for a bit of a gossip, to share some tasty snippets of news, they always say before they leave 'Be sure to tell the bees for me Hester'."

Lizzie listened, wide-eyed and suspicious. Was the woman being serious? Or was she simply having her on?

"That's why my honey wins all the prizes," Hester glanced sharply at Lizzie, aware of her disbelieving look. "My bees are the best informed bees in Cornwall."

Lizzie changed the subject quickly. "What's that funny old thing over there?"

She pointed to a peculiar object, which sat on the ground in the middle of the yard. It was a large, domed, rusty affair, some three feet wide and a foot in height. On the top there was a handle. It looked like the lid of a giant tureen.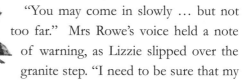

As Lizzie started across towards it, Hester Rowe lurched after her, grabbing her wheelchair and shouting, "Stop!"

"Whatever's wrong?" Lizzie asked crossly. "If you shout like that, you'll upset your bees," she said with a smug look on her face. "I was only going to take a quick peep."

The woman was composing herself. Her voice was now little more than a whisper, "This is the very heart of the secret."

"Yes, but what secret?" Lizzie begged. "Whatever it is, I promise to keep it."

Hester's eyes bored into Lizzie. "It's the pit," she said. "The secret pit."

33

The Swan Pit

Wheeling Lizzie close to the lid, Hester prepared herself for the ceremony ... the opening of the secret pit. With one dramatic sweep of her arms and chanting softly under her breath, she lifted and drew the lid aside, exposing a large round hole in the ground. Then raising her arms and her eyes to the heavens, she froze as if in supplication, her lips moving silently.

Leaning over as far as she dared and craning her neck to look into the hole, Lizzie peered down with a puzzled frown. The hole was some eighteen inches across. A ring of stones formed a rim.

She couldn't judge the depth of the pit because it was partly full of stuff— a mass of scruffy bits and pieces: what looked like fragments of old torn cloth; a spotted bird's egg; a baby's shoe; a lock of hair; a polished stone; and a weird collection of other items, some of them obviously mouldy and rotten.

The surface of this peculiar mass was several inches down from the rim. Lizzie didn't know what to think. She certainly didn't know what to say.

"This is our Swan Pit," Hester whispered. The words were spoken with reverence.

"It's lined with the skin of a whole swan. The pit has been here for so long now, that most of the skin has rotted away. But look ... you can still see some of the feathers."

"But why, Mrs Rowe? I don't understand. I'm sure it's illegal to kill a swan. Don't they all belong to the Queen? Surely you didn't kill it … did you …?" Lizzie's voice trailed away.

"No, of course I didn't, m'dear." The woman allowed herself a chuckle.

"Besides there were no Queen in they days, when this old pit were originally dug. 'Twas said by my Gran—and she knew they things—'twas said to be several thousand years old—dating back to They Prehistorics."

"Oh my days!" Lizzie gasped, amazed, yet knowing she mustn't show any doubts.

"How could it be as old as that? And why was it dug here in the first place? It must, I suppose, have served a purpose."

"Oh yes, it certainly served a purpose. Other pits like this have been found by they RKologist people … and their contents all dug out. 'Tis very wrong and a crying shame … to desecrate these sacred places."

"Sacred?" asked Lizzie. "Surely not."

Hester Rowe scowled at Lizzie. "Definitely sacred," she insisted. "That's why it's locked in here with me bees … hidden away from prying eyes … 'cos this is the only working pit left."

"Working?" Lizzie asked in surprise. "Whatever do you mean by that?"

"'Tis still a highly valued tradition." Hester nodded her head at Lizzie. "By now I expect you will have discovered that this world is ruled by men. But we womenfolk have always been powerful. Since time began there have been Wise Women. They've always had their ways and their means." Hester nodded knowingly.

"But why the pit?" Lizzie asked, bemused. "And why swan feathers? That's very strange."

"No, it isn't strange at all," Mrs Rowe responded firmly. "Surely you must have heard of Cygnus … Cygnus the celestial swan?"

On seeing Lizzie's blank expression, Hester shook her head in despair and clucked her tongue noisily.

"The swan is a very special creature … much respected and loved through the ages … a magical beast and highly regarded … an ancient symbol of grace and beauty … of innocence … spiritual evolution.

"And these 'ere Swan Pits have played their part in helping women through the ages … to fulfil their desires … and their needs.

"For example," Hester continued, "if a woman wanted a husband, she'd come and visit her local pit. A special ritual would be performed. The woman would make her wish by the pit and then drop in a little token—a kind of gift to the Swan Goddess, to encourage her to grant the wish.

"A crystal or jewel would be the best. But most of these women were very poor, so the token was often a scrap of cloth torn from the edge of the woman's best blouse, or p'rhaps torn off her skirt—or mebbe torn from an undergarment—or even a trimming of lace off her cacks."

"Cacks?" Lizzie questioned, confused.

The woman pursed her mouth at Lizzie. "Nether garments … you know," Hester muttered, impatient now. Surely, the girl couldn't be this dim.

Then seeing Lizzie's vacant expression, "Garments for your nether regions, as my old Gran used to call them."

Hester wiggled her bottom and giggled.

"Knickers," she hissed, winking broadly.

"Oh. I see. And then?" Lizzie asked, struggling to keep her face straight.

"Well then, of course, she would get her man." Hester Rowe was adamant.

"Seriously?" Lizzie asked, cautiously.

"Oh yes. It almost always works. It works for married women too—women who have longed for babies. The Swan Pit could do a lot for them. A lock of hair was the usual token. And then they would soon find they was expecting."

"How extraordinary!" Lizzie exclaimed. "I suppose … if it works … it must be magic."

34

The Lock of Hair

"Look down," Hester ordered tersely. "Do you see that lock of hair? Tied up with a faded, red ribbon? Well that came from a sweet young woman. She had one child but she longed for another. Most of all she wanted a girl, but it didn't seem to be happening. And so I brought her here to my pit.

"Mind you," she added sadly, "that were many years ago. I never did hear any more of her …"

As her voice trailed away, she gave Lizzie a long, hard stare. The glitter of her searching eyes was curtained by her drooping lids. Rimmed by fringes of thick, dark lashes, they hid her thoughts and her feelings from Lizzie. It was a strange, unsettling look. Lizzie, disturbed, suppressed a shudder.

"Now come on," Hester Rowe said briskly, "there's a powerful superstition that every time the pit is opened, a wish must be made and a token given—or else the pit will lose its power. So now you'll have to make a wish."

"Me?" asked Lizzie, horrified.

"And you'll have to give a token. You have some jewellery round your neck. A piece of that would do nicely, I think."

"Oh no!" Lizzie exclaimed, "I can't use that."

But what else could she use, she wondered? Hester Rowe stood quietly, waiting.

"We could use a button off my cardi. My friend Betty knitted this for me. She sewed on all these beautiful buttons." Lizzie showed the buttons to Hester. "They're handmade by a friend of hers, but I don't think she would mind if I used one. There are some scissors in my bag."

With the button clenched in Lizzie's fist, Hester was now poised and ready. "You can make any kind of wish you want—as long as it's not a wish to harm others. But your wish must be silent, mind," Hester warned. "Drop your token into the pit when I've chanted the sacred words. And then we must quickly close the lid. We mustn't let the wish escape."

"Sacred words?" Lizzie questioned.

"Yes, of course," Hester hissed. "My Gran were wise beyond all others. She knew every charm and spell. And she had a few of her very own specials." Hester smiled knowingly. "Highly efficacious, they be."

"I see," said Lizzie, not seeing at all.

"Now close your eyes and concentrate." With hands held high and her face to the heavens, Hester began the magic chant …

"O blessed Goddess of The Swan,
Receive our tribute to thy grace.
We speak no ill, we wreak no wrong,
Please grant our wish through time and space.
O star bright! O heavenly light …"

But even concentrating hard, Lizzie couldn't catch the rest. The spell went on … and on … and on …

When it finally drew to a close, she opened up her clenched fist. Then slowly mouthing her silent wish, she dropped the button into the pit.

"One, two, three—so shall it be …" Hester's words died away.

As Lizzie watched the button land—settling on the lock of hair—a mighty shiver ran right through her.

"Ooooooooooooh!"

35

Knockers

With the lid firmly back in place, silence reigned in the little yard, save for the endless drone of the bees: buzzing, buzzing, busy bees, coming and going from their hives.

"We must leave now," Hester's voice broke the silence. "Bees, we're going now," she called out. "We'll leave you in peace to do your good work—for which, as you know, I am always grateful."

She smiled delightedly at the hives. "Thank you, thank you, dear, good friends."

Even Lizzie murmured "Thank you." It seemed the proper thing to do. The buzzing response was gratifying.

With the door firmly bolted behind them, Hester Rowe turned to Lizzie.

"And now I want you to promise again that you will *never*, in your whole life, tell anyone about my Swan Pit."

Satisfied by Lizzie's insistence that she would never do such a thing, Hester set off down the path. On the way, Lizzie remembered something she'd been meaning to ask.

"I wanted to ask you about that cottage," she said.

"Cottage! What cottage?" Hester asked sharply, turning back to stare at Lizzie.

"The cottage along the road—by the causeway. You must know the one I mean. At first I thought it must be empty. It looks a sad and lonely place. But somebody's obviously living there. So why are the curtains always closed?"

"Living there!" the woman exclaimed, her sharp eyes fixed on Lizzie's face. "No, you've got that wrong m'dear. That cottage has been deserted for years."

"But I know I saw a face at the window," Lizzie insisted. She wouldn't give up. "There must be somebody living there."

"Oh dear! Oh dear! Oh dear!" The woman shook her head at Lizzie. "I can assure you that you're wrong. But," she added, her voice a hoarse whisper, "'tis said the place has always been haunted."

"Haunted? Surely not," said Lizzie.

"It sounds to me like you've seen a ghost. Rumour has it there are several."

"Several?" Lizzie asked amazed.

"Some might say a brave few." Hester nodded her head wisely.

"Whatever do you mean by that?" Lizzie was beginning to wish that she hadn't mentioned the cottage.

"I've heard it's a possibility ..." Mrs Rowe looked slyly at Lizzie, "that it's been taken over by Knockers."

"Knockers?" Lizzie asked. "What are they?"

"You should be asking who, not what," Hester Rowe rebuked Lizzie. "They are the little people," she added. "They are what people sometimes call pixies."

"Pixies!" Lizzie exclaimed with a giggle. "Surely you can't be serious. I certainly don't believe in pixies."

Hester clucked her tongue at Lizzie. "You wouldn't say that if you lived on the moor. If you were a man who'd worked down the mines, you would know all about they Knockers. You would have heard them underground, usually in the deepest tunnels—knock, knock, knocking, the way they do."

Lizzie tried to keep a straight face.

"Don't you mock what you don't understand," Hester Rowe glared crossly at Lizzie. "You ought to show them proper respect. They Knockers can be very tricksy."

"Tricksy? What do you mean?" Lizzie asked.

"They can be helpful if they choose. I'll give you that," Hester nodded. "But they'm lively little beggars and they'm very cunning too. You'd best keep well away from that cottage. It would be a mistake to upset them. Goodness knows what would happen to you. We might never see you again ... if they caught you ... "

Lizzie wasn't going to be put off so easily.

"But if they live deep down in the mines, why would they want to live in a cottage? That doesn't sound right to me," she insisted.

"I have heard tell," Hester whispered, "that, on very rare occasions, they do take over deserted houses. They likes tormenting passing strangers—playing fiendish tricks on them. Especially emmets like yourself—foreigners, people that don't belong."

"If they normally live in the dark … I suppose that might explain the curtains … " Lizzie said thoughtfully, watching Mrs Rowe's face closely.

"It certainly does," the woman said firmly. "They're bound to want to shut out light."

"Yes. I suppose so," Lizzie agreed reluctantly.

Determined now to change the subject, Hester looked up into the sky.

"The weather's on the change," she suggested.

"It looks alright to me," Lizzie said. "The sky's still blue. There aren't many clouds."

"All the same. You mark my words. There's a big storm on the way."

"Oh dear!" Lizzie said, concerned. "Your husband's a fisherman isn't he?"

"Yes. He's away at sea just now. He'll not be back for a week or more."

"But what about the storm?" asked Lizzie.

"Our boy and he works well together. They've weathered many a storm before. They'll find a place to ride it out. And they keep contact on their mobiles." The woman's voice was confident. "Besides, they're well protected," she added.

That seemed like a very odd claim to Lizzie. "But how are they protected?" she asked.

"You'd do best to get back indoors," the woman continued, ignoring the question. "And stay there until tomorrow morning."

It sounded like an order to Lizzie. She did her best to smile back sweetly.

"Oh, and by the way," Hester added. "I've seen a big black car in the lane. Cruising up and down past here. Were you expecting visitors?"

"No," said Lizzie firmly, "I wasn't."

36

A Fleeting Figure

Back in the cabin, over lunch, Lizzie discussed the cottage with Tom. She didn't dare tell him about the Swan Pit, but she told him about the Knockers. Though she couldn't help feeling rather silly; she knew exactly how he'd respond.

"Oh, not pixies, surely?" he laughed. "You weren't taken in by that rubbish … were you?"

"Well … not precisely pixies," she answered. "More like little, malevolent spirits. Mrs Rowe made them sound quite real."

"Real or not," Tom said, "I think you should keep away from that cottage. Something funny is going on here. I have a sense of impending danger."

"Perhaps we shouldn't go to the pub," Lizzie said in a doubtful voice.

"I think we have to go," Tom said. "But the weather's breaking up. We're going to need our waterproof clothing."

The weather broke late afternoon. Darkness fell early. A storm was building.

The rain held off but the wind blew hard. It battered the hills behind the village that led up onto the open moor, bending every tree and bush in its relentless, gusting path. It blasted the clouds across the sky, only occasionally ripping them open to hint at the huge pale face of the moon.

With the lights turned off in the cabin, Lizzie sat in front of the window, peering out into the darkness: searching for the island in vain; watching out for the flashes of lightning; listening to the distant rumbles.

A sudden chink of light from the cottage, told her the door had been opened … then closed. As the security lights came on, Lizzie caught sight of a fleeting figure, dressed in long, black, floating robes. She saw the glint of silver strands—in a mass of long, dark, flowing hair.

But … now you see it … now you don't. No sooner had she focused her eyes, than the black robed figure had vanished from sight.

"Did you see that?" Lizzie asked sharply.

"See what?" Tom asked, bemused.

That left Lizzie wondering. Had she seen what she thought she'd seen? Or was it merely a trick of the light?

37

The Smugglers' Retreat

Mauled and buffeted by the wind, Lizzie struggled along the road, which she knew would lead to the village inn. She couldn't have done it without Tom's help: without his constant voice in her ear. "Come on Shrimp. You can do it."

At last they came to the dingy old pub. Waves crashed on the shore close by. The wind howled. The rain lashed.

A horrible, ghostly, groaning sound came from somewhere overhead: the pub sign swinging in the wind. Lizzie cringed in her chair beneath. Darkly masked by the foul weather, an ugly, mean faced man glowered down from his portrait on the board.

Ignorant of the smuggler's glare, but strengthened as ever by Tom's presence, Lizzie turned towards the pub. Her hands and wrists were running with water as she tried to tackle the door. "I can do it, Tom," she insisted.

Finally thrusting it open before her, she lurched across the shallow step, rolling jerkily into the bar amidst a flurry of rain and wind. The buzz of conversation stopped. The customers, shocked, sat like statues, staring fixedly at the intruder. Nobody moved so much as a muscle.

Nervous and wet, Lizzie waited: pushing back her waterproof hood and mopping at her streaming face. Water that was filling her lap, spilled out, splashing down her legs and forming a pool beneath her wheels.

"Oh dear, Tom," she whispered quietly. "I think this might have been a mistake. We should have listened to Mrs Rowe. The people don't look friendly, do they?"

The pub bar was a murky room: black slate slabs paved the floor; the low ceiling was heavily beamed and on the beams hung brasses and mugs, shrouded by the dust of ages, festooned with skeins of draping cobweb. Flames from a wood fire lit the room. On either side of the granite hearth the walls were lined with old, oak settles on which a number of figures were sitting: some with their elbows propped on tables; others leaning back in corners, their pipes gripped firmly in their hands.

The sweet, hot, fruity smell of tobacco mingled with the stale beer odour. A pall of smoke darkened the room and, as the door swung shut with a bang, the lighted candles on the tables, stuffed into heavily wax-cloaked bottles, guttered in the blast from the door, spewing wax in all directions. Cobwebs juddered overhead.

A brooding silence filled the room, broken only by the sound of weather buffeting the door and of the crackle of wood in the hearth. Lizzie pulled herself up in her chair. She made her way across the room and smiled at the man behind the bar.

"What can I get you?" the man asked gruffly, producing a forced and awkward smile. "I'm afraid we're not used to tourists here."

"I'm not just a tourist," Lizzie said firmly.

"No," a voice piped up behind her. "We'd heard you was an investigator. Them kind of folk aren't welcome here." A murmured agreement ran round the room.

"May I please have an orange juice?" Lizzie asked the barman boldly, struggling to steady her voice. Tom, she knew, would want a beer or maybe one of those lagers he liked. She stretched up: handing over the money; smiling sweetly at the barman.

"I am hoping that you can help," she said, "in trying to trace a local man— a man you might know. He's called Bob Tregarrow."

A deathly hush fell over the room. Looks were exchanged amongst the men. As one got up and came towards her, Lizzie recognised the man: the taxi driver who'd met the coach.

She'd noticed yesterday that he was lame. Today his limp seemed so much worse. Though probably only in his late forties, his body was twisted and deformed; his face was taut and lined with pain. But his eyes were bright and strong: they shone with an almost fanatical gleam. The twisted body and shining eyes gave him a threateningly sinister look.

As he came to stand in front of her, Lizzie shrank back in her chair.

"Best not to mention that name here," the man said quietly but firmly to Lizzie.

"You're staying at my sister's place. I suggest you go straight back there now. Have a few days holiday. Then go away and leave us in peace. We knows nothing of that man. And we've no wish to know, have we, lads?" he asked the assembled company.

"No. No, Wesley." A chorus of voices.

"I see," said Lizzie thoughtfully. Tom's presence gave her confidence. She sat quietly sipping her drink. A gentle chatter built up in the room as the men relaxed back in their seats.

"Does anyone live over there on that island?" Lizzie asked in a loud voice.

The chatter stopped. The barman stared, his face hardening into a scowl. "Live on that island? What do you mean?"

"I thought the man that we're looking for might be living on the island,"

Lizzie said. "I'm sure I could manage to cross the causeway. It looks quite sound to me," she added.

"Whatever you do, don't go out there." The barman was almost begging her. "The tide is treacherous in these parts. It's what we call a rip tide. One minute you think you're safe. Next minute, you're floatin' away."

"We've done our best, haven't we lads?" Wesley broke in. "We always advise visitors. But the daft ones don't take any notice. That can be a big mistake." He glowered threateningly at Lizzie. A hiss of agreement filled the room.

"Three people have drowned on that causeway," another man butted in. His comment was followed with a chuckle, as if the deaths had given him pleasure.

"I'd be very careful," Lizzie insisted.

"My son Wesley is quite right." An old man got up and came towards her. "It is a very dangerous place … and not just because of the tide …"

The man nodded his head sagely, his mouth pursed, his eyes screwed tight. "You won't have heard the story, I s'pose? Your being a stranger in these parts … your being what we call an emmet."

The sickly smile made Lizzie shudder. "What story?" she asked uncertainly, trying to control her wavering voice.

"It's not a very pleasant story, but since you ask, I suppose I should tell you

… about the creature that lives on the island …"

"Ahh … Ahh … Ahh … Ahh!" A heavy sighing filled the room. Lizzie could feel Tom's comforting grip tightening on her stooping shoulders.

The old man paused and looked round the room. Wesley came forward to take up the story.

"I've seen it with my own eyes," he cried out in a shrill voice, his face contorted, his eyes shining in the light from the glowing fire.

"'Tis a poor, tormented creature … huge and hairy … a savage beast …"

From somewhere at the back of the room, a horrible howling noise rose up.

"Howooooo … Hooooooooo … Howooooo … Hooooooo …"

On and on … a chorus of howls. It started low then grew … and grew, as each man added his voice to the rest.

When the howling finally died, every eye was fixed on Lizzie. Wesley was looming over her. His face was twisted. His eyes gleamed. His voice had sunk to a hissing whisper.

"'Tis not quite man … and 'tis not quite wolf … "

38

The Wolfman

As Wesley fell back into a chair, seemingly overcome by emotion and by his claims for the savage beast, his father patted him on the shoulder.

"You're right, boy," the old man said. "'Tis, to be sure, a savage beast."

Then he moved across to Lizzie: bending down towards her chair. Brown and shrivelled like a walnut, his deeply lined face was too close to her own: so close she could smell his sour breath, tainted with tobacco and beer. Sharp, beady eyes bored into her.

"But be he man? Or be he wolf? Or be he maybe some … and some …?" the voice croaked hoarsely in her ear.

"We're not trying to frighten you, maid. We're just a bit concerned for your safety. Some very strange things have happened out there."

A murmur ran around the room: "Very strange things. Yes, very strange." The men all nodded to each other.

"I'm not afraid of wolves," said Lizzie. "I think wolves are beautiful creatures. Whatever you say, I shall go to the island," she insisted stubbornly, in the boldest voice she could muster.

"Come on Lizzie. I think we should go." Tom's voice was in her ear.

"No. I'm not leaving." She was determined.

The old man bent down even closer.

"It's only right for us to warn you," the stage-whispering voice hissed. "You must beware! Beware The Wolfman!"

"The Wolfman ... The Wolfman ... " the words were slowly taken up, till every man in the bar had joined in. A loud chanting filled the room. Despite the small number of men, their voices sounded like a choir. And yet their chant was full of menace.

"The Wolfman ... The Wolfman ... beware the hungry, evil wolf.

"The Wolfman ... The Wolfman ... beware his shining, ripping teeth."

The words were repeated over and over, building to a sickening crescendo.

Lizzie sat frozen, gripping her wheels.

As quickly as the chant had begun, so it came to a sudden halt. An eerie silence filled the bar. The men sat fixed, still, watching Lizzie.

Suddenly one of them sprang from his seat. Lizzie started in her chair, the sudden movement crashing her nerves.

"Hark! Hark!" the man stood rigid, pressing a finger to his lips. "Sometimes we can hear his howl, even above the voice of the storm."

Taut faces were raised to listen.

"Ah yes! Ah yes!"

The chorus of voices built again.

"'Tis the howl of the wolf. The howoool of the wolf! The howl! The howl! The howoool of the wolf!

"Howool … Howool … Howool on the winnnnd …"

Lizzie's fragile body shook.

"Some say he has a taste for maids," one of the man suggested with relish, when the chorus had died away. "Perhaps their flesh is more tender and juicy."

"Of course, he might not fancy you," Wesley added thoughtfully. "You don't look plump enough to me?"

"On the other hand," Wesley's Dad said, "I s'pose you'd be quite easy to handle, fixed as you are in that contraption."

Then more shouts from around the room.

"What they calls convenience food."

"Ready prepared and easy to manage." The snorts and the laughter were sickening.

And then another voice came from the back: "More like meals on wheels, Wes."

Raucous laughter filled the room. Lizzie couldn't take any more. All she wanted was to escape: to get away from these hateful men.

"Leave your drink. We must go now." Tom's whispered voice was urgent.

The storm still raged on out at sea. Struggling back along the road, they stopped for a breather on several occasions. Lizzie turned her face to the island and listened oh so carefully.

Was that only the voice of the storm? The wind whipping along the shore? Or was it the howl of the wolf on the wind?

39

The Strange Pebble

Lizzie slept fitfully that night, waking up on several occasions, thinking she could hear the wolf. His howling seemed to fill her head, waking her with a horrible jolt. But was it real or only a dream? She puzzled, as she lay rigid and trembling.

The following morning dawned clear and bright. The storm had obviously blown itself out; only a few scattered clouds remained. Lizzie made a pact with Tom. No matter what Mrs Rowe said at breakfast, they wouldn't discuss the horrid experience—in the pub the night before.

In the event, nothing was said.

"It seems probable," Tom suggested, when they were back in their cabin again, "that Hester Rowe doesn't yet know about our evening jaunt to the pub. You told me you saw her going out."

"I can't be sure it was her," Lizzie said. "Although I know I saw someone … or something."

"Not one of your famous manifestations?" Tom teased with a chuckle.

But Lizzie found it hard to smile.

"I noticed something else in her kitchen. That stone in the window. Did you see it?"

"No. I was too busy eating my breakfast. What about those sausages then? I've never eaten such fabulous bangers. Made by her pig keeping friend, Mrs Rowe said, and flavoured with the herbs from her garden."

"Yes, delicious," Lizzie responded. "But let me tell you about that stone. It was a large, smooth, rounded pebble, maybe two or three inches across and hanging from a string in the window."

"How could a smooth pebble hang from a string?" Tom asked doubtfully.

"It could easily hang from a string, because it had a hole right through it."

"You should have asked Hester about it?" Tom said.

"I opened my mouth meaning to ask," Lizzie said quietly and thoughtfully, "but something stopped me. I don't know what. I told you I asked her about that cottage."

"Ah yes. The haunted cottage," Tom said. "She didn't like you asking, did she?"

"No," said Lizzie, "she didn't like it. I felt she was making it clear to me that I shouldn't ask any more questions."

40

The Book

Whilst Tom went off on his morning run, Lizzie pottered about on the road that ran along beside the beach. It was her habit each day after breakfast to go and take a look at the causeway; to note the time and the height of the tide, whilst keeping well away from the gate that led into the haunted cottage.

With the passing of the days, she was becoming more and more certain that the island held some secret. Any mention of the place seemed to provoke an extreme response. The locals must be hiding something.

"But surely it can't be a Wolfman can it?" Lizzie wondered what Tom would think.

"No," his voice had sounded scornful, "but they might be smuggling. The haunted cottage might be involved. They might be storing drugs or guns there. Whatever you do, you must be careful. Smugglers can be very violent, if their lucrative trade is threatened."

Every day on her morning 'run', she stopped her chair at the top of the ramp and did her best to examine the island, starting from the left-hand end and working her way along the shore: peering closely at every detail; then back across the rocky slopes; then along the jagged skyline.

After several days of this, Lizzie was no further forward. No matter how hard she concentrated, she never spotted any movement—apart from the circling birds in the sky—or indeed any feature of interest. She only ended up with a headache.

If only she had those binoculars. They must be somewhere in the cabin. She made her way back, determined to find them. Perhaps they'd fallen on the floor and been kicked away under a bed—or maybe even under the sofa.

Back in the cabin she started to search: in the drawers and all the cupboards; along shelves and the small bookcase; under all the furniture—not easy if you're stuck in a wheelchair; behind and under every cushion. But, despite hunting high and low, she couldn't find the binoculars. They had simply disappeared. Surely they hadn't been stolen … had they?

She only found one thing of interest. A book had appeared as if from nowhere on the table beside her bed. Lizzie read the title out loud: '*Myths and Legends of Old Cornwall.*'

When it came to bedtime each night, Lizzie was faced with a dilemma. With the beach so close to the cabin, she would have loved to open her windows: to be able to lie in her bed at night and listen to the voice of the ocean … the ceaseless whooshing of the waves, lulling her gently off to sleep.

But having lived in fear of the villains, she had grown security conscious: closing her curtains early each night; making sure windows and doors were locked. Even in this most remote place, where there was little risk of those men turning up and causing problems, Tom insisted on this regime. And so, with all the windows closed and with them being double glazed, the sound of the ocean was muted and distant.

Tucked up in her bed that night, she couldn't resist picking up the book. She flipped idly through the pages, enjoying a chapter on the Knockers—the pixie people who lived in the mines. They could, so it seemed, be kind and helpful. They showed the miners where to dig to find the richest deposits of metals. The men, in their turn, rewarded them by leaving tasty snacks and pasties, which they hoped would please their helpers.

But the Knockers had a different side to them. If they weren't treated with proper respect, they could become aggrieved and bad-tempered. Whistling, Lizzie learnt, drove them wild.

She was making a mental note not to whistle near the cottage, just in case Mrs Rowe's stories were true, when a page of the book caught her attention, marked as it was by a yellow sticker.

The chapter was headed 'The Green Man'. It was an intriguing story. And it was illustrated too. Some of the pictures were very strange. When she finally closed the book and lay down hoping to get to sleep, Lizzie was soon beginning to wonder if reading it late at night had been wise.

Sleep, when it came, was light and troubled. Her usual nightmares and even

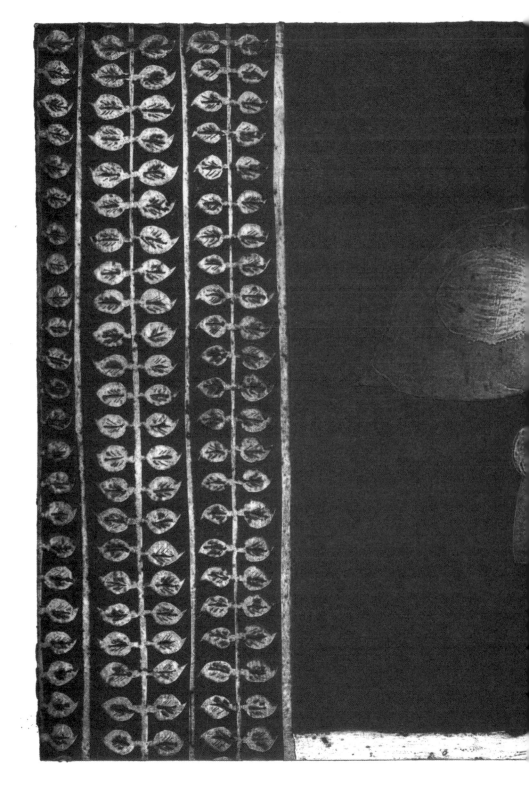

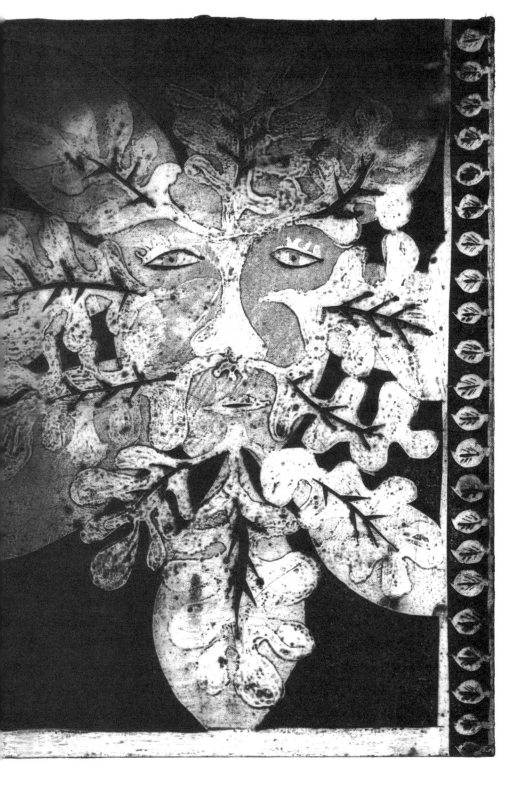

the wolf were driven away by woodland spirits, chasing her through a forest of oaks; by haunting voices amongst the trees from which there seemed to be no escape. As she struggled through the undergrowth, her wheels ensnared by roots and branches, twig-like fingers reached towards her … entangling in her long, loose hair … tap, tap, tapping against her skin.

At the dead of night, she woke with a start—hot and sweating, shaking with fear. She could hear it now—a gentle tapping—little more than a twig or leaves moving against the windowpane. The more she listened, the more she wondered. Nothing big grew close to the window: no bush or tree, which might touch the glass.

She dozed and woke … and dozed and woke … until in the end she could stand it no longer. The tapping was growing more insistent. She couldn't ignore it any longer.

"I'll have to go and look," she mumbled, switching on her bedside light, reaching for her fleecy top and for her cosy lambskin slippers.

Shifting from the bed to her chair, she wheeled herself quietly across the room. She didn't want to wake up Tom. In front of the curtained window, she paused.

"Of course there can't be anyone there," Lizzie said sternly to herself. "Anyone moving near the cabin would have triggered the two floodlights. And that clearly hasn't happened."

"Here goes," she murmured to herself, grasping and drawing the curtain aside, gritting her teeth and holding her breath. But there was nothing to be seen: only the blackness of the night and a few, small, distant stars.

"Phew! Thank goodness for that," she sighed, a wave of relief flooding over her.

But just as she lifted up her hand to pull the curtain closed again, a figure sprang up before her eyes. She gasped and reeled back in her chair. Lit by the light from within the room, a ghastly face looked in on her.

The head of the figure pressed close to the window. The nose was flattened, wide and shapeless. Dark eyes stared from the bright green face. The sculptured lips of the wide mouth curved in a knowing and grotesque smile. Instead of hair the head grew foliage. And where a normal person had ears, oak leaves sprouted out of the scalp.

"Ahhh!" Lizzie gasped in disbelief. Her eyes widened. Her mouth gaped. She could feel and hear the beat of her heart, drumming loudly in her head. Racing ever faster … faster.

The Green Man stood glaring at Lizzie. She sat unblinking, bewitched by the sight, only finally finding the courage to grab the curtain and swish it across—to shut away the horrible vision.

Wheeling her chair back close to her bed and to the comfort of the lamp, she sat rigid … clutching Crocker … trying to calm her shaking body.

Her eyes were fixed on the curtained window. Occasionally they slid to the door. Had she remembered to turn the key?

41

Ghostly Footprints

izzie sat staring at the door. In the gloom of the half lit room, she couldn't be sure about the handle. Had she seen it turning gently?

She held her breath and waited. Waited. She didn't want to call for Tom. She knew how soundly he was sleeping.

"Please, please let the door be locked!" the words were pounding in her brain.

Finally, when nothing happened, she breathed an enormous sigh of relief. Yet the horrible vision was stuck in her mind. Could this be what Hester meant? A terrifying manifestation, invoked by someone with those powers? If so, it must certainly be a warning.

Her eyes sought comfort from Tom's sleeping form. In the morning she'd tell him about it. Doubtless he would give her a lecture.

Even though sleeping in her chair was an almost impossible option—

because there was no support for her head—Lizzie dared not go back to her bed. So she laid a pillow on the table. Slumped forward across it, tucked round with a blanket, she catnapped through the rest of the night, with Crocker lying by her side.

When dawn broke she roused herself, made a comforting cup of tea, then transferred carefully back to her bed: anxious to shift from her cramped position; to stretch out as best she could; to rest her aching shoulders and neck.

"You shouldn't read books like that at bedtime," Tom lectured her firmly later, when she told him the horrible story. "And where did the book come from in the first place? And who would have put it beside your bed?"

"I've no idea," Lizzie answered.

"Was it a dream, perhaps?" Tom suggested. "You always suffer from nightmares, don't you?"

"No." Lizzie was sure. It had not been a dream.

She was unusually quiet over breakfast. Mrs Rowe was watching her slyly. "I hope you slept well?" she enquired with a smile.

"Yes, very well, thank you," Lizzie insisted.

On their way back from breakfast later, they stopped on the grass in front of the cabin and focused on the narrow flowerbed that ran along beneath the window. They couldn't be certain, but they wondered: could they detect a flattened area in the bed below the window —where someone or something might have been standing? And were those fresh leaves on the ground? Oak leaves, severed from their branches?

Ghostly feet wouldn't leave their mark. Ghostly figures didn't drop leaves. And yet there was another problem. Any normal human being would have triggered the two floodlights.

"Someone is trying to frighten us, Lizzie," Tom said later over a coffee.

"Yes," she answered. "And they're succeeding." She couldn't hold back a convulsive shiver. "I hope it won't come back tonight."

"We mustn't allow them to drive us away," Tom's strong voice was so insistent.

"No. Of course not," Lizzie agreed, doing her best to sound positive.

But even on such a beautiful morning, with the golden sun in a wide, blue sky, she trembled at the memory—of the terror that had seized her—when that figure had sprung into view.

42

Red Rag to a Bull

"I wish I'd booked the cabin for longer. We only have a couple more days," Lizzie said later, sounding troubled. "We're nowhere near achieving our goal. I think we'll need more time, don't you?"

Tom agreed. They would need more time.

"I'll ask Mrs Rowe to come over and see me," she said. "And then I'll ask for an extra week. Of course she might not be able to do it. She may already have a booking."

"And, even if she doesn't," Tom said, "I don't think she'll want us to stay any longer."

But when it came to it, Tom was wrong, although it was clearly touch and go.

When he'd gone off for his morning run, Hester came across from her cottage, bringing a tin of home-made goodies. She and Lizzie sat at the table chatting over a cup of coffee and crunching on the delicious biscuits.

"There's something I want to ask you," said Lizzie, sliding her wallet out of her pocket and placing it casually on the table.

"You ask away, m'dear," Hester said. A barely perceptible shift of her gaze beneath the heavy droop of her lids told Lizzie that she'd noticed the wallet.

"I'd like to book another week, please," Lizzie said unexpectedly.

"Oh yes?" the woman said doubtfully, shifting uncomfortably on her chair and avoiding Lizzie's eyes.

"But perhaps you already have a booking?" Lizzie suggested, waiting and hoping.

"Well … no … I don't think I have. Although I would have to check in my diary …"

Hester was obviously tempted. She strummed her fingers nervously. Her eyes strayed to the bulging wallet.

"And I'd have to check with Wes," she said.

Lizzie dreaded Wesley's input, which she thought was bound to be negative.

"I'm sorry," she said in an innocent voice. "I hadn't realised that your brother was involved in your letting business. I thought it was you who owned the cabin. But, of course, if Wesley's your boss, you must certainly ask him first."

It was like a red rag to a bull. Hester Rowe's body stiffened.

"Of course it's my cabin and my business," she snapped back, glaring crossly at Lizzie.

Her mouth was pursed with irritation. Her fingers strummed even faster. "And Wesley is certainly not my boss."

"It will only be a few extra days," Lizzie said persuasively. "I do so love your beautiful cabin. I'll pay you all the money up front."

She reached across and picked up her wallet. Then drawing out crisp twenty pound notes, she counted them loudly onto the table. She even added an extra note, before sliding the pile towards the woman.

Mrs Rowe was clearly torn. Her eyes lit up at the sight of the money. Her fingers stopped their incessant strumming. As they crept towards the notes, Lizzie held her breath and waited.

Not till the money was double checked, folded and tucked safely away within the confines of Hester's bosom, did Lizzie feel that she could relax. Later, delighted with the result, she and Tom had a good laugh together.

"How could you do it, Shrimp?" he exclaimed. "And still manage to keep a straight face? But I don't fancy our landlady's chances when dear brother Wes finds out. I wouldn't want to be in her shoes. I think he's going to be furious, don't you?"

"I'm sure you're right," Lizzie said.

"I only hope that his seething fury doesn't trigger something nasty—some unpleasant action against us," Tom said in an anxious voice.

"He may seem slightly built," he continued, "and he's certainly very lame. But he has a fanatical gleam in his eye. I think he could be a ruthless man … if somebody pushed him a bit too far."

43

An Almighty Row

L ater that same afternoon, with all the doors and windows wide open, both in the cabin and the cottage, Tom and Lizzie could hear loud voices—the noisy row that was bound to ensue when Hester gave her brother the news about her extended let for her cabin.

Lizzie sat out of sight in the cabin, keeping well back behind the curtains, doing her best to hear what was said. She couldn't catch all the words, but it was clearly a lively row.

"How could you be so stupid, woman?" That was Wesley's angry voice.

"I'm sorry, Wes," his sister whined.

"I knew that cabin would be a mistake. We don't want all these foreigners here. It's dangerous. You know it is."

"But don't you see, Wes? We needs the money."

"Needs the money! What for?" Wesley's angry voice was dismissive.

"It's all very well for you," Hester snarled, "your garage business is doing well, what with the taxi work and all. But Fern and me—we're struggling, even though he works all hours. The fishing's been so poor of late—what with the newfangled regulations, and the dreadful weather we've had—all our catches have been down. We're losing money hand over fist. My cabin is our only hope."

"I don't understand you, Sis." Wesley sounded exasperated.

"It's only one more week, Wes," Hester did her best to persuade him. "And … there's something about the girl. I can't quite pin it down … but there is."

"Not even with your 'special powers'?" Wesley's voice was full of sarcasm.

'Special powers'. That phrase again. Lizzie caught the words quite clearly.

" It can't be fun in that contraption," Hester's voice continued firmly. "But she always has a smile. I can't help feeling sorry for her. And she loves my little cabin."

"Sorry? Huhh!" Wesley mumped. "And she loves your little cabin?"

Wesley's scornful voice continued. "She's wrapped you round her little finger. Had you thought that she might be a fake?"

"A fake, Wesley! What do you mean?"

"We've heard these kinds of stories before," Wesley stormed on grumpily. "People tromping around in wheelchairs when, in fact, they don't need them."

"Oh, if only," Lizzie muttered, listening with a wry grin.

"It might be some silly trick she's playing. She might be testing out your cabin. And when she reports to the County Council, they'll probably come and close you down."

"Oh surely not," Hester whimpered.

"Or she might be an undercover agent. Somebody from MI5. Had you ever thought of that?" Wesley asked impatiently.

"Oh dear no, Wes. That I hadn't."

"MI5? Good grief!" Tom murmured.

"And then we've the problem with that car …"

There was a pause. Lizzie waited.

Then suddenly Wesley's explosive voice: "Have you totally lost your senses? Why are all these windows open? Anyone could hear what we're saying."

"Oh dear!" Lizzie exclaimed disappointedly, as Wesley slammed the windows shut. She closed her eyes and concentrated, struggling to catch the words. But although she could hear the sound of voices, she couldn't work out what they were saying.

"There is a problem with those … people." Wesley continued out of hearing. "I've seen that car parked up on the headland. I'm sure it's the one we've seen before—the big one with the blackened windows."

"Blackened windows?" his sister questioned. "Why would they have blackened windows?"

"Villains like to have those windows," Wesley answered, nodding knowledgeably. "They feel more secure if they're hidden from sight."

"Villains?" Hester exclaimed in amazement. "Whatever will you be telling me next?"

"We've spotted the car now twice in the village. And Walter recognised the vehicle. He's seen it in town on several occasions—over the past year or two. He's afraid they're closing in."

"Why yes. I think I've seen the car," Hester responded thoughtfully. "I've seen it cruising past here. I even asked the girl about it—if she was expecting visitors? She looked quite innocent. Surprised."

"Hmm!" Wesley snorted loudly. "We need a solution for that girl—something permanent I think."

"You're not up to all your old tricks again … are you?" Hester's voice was suspicious now. "You and your Dad and those wretched lads?"

"I haven't worked all these years to have her come and spoil our game. Just some little slip of a maid," Wesley exclaimed in a bitter voice.

"Just leave her to me," his sister begged.

"Well, isn't that just what I *have* been doing? And are you having any success? Quite the opposite, I should say. Now she'll be staying here even longer. She'll be poking her nosy nose even deeper."

"There's something funny going on," Hester murmured thoughtfully. "I only wish I could work it all out. I think she has a part to play."

"She's not going to play any part in my action," Wesley insisted with a snort.

"Just you make sure you look after her proper." Hester eyed her brother sharply.

"The only part she'll play for me," Wesley muttered to himself, unheard even by his sister, "is a speedy and final departure. And the sooner the better, I say."

44

A Trip is Planned

n the following morning, to Lizzie's surprise, just as they were finishing breakfast, Wesley came to call on his sister.

Lizzie sat observing the man, whilst she chomped her way through a chunk of fresh bread—thick with butter and crunchy with honeycomb. She guessed that at some time in his life he'd had a terrible accident. He wasn't as badly off as she was—at least he was still up on his legs—but his every move seemed difficult. His face was lined from years of pain. Lizzie wondered what had happened. But she didn't dare to ask.

"There Sis," the man said. "Hedley asked me to give you this rabbit. It's skinned and cleaned and ready bagged. I think it ought to go straight in the freezer."

"Thank you Wes. How very kind," his sister told him with a smile. "There's no time like the present," she said. And taking the rabbit, she left the room.

When she had gone, Wesley turned to Lizzie. He was looking surprisingly friendly.

"The lads and I have been thinking," he said quietly, "about your important investigations. We know there's a chap living up on the moor. Very few people have ever met him. But," and he lowered his voice to a hiss, "we all reckon that he's your man. The one you said you were looking for … ?"

Lizzie gasped in delighted amazement.

"If you like, I could take you to meet him," Wesley continued with a smile.

"Oh yes." She nodded excitedly.

"It can be our little secret," Wesley whispered close to her ear, tapping the side of his nose with a finger and watching out for his sister's return.

"'Tis a wild and desolate place. My sister hates me going there," he added by way of explanation. "We wouldn't want her to stop us—would we?"

He raised a finger to his lips and then, as his sister returned to the room, he said in a perfectly normal voice "I'll pick you up in half an hour. The weather isn't up to much, but I thought you might like a bit of a drive."

"That's a kind thought Wes," Mrs Rowe said. "As long as you keep well away from the moor." She gave her brother a warning look. "You won't see much up there today anyway, not with the weather closed down like this."

"We'll go for a run along the coast. I expect you'd like that, wouldn't you?" He winked at Lizzie: a shady, surreptitious wink, when his sister's back was turned.

"Yes. That's a lovely idea," she answered.

When they got back to the cabin she said "Isn't this exciting, Tom?"

"Yes," he replied. "I *think* it is. But I wonder why he's changed his mind … and decided to help us after all?"

"Perhaps he's feeling guilty," she suggested, "after being so unpleasant."

"Hmmm … perhaps," Tom muttered doubtfully.

45

The Lake

The weather had indeed closed down. As they drove towards the moor, a thick mist, more like a fog, blanketed the countryside. Lizzie and Tom would never have guessed that a May morning could be so foul. The further they went, the worse it became.

Having expected beautiful views of rocky tors and tumbling streams, Lizzie was naturally disappointed. The clouds were so low; the light was so poor. And Wesley's headlamps didn't help. They only lit a wall of fog.

The narrow road, bordered by boulders, wound its way across the moor. Banks of gorse loomed either side. Their would-be stunning, yellow flowers were dulled and dimmed by the dingy light.

No other traffic moved on the road. Lizzie lost all sense of direction. They might be almost anywhere.

Wesley wove his way slowly: through the dank, crepuscular gloom, having to stop from time to time to avoid the shaggy, long-tailed sheep. Seemingly unaware of danger, they lay almost in the gutter or cluttering up the road itself. Even those with tiny lambs took no notice of the car. Only the hooting of the horn cleared a pathway through the animals.

The voice of the horn, strangely muted, shifted other ghostlike grazers. Desultory groups of wandering cattle, with their thick pelts drenched with dew, jostled surprisingly close to the car: big, black, lumbering beasts with their broad, white, woolly waistbands.

"Belted Galloway," Wesley mumbled.

And there were Highland cattle too. They were huge, impressive creatures, their long, dangling, chestnut coats, swishing rug-like around their legs. As they ambled slowly away, they swung amazingly long, curved horns—sometimes narrowly missing the car.

As Tom whispered quietly to Lizzie, "They seem out of place on a Cornish moor."

Yet Lizzie loved the chunky calves with their fluffy, golden coats; their curling tongues and wet noses; their huge eyes, fringed by sweeping lashes.

The spectral forms of moorland ponies, drifted across the road ahead.

"Oh look!" Lizzie exclaimed, delighted. "Look at the mare and the dear little foal."

Eventually they left the road. A flat and seemingly endless track led them on across the moor, now peculiarly bleak and bare: on and on, down a steady incline, towards a wide, cloud-shrouded basin. Lizzie could sense rather than see the darkly spreading sheet of water.

"Wow! What a fabulous place …" Lizzie heard Tom's hoarse whisper. "It's very King Arthur, don't you think? I've read that he ruled in this very region.

This could be the legendary lake.

"Any minute now," he continued, "you'll see a hand emerge from the water. You'll see The Lady of the Lake reaching out for Excalibur. Her long and slender arm will stretch up, 'clothed in white samite, mystic, wonderful'. Do you remember the poem Lizzie?"

But Lizzie knew it would not be The Lady. As the car cruised past the lake, she pressed her face up close to the window, peering out through the rain splattered glass.

Cloud hung low on the peat-dark lake. It drifted on the water's surface, swelling and rolling then welling up, together with the sound of the music that was already filling her brain: sighing strings and the song of the cello—subtle, rounded, delightfully mellow.

Lizzie held her breath and waited: listening for the soaring voice of the plaintive, reedy horn that always ushered in her swan.

And here he came with wings arched high, gliding majestically out of the mist, like a galleon in full sail, his stark, white feathers glowing brightly. The long and powerful, sinuous neck carried the elegant, bright-eyed head. The golden beak and the emerald eyes were turned as ever in her direction.

As the music faded and died, billowing clouds engulfed the swan, stealing the vision from Lizzie's sight. She sank back, sighing heavily. The music was still a mystery to her.

When she'd been a little girl, Lizzie had fancied becoming a dancer. Swan Lake had been her favourite ballet. But although she had the lake and the swan, this music didn't belong to that ballet. It had a more haunting, spooky wildness. The sound of it always made her tremble.

"Your friend the swan?" She heard Tom's voice.

"Oh yes, my friend the swan," she answered. "I'm sure that he has a special name. Why is it that I can't remember?"

'Never, Never Go into the Circle ... '

Wesley changing gear roughly, brought her back to reality. The lake was far behind them now. They were climbing higher onto the moor, swamped by the ever lowering weather.

The darkly sullen light persisted. But then, quite unexpectedly, sunlight cleaving the heavy cloud provided a glimpse of open spaces: a seemingly enchanted upland.

"Ooh!" Lizzie gasped aloud.

Grasses, wild flowers and thistles were draped with a mesh of woven silk: the webs of countless tiny spiders. Their heavily dewdrop spattered work, reflecting the light from the shafting sun, resembled a diamond encrusted carpet.

"It's just like magic, Tom," she whispered.

Then she suddenly noticed the figures. A large number of tall, grey stones stood with their feet sunk deep in the carpet. Hester's words came back to her. 'Never, never go into the circle ...'

"Stop, please," Lizzie cried in fright. "Don't let's go this way," she begged.

But Wesley pressed on, despite her cries. As their wheels defiled the carpet, a jolt made Lizzie gasp with pain. They'd strayed across some hidden threshold. They were driving into the circle of stones.

"This isn't right. We shouldn't be here. This circle belongs to the ancient past." Lizzie was almost sobbing now.

'To the past ... the past ... the ancient past.' The echoing chorus filled her head.

Leaning forward as best she could and pressing her face to the windowpane, Lizzie peered out through the gloom at the stones. Was it her imagination, or were they moving? Closing in? As if they were drawing her into their fold ... as if they might never let her go ...

As the car slipped past the central stone, she turned her head to peer more closely.

"Ahhh! It's the magic symbol," she whispered, reaching out for Tom's hand.

Long since carved in the face of the stone, the faint lines were weathered and worn. But they were none the less clear to Lizzie. She'd seen that strange pattern of lines before. The recognition made her shudder.

Yet, even as she focused her eyes, the swirling mist took over again. Just as quickly as they'd appeared, the stony spirits vanished from sight: first cloaked by the swirling mist, then merging with the descending cloud.

The car was climbing slowly now along a rough and winding path. The endless jolting made Lizzie feel queasy. Peering out through the gathering gloom, she could just make out the lines of a tor. It was peopled by hordes of granite chunks that nestled in the grassy slopes. It was topped by an amazing structure.

Gigantic stacks of huge, flat boulders were placed and balanced carefully, as if by some almighty hand. They towered high above the car, as it ground its way slowly across the slope. Distorted by the swirling mist,  they looked as if they were on the move: rearing up and tipping. Tipping. Poised to tumble down the hill, crushing and mangling all in their path.

Lizzie cowered in her seat, closing her eyes and gritting her teeth: fighting down the waves of nausea; hearing in her mind again, the crashing, the smashing, the tearing of metal.

Tom's voice was reassuring. "I'm here for you, Shrimp. You'll be OK."

Suddenly the car stopped.

"This is the old mine," Wesley announced.

47

Raucous Voices

The car had stopped on a flat open area. Lizzie soon found herself out of the car and sitting ready in her chair. The chilly air crept damp around her. An eerie silence pressed close; the only sound the occasional clink that came from the hot and resting engine.

Away to her left and yet towering too close, there loomed an old and ugly building. Moisture ran down the rough-cut granite. Pennywort and ferns sprouted. Dark holes gaped in the crumbling walls. A huge chimney rose from the building, its top hidden in lowering cloud.

"That's the old engine house," Wesley declared.

"And there's the cottage you're going to visit. That's where the mine Captain used to live." He pointed towards what looked like a dwelling, perhaps some forty yards away.

Lizzie glanced nervously at the cottage. What she could see of it through the fog looked dingy, almost tumbledown. It certainly didn't look inviting.

Noticing her hesitation, the man continued persuasively, "Of course I haven't met the hermit. He keeps himself to himself, do you see? But the lads all think that he's your man." Wesley nodded encouragingly, his lined face twisted into a grimace, probably meant to be a smile.

"I see," said Lizzie doubtfully. "But if he keeps himself to himself, he might not welcome visitors."

"My good sister did hear tell that the hermit likes people dropping in. So I'm sure he'll be happy to see you," Wesley insisted.

Faced by such a desolate scene, Lizzie's enthusiasm was fading. The cold and damp were getting to her. They seemed to be seeping into her bones. She longed to leave this depressing place. She longed for a comforting hot drink of tea.

"You don't have to stay long," Wesley wheedled. "Just long enough to meet the man. To make quite sure that it's Tregarrow. He'll probably make you a

nice cup of tea," the man added, noting her shiver.

"What do you think, Tom?" Lizzie whispered.

"It's yet another challenge," he answered. "But come on Shrimp. I know you can face it. And I'll be with you. We'll face it together."

With Tom's words ringing in her ears and his comforting hand on her shoulder, Lizzie started towards the cottage, which stood on its own across the clearing. She could just make out the ragged remnants of an old and broken fence, enclosing what must have been a front garden. A gate hung on a single hinge, rotting and propped at a drunken angle.

The garden itself was a wilderness of overgrown ramblers, choked by nettles. But the path to the door was clear enough. It was almost spotless, Lizzie thought, as if it had been recently brushed.

As they started along the path, raucous voices broke the silence. Startled, Lizzie stopped abruptly. A large flock of squawking birds rose from somewhere on the roof. Their black wings beat the heavy air. They circled angrily over her head, diving and swooping alarmingly close. They reminded her of a horrible film that had frightened her as a child.

She could see the gunmetal grey of their beaks, stabbing oh so close to her face. She could see the orange rims of their eyes. Shaken, Lizzie cringed in her chair, hoping and praying they'd soon go away.

She paused, breathless, on the doorstep, staring at the closed door. The paint had peeled from the rotting wood, showing a succession of colours, all of them now long since faded, but hinting at blues and red and yellow. Yet Lizzie noticed to her surprise that the brass doorknob and the knocker were clean and bright—as if they'd been polished.

Leaning forward and reaching up she could only just manage to lift the knocker. She sat still, holding her breath and waiting, trying to steady her shattered nerves. This ought to be a thrilling moment. So why did she have this creepy feeling?

Was it perhaps the weird brass knocker? She hadn't noticed it at first. But now, as she sat there waiting and staring, the peculiar figure caught her eye: a strangely twisted, pixie like person seemed to be scowling down at her.

"It looks like one of those beastly Knockers," Lizzie muttered nervously.

"A Knocker knocker," Tom joked in her ear.

But Lizzie found it hard to smile. She couldn't take her eyes from the figure. The face had such a strange expression.

"It has a familiar look," she hissed.

When nobody came to answer the door, Lizzie knew she must knock again. With some reluctance, she reached for the knocker. Lifting it gingerly in her hand, she knocked as boldly as she could.

Was that an answering voice she could hear? Somebody calling out 'Come in'?

"Oh Tom … do you think it's our Dad?" she whispered. "Could it possibly be him?" Her voice was shaking with excitement.

"We'll only find out by opening the door." Tom could be so down to earth.

The doorknob turned easily. The door swung quietly when Lizzie pushed it. The hinges must have been well oiled, although it would only open so far.

Tipping her wheels, she crossed the threshold. Then slipping in through the awkward gap she found herself in a darkened room. The air was dank. She could smell the mould.

To her left she could see the outline of a window, but it was clearly closed and shuttered. With only the half opened door behind her and no proper source of light, the details of the room were hidden.

"But there must be somebody living here," Lizzie murmured happily, lifting a hand to shield her eyes.

Across the room, a door was ajar. A pencil-thin shaft of light was shining directly into her face. And there was something else as well. Lizzie could hear the sound of music coming from the open doorway: maybe an old-fashioned gramophone. Or it might be a radio. Whatever it was, it sounded homely.

She set off across the room … with confidence … towards the music and the light.

48

The Trap

Only Tom's frantic cry saved Lizzie. "Stop! Stop! Shrimp! Stop!"

At the very last moment she realised. Where the floor should be, there was no floor. The cottage must have been undermined. Part of the floor had completely collapsed. She was teetering on the very brink of a black and yawning chasm.

As her wheelchair ground to a halt, chunks of old and broken slates were scuffed over the rim of the pit. Lizzie could hear the sound of those fragments: falling, falling, clunking, splashing, into the ruined mine far below.

She sat frozen, gripping her wheels. The music stopped. Silence reigned. And then she heard a peculiar voice: softly sinister, gently persuasive.

"Come, my dear. I am waiting for you. Do please come and have tea with me? I'm so looking forward to meeting you."

The hair rose up on Lizzie's neck. Her hands trembled. Her heart beat fast.

"Quick Tom! We must escape." Lizzie's voice was desperate. "It's a trap. I know it is."

Poised as she was on the edge of the chasm, she hardly dared to move at all—even so much as a little finger. Shaking with fear and gripping her wheels, her knuckles white, her face taut, she could feel the crumbling rim of the pit giving way beneath her weight. In the silence of the room, she could hear the rattle and clatter of debris, bouncing off the rocky walls. One more inch and she'd be gone—down into those cavernous depths.

Lizzie had never been good with heights. Even the thought of a drop below her could make her feel horribly sick and wobbly. The ghastly sensation came creeping now: a clutching terror in her stomach; rising up and suffocating; turning her muscles into jelly … demolishing her power to escape.

"Help me Tom … please …" she begged, her voice a fragile rasp of despair.

"Come on Shrimp …" she heard his voice. She felt the power of his guiding hands, as gripped by horror, she eased herself back … slowly, slowly away from the brink, terrified lest she lose control and find herself sliding forward again.

Backing out through the half open door, she struggled with the narrow gap. Yet she dare not turn her back on that room. The horrible thing with the luring voice might come creeping up on her … without her even seeing it.

"Quick! Quick Tom," she sobbed aloud.

As she swung her chair and set off down the path, hideous laughter filled the cottage. A chilling cackle followed her, as she rushed out through the gate and started across towards the car.

But Lizzie's troubles weren't over yet. Wesley was preparing to leave. She could see the man's face in the wing mirror, checking the scene behind as he turned. She could see what looked like a satisfied smile.

When her wheelchair loomed into view, the smile was wiped from Wesley's face. His mouth dropped open. He stared in amazement.

"I think he's going to abandon us, Tom," Lizzie cried in desperation, speeding herself towards the car.

Wesley was obviously revving the engine and preparing to drive away. At the very last moment, he slammed on the brakes. Then climbing painfully out of the car, he came reluctantly back to help her.

"Just turning the car around ready," he said, with a forced and sickly smile, his mouth pursed, his eyes screwed.

"Did you have any luck?" he asked, grunting as he loaded her chair.

"Did you find the man you wanted? I felt quite sure that you would," he said, climbing back into the driving seat.

Lizzie felt sure that he knew that she wouldn't. She sat very still in the back of the car, trying to steady her shaking body.

"Come on Shrimp. You're safe. I'm here." Tom's consoling words brought comfort.

But Lizzie wasn't feeling safe. She tried to recall Wesley's earlier comments. What was it the man had said? 'The hermit likes people dropping in'.

Glancing up from time to time, she watched the face in the rear-view mirror. The smiling mask hid something unpleasant. Disappointment, Lizzie thought, tinged with another emotion—cold fury.

Tom had been right. This was serious stuff. What one might call deadly serious.

As they made their way down the village street, Lizzie noticed a big, black car parked in front of the Post Office shop.

"Flipping emmets!" Wesley growled, negotiating the narrow gap. "With them girt big, fancy cars, hogging the road and causing trouble. Folks with much more money than sense! Look at the length of that there thing. And all that horrible blackened glass? 'Tidn' proper, that's what I say."

49

A Shadow Falling Across Her Face …

On the following morning, Lizzie pottered around in the cabin. Although the weather wasn't warm, she'd known that Tom would love a swim, so she'd sent him off to the beach with his towel.

"You must make the best of the fine weather. For all we know, it may change again," she'd said.

"As long as you'll be alright on your own?" After yesterday's grim adventure, Tom was bound to be concerned. They'd sat up long into the night, mulling over the whole affair. But Lizzie was fully recovered now, from what she acknowledged had been a near miss.

"I'll be fine," she reassured him. "I promise you that whatever happens, I shall stay here, safe indoors. There'll be no gallivanting today."

Lizzie smiled to herself at the word. It had been one of her mother's favourites—old-fashioned, passed on from their Granny. And now, in her turn, she was using it too.

"Take your jacket," she called to Tom. "There's a chilly wind. You're going to need it."

She knew what the reply would be. "I don't need a jacket. I'm warm. Don't fuss." She'd heard that a few times in her life. It was her brother's standard answer if anyone asked him to wear warm clothing.

Lizzie imagined him on the quay, wearing only a T-shirt and shorts. Goodness knows how he managed like that. She'd be frozen without a coat and long trousers.

Hester came and knocked at the door.

"I'm off to do my shopping," she said. "Is there anything I can get for you? You're not too nervous here on your own?"

"Of course I'm not." Lizzie tried not to snap. "I can manage perfectly well. But when you come back through the village, could you please bring some more fish and chips?"

"Indeed I will," Hester answered. "And some of they girt big pickles too," she added, licking her lips with a flourish, making a loud slurping noise and smiling broadly with delight at the thought of the crunchy pickles. Then she went off down the path. Lizzie could hear the sound of the car, pulling slowly away down the lane.

She sat quietly, thinking of Tom: doubtless out there making enquiries, but mostly enjoying the sea and the sand. She loved to think of him on the beach. She'd heard that the very best place for a swim was another half an hour's walk away on the other side of the village. Without her presence to slow him down, he would be free to roam at will. That beach would be well within his reach.

She could visualise him now: running on the firm sand, his dark locks blowing in the breeze. Then swimming happily in the sea: his strong arms cleaving the turquoise water; his hair held back by that wide, red band.

Lizzie had always loved swimming too. It was Tom who had taught her the butterfly stroke when she was only twelve years old.

"It strengthens your upper body, Lizzie, especially your arms and your shoulders. You should do it more," he would urge.

Lizzie had done her best for Tom, but she had always found it a struggle. Now she was endlessly grateful to him; her arms and her shoulders were stronger than average. And that, she had found, was a huge advantage in her present circumstances.

She would have loved to go for a swim; and she'd already been tempted to try. But common sense told her that would be mad. And she knew she must keep her promise to Betty.

Having made herself a coffee, she sat contentedly in the doorway with dear Crocker on her lap and reading one of her favourite books. It was set in a secret valley in Cornwall. She'd read it a couple of times before, but she wanted to read it again. She always noticed something new; always found it comforting.

Despite the crisp and salty breeze, warm sunshine streamed through the open doorway. Lizzie dozed comfortably in her chair. She didn't hear the approach of her visitors. A shadow falling across her face was the only warning of their arrival.

Jolted awake, she looked up in surprise to see two figures filling the doorway. Standing with their backs to the light, she couldn't see their faces at first. But their outlines were unmistakeable: one a huge hulk in an ill-fitting suit; the other so neat and smartly dressed with diamonds flashing as he moved forward.

Lizzie started in her chair, suddenly gripped by fear and dread. Not one word was spoken to her. The men weren't messing about this time. They moved quickly into the room and, with only a nod to each other, went immediately into action: the smiling man checking round the room, rifling drawers and stripping the wardrobe, while the other one attended to Lizzie.

He threw her precious book aside. It struck the wall then fell to the floor, the cover torn, the pages mangled. Lizzie could have wept at the sight.

And then her precious Crocker was grabbed.

"Oh no!" Lizzie winced and moaned as Crocker was trampled underfoot.

She clung on tight to the wheels of her chair. But she was no match for the man. He wrenched her fingers away from the chair and lifted her bodily into the air, casually tossing the chair aside. Then carrying her clutched against his chest, as if she were no more than a doll, he swept her away down the garden path.

Lizzie hated being carried. It was bad enough being stuck in her chair with her feet propped on the rail. But when she was picked up and carried along— that was the thing that she hated the most: the dangling of her useless limbs; the feeling of utter helplessness.

Being carried by this man was foul. His head loomed much too close to hers. His breath was putrid. His body stank.

Lizzie thrashed her arms and yelled. But even as she screamed for help, she realised that shouting was pointless. Hester had gone to do her shopping. There was nobody there to hear her cries.

50

Hip Chick to the Rescue

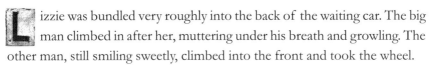izzie was bundled very roughly into the back of the waiting car. The big man climbed in after her, muttering under his breath and growling. The other man, still smiling sweetly, climbed into the front and took the wheel.

She closed her eyes and gritted her teeth. The huge body pressed so close. The ghastly smell was overpowering. She could feel her stomach churning. Any minute she might be sick.

"You mess this car and you're in dead trouble," the threat was muttered savagely.

The man's breath wafted over her. She bit her lip and clenched her fists, clamping them firmly to her mouth, sealing her nostrils as best she could and trying to breathe through the sleeve of her shirt.

They hadn't been going for many minutes, when Lizzie heard the driver cursing. The car ground slowly to a halt. A vehicle blocked the road ahead.

This was a typical Cornish lane, little more than eight feet wide with high stone banks on either side. Such lanes have occasional passing places, widened for the modern traffic. But a driver may have to back up for a mile in order to find a place to pass.

From her seat in the back of the car, Lizzie could see enough through the windscreen to recognise the plump figure that was dancing along the road towards them. Hester Rowe, in a nervous state, was soon knocking on the darkened glass. The driver lowered the window—an inch.

"Good morning, Madam," he said, with his usual honeyed smile. "Would you please move your car—and quickly."

"Oh sir. I'm sorry, that I am," Mrs Rowe gasped in a fluster. "I wouldn't have had this happen for the world. But my poor old car … she's got a flat tyre. I have been telling my husband for ages and ages that dear old Bertha needs new tyres. But what has he done about it? Nothing! Just like a man … if you'll excuse me …" she bobbed and beamed apologetically, suddenly realising what she'd said.

It all struck Lizzie as rather strange. Hester seemed to be acting a part. Could it be that she knew of her plight? That somehow she knew that Lizzie was there?

"I've rung my brother. He'll soon be here," the woman smiled reassuringly, waving a very smart mobile phone.

"I don't know how we'd manage, do you, without all these newfangled gadgets?"

Lizzie craned her neck as far as she could. She couldn't see the woman clearly, but she could certainly hear her words.

"This 'ere case came all the way from London," Mrs Rowe boasted. "'Twas bought 'specially for me by my clever nephew, Denzil. He has an eye for class and fashion," Mrs Rowe confided with pride.

"All the hip chicks have one like this," she assured her captive audience. "That was why he got it for me—to keep his Auntie in the fashion."

If Lizzie hadn't been so frightened, the thought of Mrs Rowe as a hip chick would have reduced her to helpless giggles. But, as it was, she bit her lip harder.

"This 'ere phone can take photos m'dear," Mrs Rowe told the nice, smiling man. "And they are surprising clear. I could take one now," she said obligingly, "a picture of this fine big motor."

Lizzie felt the big man freeze.

"Oh no ..." she groaned in despair. That certainly wasn't a wise suggestion.

With one hand clamped over Lizzie's mouth, thrusting her firmly back in her seat, the big man slipped his other hand swiftly into the front of his jacket. He seemed to be grasping hold of something ... and beginning to draw it out ...

But the other man had noticed the move. He turned in his seat. His mouth smiled sweetly.

"Not just now, Sid," he warned gently. "There's more than one way to kill a cat ... especially a silly old cat like this one. Just you leave it to me, dear boy."

He lowered the window and smiled at Hester.

"Don't upset yourself," he said kindly. "We can go round another way. It isn't a problem, I assure you."

Then, as if it were an afterthought: "That is a very beautiful phone. I haven't seen one like that before. May I hold it for a moment?" he asked with one of his extra sweet smiles.

"Of course, m'dear." Mrs Rowe primped, beaming with delight at the man and handing her phone in through the window.

Lizzie, suspecting what might happen next, knew that this was her only chance. Taking a big breath in through her nostrils and opening her mouth as wide as she could, she sunk her teeth in the filthy hand.

As the man recoiled in pain, Lizzie lurched upright in her seat.

"Mrs Rowe! Help!" she screamed loudly, leaning forward as far as she could, frantically waving her arms at Hester.

The woman didn't seem surprised.

"I thought I might find you here, Miss Stevenson! What *are* you doing? And are you alright?"

"Kidnapped ..." Lizzie managed to shout, before the filthy bleeding hand was clamped back firmly over her mouth and the window was smartly closed.

As the car began to back, Mrs Rowe was dancing in fury, shouting and banging on the windows. She was surprisingly quick on her feet and doing her best to keep up with the car. Lizzie watched with increasing horror as the driver kept swinging the wheel—doing his very best to catch her and squash her into the stony bank.

"There dear boy," the smiling man laughed, when they had backed well away from the woman. "It was easy, wasn't it? No need for any unpleasantness."

"I told you she was a silly old cat," he added with a smile of satisfaction.

"But look boss!" the big man shouted, pointing excitedly out through the windscreen.

"Blimey! What's she doing now?"

51

Bullocks

Hester Rowe was standing still in the middle of the road. She must have released her long, black hair. It floated out wildly around her shoulders—a great mass of dead straight locks with the tips of the hair just curling up. With her arms held wide and high in the air, she was gazing fixedly into the heavens. Lizzie couldn't hear the words, but she could see the woman's mouth working.

"Don't take any notice of her. I told you she's a silly old ..."

But the smiling man never finished the sentence. The car came to a grinding halt.

"What next?" Lizzie moaned. "Help me someone. Please help," the words were pounding in her brain. She couldn't see out of the back window. But could she hear the sound of cattle?

The smiler's language was unrepeatable. A large herd of well-grown bullocks filled and blocked the lane behind. Beyond the bullocks a massive green tractor now hove noisily into view with farmer Hedley at the helm. It was his new and cherished John Deere—something that he'd always wanted and had only finally attained after years of careful living. Rather too careful, Dority thought … starved of hats and holidays.

The animals jostled behind the car. They started licking the rear window. It looked as if they were doing their best to rearrange the rear window wiper. The big man sagged and began to moan.

"Whatever will the boss say? You know what he's like about this motor. One dent or scratch … and we'll be mincemeat."

Even the smiler was looking anxious; his permanently upturned mouth was straightened in a grimace of anger. He was twisting and turning in his seat, trying to work out what to do next. Eventually he eased the car forward as far away from the bullocks as possible.

But he couldn't go very far. For around the corner came Hester Rowe, waving a long French stick of bread. Lizzie could see her clearly now, brandishing what she must suppose was the woman's only weapon: perhaps the supermarket's finest … rigid, hard and tough as old boots.

Lizzie could hear the woman's shouts. "Stop them Hedley. They've kidnapped the girl … and, what's more, my telephone … I can't lose that," she wailed loudly.

"Don't you let them get away," Hester screeched at the top of her voice, dancing wildly in the road and making vicious stabbing gestures towards the driver of the car.

It was such a ludicrous sight, Lizzie felt a giggle rising. And yet she feared for the woman's life. These men were thugs. Hardened criminals. They wouldn't stop at anything—anything that might aid their escape—like crushing a defenceless woman.

Lizzie looked at the furious face reflected in the driving mirror. She'd originally thought that the face was kind. The full mouth was always smiling and there were crinkles round his eyes. But now she could see that the eyes were evil: snake-like almost in appearance; lacking any depth or warmth.

The bullocks had crept up close again. And they were soon resuming their games. They rubbed themselves on the back of the vehicle. They tasted anything of interest: slurping with their sloshing tongues; trailing saliva across the window.

The road beyond Hester's car was better blocked now than before. The breakdown truck had just arrived, with Wesley waving wildly at Hester. Meanwhile Hedley had arrived and was knocking on the car window: waving a pickaxe shaft in his hand.

"Let's do this nicely shall we?" he called out. "Just open this door. Now!" he commanded.

Hedley was a short, slight, figure, almost dwarfed by the size of the car. But his voice was strong and steady. And his cap sat firm on his head.

A very old and battered pickup now pulled up behind the tractor. A tall and burly lad got out. He made his way quietly through the bullocks.

"Give us over that pick shaft, Dad," he said.

"Careful, Digory," Hedley warned. "I don't much like the look of they folks."

"Tha's alright Dad. Don't thee worry." He raised the pick shaft over his head.

"Best open this door," he shouted loudly, "or else … I'm going to smash it in."

Lizzie heard the door lock click. The smiling man must be seeing sense. But the stinker wasn't giving in. With one hand holding her back in her seat, he slipped the other inside his jacket and then, as the young man opened the door, she saw the cold, grey steel of the gun. Digory paused. He'd seen it too.

"No Sid," a quiet voice intervened. "Put it away now. There's a dear boy."

"Come on maid," Digory ordered, opening the door as wide as he could.

"There's not a lot of room in this lane. You hang on tight around my neck. We'll soon have you out of there."

"Goodbye … for now," Snake Eyes said, giving Lizzie a sickly smile. "I have no doubt we shall meet again."

"Oh yes," the hulk growled close to her ear. "We will get you in the end. Remember—you are already broken. We are indestructible."

With Lizzie clinging on round his neck and burying her face in his collar, the young man carted her quickly away. The bullocks parted to let them through. Bruised, exhausted and shaking badly, she was lifted up into the tractor.

"You'll be more comfortable here with me," the older man said with a grin and a wink. "You'll not want to travel with that young madman." He nodded and laughed across at his son.

"Thank you," Lizzie murmured weakly.

"Phew!" gasped Digory, with a grimace, as he settled her into a seat. "There's some powerful whiff in that car! My beasts are better perfumed than that. I wonder you wasn't 'sphixiated."

Lizzie did her best to smile. She'd never been in a tractor before. Seated in the passenger seat, it was amazing how much you could see.

Wesley, who'd slipped away to turn round, was busy loading his sister's car onto the back of his breakdown truck. Mrs Rowe was dancing attendance: still bemoaning the loss of her phone; still brandishing the loaf, though Lizzie couldn't hear her words.

"Please, Wes. Let's go back and get it?" Hester Rowe was begging her brother.

"No," Wesley said "We can't do that. Those men are dangerous villains. You're lucky to get away with your life."

"But it's my Beauty … my Treasure," she wailed.

"Well, I'm afraid you've lost it now. But rest assured," Wesley grimaced, "we'll have our revenge. I'll see to that. Yes and soon. You see if we don't."

"Yes." Hester was calmer now.

After a few moments careful thought, she swung around to face the black car. She focused her piercing eyes on the villains. Striking up a rigid pose with one arm flung up into the sky and using the bread stick like a wand, she stabbed it four times in their direction. Lizzie could see her mouth working furiously.

Then she turned calmly back to her brother.

"You're right, Wes," she said with fervour. "We will have our revenge … and soon."

52

A Bit of Invoking

The following day found Lizzie resting. She'd been having a tussle with Tom: insisting he should run as usual; insisting that she'd be OK. She knew how worried he'd be about her. But she needed the time on her own. She had a lot of thinking to do.

Hester Rowe came to call. She was wearing a truly amazing jacket. Lizzie could see it was hand sewn patchwork.

The juxtaposition of unlikely colours gave it a rich and jewel-like quality: blues, greens, purples and reds, oranges and striking yellows—all the colours of the rainbow. Many clear, plain coloured fabrics were interspersed with floral patterns: the delicate pinks of dainty rosebuds; flamboyant mauves of stately iris; the subtle greens of vines and ferns. The overall effect was stunning.

Hester sat down at the table, staring closely at the girl.

"How are you doing today?" she asked. "You must have been some shaken up." Her eyes seemed especially bright and watchful.

"Yes. But I'm feeling better today. And I want to thank you very much. I hate to think what would have happened—if you hadn't had that puncture. What an amazing piece of luck."

"Ah yes. My lucky puncture …" Hester mused with a glint in her eye, nodding her head and winking at Lizzie.

Lizzie gaped at her in surprise.

"You don't mean to say ..." she exclaimed in amazement.

"No I don't," the woman snapped, before Lizzie could finish the sentence. "As if I'd ever do such thing."

"But did you have a puncture or not?" Lizzie was determined to know.

"Well ... in a manner of speaking ... I did ... and in a manner of speaking ... I didn't."

"I see," said Lizzie, not seeing at all.

"As I said to Wes last night, 'tis maybe the fault of them diddly valves. I told him it was poor design. But he didn't seem to agree.

"Temperamental things, they be. They can't even take so much as a twiddle. Just a little twist or two and all the air comes rushing out. I don't think that can be right, do you?" Her face was the picture of innocence.

"I don't know ..." Lizzie said doubtfully.

"That sort of thing can just happen, you see," Hester Rowe insisted firmly.

Lizzie sat staring at the woman. A sudden question came to mind.

"What about the bullocks?" she asked.

"Bullocks, m'dear? What do you mean?" Hester asked, appearing surprised.

"I wondered how you brought those bullocks," Lizzie said, choosing her words with care. "They appeared at such a convenient moment. It's hard to believe they just happened on cue. Perhaps you were doing a ... bit of invoking?"

"Invoking bullocks? Whatever next?" The woman rolled around with laughter. "I think they'd take a lot of invoking," she finally managed to wheeze between laughs. "Such big stubborn beasts, they be.

"I knew that Hedley was planning to move them," she continued. "But I wasn't quite sure when that would be, so I summoned them up ... a bit quick like."

"Summoned them up?" Lizzie asked.

"What do you think of my coat then?" Hester changed the subject abruptly.

"I think it's beautiful," Lizzie said. "I'd love to have a jacket like that."

Hester sprang up and gave a twirl, showing off the back of the jacket.

"What a stunning bird!" Lizzie gasped, admiring the brilliant, silk-white swan embroidered on a purple panel, set in the centre back of the jacket.

"As I know I've told you before, the swan is a magical, mystical beast," Hester hissed, her voice a whisper. "He is the harbinger of Spring. And there are many ancient tales—including some stories of shape-shifting swans."

"Shape-shifting swans? Whatever are they? Please tell me the stories," Lizzie begged.

"I haven't got time now," Hester said firmly. "But they're stories where maids can change into swans and fly away to another life. Have you never heard of The Swan Maidens?"

"If only I were a swan maiden," Lizzie said, in a miserable voice, "I would shape-shift myself right out of this chair."

"My Gran made this wonderful jacket for me," Hester changed the subject again.

"Did she?" Lizzie exclaimed. "How clever. It's beautifully designed and stitched." She gazed in awe at the intricate patterns. "It must have taken her ages to do." Her voice was full of admiration.

"My Gran was a wizard with her needle," Hester said with pride in her voice. "She made it for my seventeenth birthday. Her Gran had done the same for her—stitched her a birthday jacket like this.

"It's one of my earliest memories," she continued, "seeing my Gran in her patchwork coat. Hearing her gentle, kindly voice explaining the harmony of the colours, telling the meaning of the patterns. I still have her old and treasured jacket, safely tucked away in my wardrobe. I could never throw it out."

She sniffed loudly and mopped her eyes on the cuff of the beautiful jacket. Lizzie handed her a tissue.

"I was so thrilled when I unpacked this jacket," Hester continued, in between sniffles. "I've never forgotten Gran's special message. It was on a very pretty card that she had slipped in the bag with the jacket.

"Here is your Coat of Many Colours
Feed on the Harmony
Wear it with Love
Let its Magic Guide your Steps …"

"I shall be seventeen soon," Lizzie sighed.

"I doubt if your Gran will make you a coat, but I 'spect she'll give you something nice" Hester said encouragingly.

"I don't see my Grandmother," Lizzie said sadly.

"I didn't come here to talk about coats." Hester's voice was brisk now. "I came to talk about your future."

"My future?" asked Lizzie. "What do you mean?"

"It isn't safe for you here," came the answer. "I don't think you should stay any longer. In fact, I've decided. You'll leave tomorrow. I'll pay you back the money I owe you."

"Oh no. Please …" Lizzie begged.

"You need the safety of your own home." The hooded eyes were fixed on Lizzie. "Wes tells me there's a coach tomorrow. He will take you into town. Whatever happens, you'll be on that coach."

53

A Frightening Decision

After Hester Rowe had gone, Lizzie sat in her chair, thinking. She had so little time to act, but act was what she would have to do. Somehow she must find the strength. Somehow she must find the courage.

The trouble was she was very tired, having been woken every night by that spooky, distant howling. Was it only in her dreams? She could never be quite sure. It sounded horribly real at the time.

Lizzie had always found it odd that when the visions came in the night and the glorious music started, even though it woke her up, she was pleased to see her swan. And when the vision had faded away, she would settle happily back to sleep, murmuring, "Thank you my beautiful friend."

But the situation was falling apart now. The nightly visions were troubling her. And even her daytime lapses had changed.

As soon as the music flooded her brain and her fabulous swan came gliding, the ghostly howl of the wolf would begin. And yet it was peculiar. For the howling blended with the music, as if the two were in harmony: the wolf who was clearly threatening her and Lizzie's special friend—the swan. Or maybe he wasn't a friend at all.

The bird seemed strangely bigger now. He glided through the mist towards her, across the wine-dark, glassy waters with wings arched wide and held aloft. And as he glided ever closer, his sinuous neck came snaking towards her.

His plumage shone. It dazzled Lizzie. His emerald eyes bored into her.

Then one night something horrible happened. Lizzie was sleeping peacefully, when the music had begun and the vision was due to appear. But instead of her beautiful, pure white friend, a huge, black swan came gliding towards her.

The bird was too close. He loomed above her. His gleaming neck was twisting and turning. His golden eyes were glowing brightly.

Lizzie woke up shaking with fear, unable to sleep again that night. It was confusing. Frightening. She didn't think she could take much more.

And now there were plans for the bus tomorrow. They were being sent away. They had failed in their vital quest. That was the final straw for Lizzie.

"Whichever way we look, there's danger," Tom tried hard to counsel Lizzie.

"Yes," she answered in near despair. "We obviously cannot trust the locals. And then, of course, there are the villains. I bet they haven't gone away. They're bound to be lurking out there somewhere … "

"Yes, I'm afraid you're right Lizzie," Tom agreed uncomfortably. "I think it's just a matter of time, before they have another go. I think we ought to go back home."

"I won't give in," Lizzie insisted, banging the wheels of her chair with her fists. She'd never had such a row with Tom: such an argument—a struggle of wills.

"Then we'll talk to the local police," he told her. "The situation is far too dangerous. We can't continue to act on our own."

"But don't you see, Tom?" Lizzie argued. "I think that would be dangerous too. Everybody here is related. If we spoke to the local police chief, we'd probably find he was Wesley's cousin or his old friend … or his uncle. I bet the police would send us away … and then we'll never solve the mystery."

"We only have one option," she said, "to cross the causeway after dark."

"But that would be madness," Tom insisted. "You'd never make it in your chair."

Lizzie chose to ignore his words. She told herself there was no other way. She knew they'd be stopped if they crossed by daylight—either by Wesley and his gang or by the evil and dreaded villains. Either would be disastrous. It was a toss-up, which would be worse.

Besides, she'd been keeping a daily chart. And she'd got it all worked out. The tide would be right just after midnight and there would still be moonlight too, to enable her to find her way. That was the time to leave for the island.

And so, despite their argument, she made a truly frightening decision. With or without Tom's precious blessing, she'd slip away at dead of night.

Even as she made the decision, she shocked herself by the gravity of it: by the possible repercussions of acting completely against his advice.

And yet it seemed the only way forward ... if she could get herself together. She thought of her father's amazing citation and of his courage against all odds. She thought about the Victoria Cross, safe in the bank and in its box: snuggled in the silk-white satin; hanging on its blood-red ribbon.

As Robert Thomas Tregarrow's daughter, she must and she would find the strength and the courage. She would conquer her fears and go to the island ... no matter what horrible secret it held ...

54

Across the Causeway

Lizzie was feeling very nervous, lying in the darkened cabin, fully clothed, on top of her duvet, waiting for the crucial time. Gazing across to Tom's bed in the corner, she tried to make out his sleeping figure: the form of his beloved head; his tousled hair; the line of his chin; his eyes closed peacefully in sleep.

"I'll prove to him that The Shrimp *can* do it," Lizzie murmured to herself.

As midnight approached she sat in the doorway, staring out towards the island, trying to face the challenge ahead. Telling herself over and over, "My destiny lies on that island. If I'm going, I must go now."

With a backward glance and smile towards Tom, she swivelled her chair and closed the door softly. She eased her way carefully down the ramp. Her wheels ran silent on the path that crossed the garden and passed the cottage. All she could do was to hope and pray that Mrs Rowe was sleeping soundly; that no one would see the security lights that lit her way out through the gate.

Making her way along the road towards the slope that led onto the beach,

Lizzie focused on her quest. She glanced only once towards the gate that led in to the haunted cottage. She dared not think about those ghosts: the line of little tricksy people who might come dancing out from the shadows and overtake her in her chair.

She gritted her teeth. She turned away, murmuring softly as she did so, "Please, please God give me courage." Lizzie had never been very religious, but now she knew she needed help.

The family motto came back to her. She muttered it over and over and over. "Ever Courageous and Persevering. Courageous. Courageous. Persevering …

"Thank goodness for a clear, calm night." Moonlight lit the path of the causeway. It stretched ahead of her, smooth, enticing: a pale line of gleaming pebbles, leading from the beach to the island; cleaving the ocean; drawing her forward.

Negotiating the causeway was tricky. "I know this won't be easy," she mumbled, "but I know that I can do it."

Stretching on beneath the stars, the surface had looked deceptively even; the pebbles smooth and orderly. In the event it was all very different: the surface, which had looked so encouraging, was turning out to be far from friendly. Boulders did their best to trip her; and there were soggy, sandy patches, which seemed intent on trapping her wheels.

"Come on Lizzie," she muttered aloud, remembering her trainer's words.

Peter had been such an inspiration. "Face The Challenge. Go on! Go on!"

Lizzie had thought she was making good progress until she was nearly halfway across. It was then that she heard the terrible voice. She stopped in her tracks, frozen with fear. This was no dream. The howling was real: a terrifying, blood-curdling sound.

"Howoooooooooo! Howoooooooooo!" The voice of the wolf rose and fell, drifting on the wind towards her.

She peered ahead towards the island. The castle with its battlements grew as a solid mass out of the rock. The outlines of crumbling turrets were jagged and sharp against the sky. Was it her imagination, or could she see the form of the creature: a silhouette, black against the moon? Its muzzle lifted towards the stars?

The howling seemed to freeze her mind. Oh how badly she needed Tom's voice … 'Come on Shrimp. You can do it.'

Perhaps she ought to turn and go back? But then she would have to admit defeat.

She couldn't give up. She'd heard it too often. 'Face The Challenge! Go on! Go on!'

55

Oh Legs! Legs! Why Won't You Work?

Crossing the causeway had taken Lizzie so much longer than she'd expected; and it had taken more energy too. By the time she was closing in on the island, with only a hundred yards to go, the tide had turned and was catching her. Her wheels were binding in the gravel. Encroaching waves were lapping her feet.

Lizzie couldn't understand why. Perhaps she'd got the timing wrong. Perhaps her watch was running slow. She'd never considered that possibility. She'd just assumed when she'd seen the causeway—a safe and glistening track to the island—that the tide was going out—as it should be.

At first her mistake didn't bother her too much; her feet couldn't feel the cold of the water. But the waves were soon swilling round her ankles. And the water was rising fast.

No matter how hard Lizzie tried, she simply couldn't move herself forward. Soon the water was up to her knees and towing her away from the causeway. She fought and struggled and heaved and sobbed, muttering over and over and over: "Come on Shrimp. You can do it. Always courageous … persevering … Come on! Come on! You *can* do it …"

With the waves now lapping her chest, Lizzie was floating away from her

chair. In desperation she tried to hang on. But even her arms seemed useless now. Her freezing limbs were shaking with cold; her useless legs were more than a hindrance; her feet in their trainers a total disaster. Her soaking wet clothing was weighing her down.

"Oh legs! Legs! Why won't you work! You useless, useless, stupid legs," Lizzie sobbed in her frustration.

Gasping and struggling as she sank, she heard a snarling, growling shout and then she saw a horrible sight. A shadowy form lurched along the shoreline. Diving quickly into the ocean, it started swimming in her direction.

Was it man? Or was it wolf? Lizzie knew it must be the Wolfman.

Still gasping and struggling wildly, she saw the creature moving towards her, its eyes aglow from the light of the moon. On and on it came … ever closer. Lizzie, almost choking now, saw the big jaws open wide … saw the flash of sharp, white fangs, illuminated by cold moonlight as the creature lunged towards her. Grasping her without mercy, it towed her swiftly towards the shore.

Coughing and spluttering, barely conscious, Lizzie grovelled on the beach.

"Lie still! Lie still!" a hissing voice growled very close to her ear.

A hairy nose was pushed in her face as the Wolfman gathered her up in his arms and, lifting her bodily from the ground, he sped her away towards his lair. The strong arms held her like a vice. The hairy face loomed over her.

"Tom. Tom," she sobbed in despair. "Oh Tom where are you? I need you now."

How could she have been so stupid? How could she have ignored his advice?

As she was swept through an open doorway, looking up she glimpsed that shield carved in the granite of the wall. It should have been a positive symbol. But all her courage had long since left her. She lay now like a broken doll in the arms of the horrible beast. As the door clanged shut behind, she knew that this was it … the end.

Lizzie was shaking convulsively: shaking both from cold and terror as, sweeping down a flight of steps, the man or creature—whatever it was—strode on speedily, clutching its prey: on down long, black corridors, illuminated by lighted brands—reminiscent of gruesome films based on medieval horrors.

Sickeningly distorted shadows danced along on walls and ceiling. Witches and ogres. Fiendish figures.

Groaning with horror, Lizzie fainted.

56

In the Wolfman's Lair

When Lizzie regained consciousness, she found herself lying on a sofa in a dark, low-ceilinged room. The only light came from a fire that blazed in a primitive, stone built hearth. An enormous animal stood close by, outlined black against the flames. A huge and very shaggy wolf.

Barely conscious and shaking with cold, Lizzie shuddered in despair. The man had morphed back into the wolf. There was no escape for her now.

There was nothing that she could do, except to lie as still as she could, trying to control her shaking body, her eyes fixed on the ferocious beast. Yet the more she looked, the more she wondered. The animal didn't look quite right. The tail was wrong for a start—she could see that.

'But be he man? Or be he wolf? Or be he maybe some … and some?' She remembered the words of that hateful old man.

Lizzie shut her eyes tightly. If only this could be one of her dreams? But when she opened her eyes again, two hairy faces were close to her own. Silhouetted against the fire, there seemed to be only one difference between them: one of the heads had long pointed ears.

The creature stood very close … body tense … eyes watchful … ears swivelled to the sides. She tried to avert her eyes from its stare, whilst at the same time noticing the strangely curling tips of its ears. She'd never seen ears like that before.

She closed her eyes again in despair. Then peeping out through screwed up lashes, it struck her that the second head did look … almost … remarkably … human. It was much hairier than was normal, but it had a human nose.

"Oh … no …" Lizzie moaned. This was the Wolfman and the wolf. Helpless and shaking, she cringed on the sofa.

"Don't be frightened. You're safe now." The gentle words drifted over Lizzie, slowly dinning into her brain.

"Weird. Yes weird," she thought to herself, with her eyes still tightly closed. The Wolfman sounded quite well spoken. The voice was almost … but not quite … familiar.

"Get back, Duke. Let's give her some space," the voice continued strongly now.

The man stepped back away from her. Beside him there stood an enormous dog. The biggest German Shepherd Dog that Lizzie had ever seen in her life. A tall, rangy, long haired animal. The two stood staring down at the girl.

"No! Please Duke. Don't do that," the man's voice reprimanded, as the dog began to shake.

Beads of water flew towards Lizzie. Illuminated by light from the fire, the droplets added a fantasy quality to what was already a very strange scene. Lizzie couldn't work it out. She didn't know what was happening.

"Feeling … very sick," she gasped.

The man sprang quickly into action, returning with a bowl and a towel. "We've got to get you out of those clothes. How much can you do for yourself?"

"Normally … everything …" she stuttered. "But … I'm so cold … so very weak … I can hardly lift my arms. Oh dear … oh dear … oh dear …" she sobbed.

The man stood deliberating.

"I think you're at serious risk," he said, "at risk of hypothermia."

"Yes … life threatening," Lizzie agreed. "I promised … I'd keep out of the sea … but I've broken my promise," she wailed, tears streaming down her face.

"I'm going to lift you off the sofa. The cover's soaking wet," he said, "I'll need to find a dry blanket, before I put you back again."

Gathering Lizzie up in his arms, he laid her gently on the floor. The enormous dog stood looking down at her.

"Keep back, Duke," the man ordered, stripping the cover off the sofa and spreading a blanket in its place. The dog retreated to lie by the hearth, where he remained alert and watchful.

"I know this isn't PC," the man said, undoing Lizzie's sodden jacket, "but we've got to get you dry and warm … fast!"

"Don't care," she hissed through chattering teeth. " … got used to … being pulled about … you have to … when you … end up like this. Besides," she did her best to grin, although it was a feeble attempt, "PC … definitely … not my thing."

"At least you are only wet with water. I've coped with worse on the battlefield," the man murmured under his breath, as he continued stripping her clothing. "I'm going to have to cut off your trousers—I think that would be easier. And then you'll need a brisk towelling down."

"No! Please!" Lizzie begged sharply. And then, ashamed of her brusque response, "Sorry … mustn't do that … I'm afraid … skin too fragile … can't be rubbed."

"I see," the man said, looking surprised. "Then we'll get you into these jog pants and shirt … much too large, I'm afraid," he mumbled, as he struggled with the clothing. "And we'll wrap you up in this nice, warm blanket."

Back on the sofa, propped against pillows, wrapped in the blanket like a cocoon, with a towel turbaned around her head, Lizzie was starting to feel a bit better. She worked her arms as best she could, anxious not to graze her skin, yet knowing that any activity must, surely, help to warm her up. She leant forward and patted her legs, but only very, very gently.

A heap of wet garments lay on the floor.

"Sorry," she mumbled apologetically. "I'm giving you … a lot of trouble."

The man gave her a searching look. His face was stern as he scooped up the clothing and took it with him out of the room.

Lizzie couldn't wait any longer. When he returned she just had to ask:

"Are you Robert … Thomas … Tregarrow?"

The man looked very taken aback. His face hardened. He stared at her.

"Why do you ask that?" he demanded. "And who are you, anyway?

As if he sensed the sudden tension, the dog rose slowly from the mat, advancing stealthily towards her: tail down, head thrust forward, ears pinned back against his skull, body low and menacing. Although her voice was thin and frail, Lizzie did her best to stay calm.

"My name's Lizzie Stevenson," she whispered. "But I think my mother changed her name. I don't think that's my real surname.

"When my father disappeared, my mother didn't know she was pregnant. I was born when Tom was three, or more accurately, nearly four. I believe my mother's name was Allison, although we knew her as Jennifer."

Lizzie was watching the man's face closely. "Does that help you, I wonder?" she asked, noticing his body stiffen, his eyes widen in amazement.

The man was staring at her now. He narrowed his eyes: a strange look.

"Well?" she insisted. "Does it help?"

"Oh yes," he murmured finally. "Yes, I can see that you're Allison's daughter. The line of the brow … the eyes … the mouth."

The man was peering closely at her. "You're so much like her. It's uncanny."

Crouching down beside the sofa, he cradled her ice-cold hands in his own. Lizzie, unnerved, sat very still. She could see there were tears in his eyes.

"I've missed her so much," the man moaned. "And I've missed my little son—although I expect he's enormous now." He smiled expectantly at Lizzie.

It was what Tom would call a result. But Lizzie didn't know how to react. What could she possibly say to this man … the man who was obviously her father. And how would she tell him … all her news?

57

Tomato Soup

"A hot drink, that's what we need." The man got up clumsily and went across towards the hearth, wiping his eyes with the back of his hand. "Do you like tomato soup?"

"Oh yes," Lizzie murmured weakly, "very much. It's my favourite." Her shivering was easing now. But she was still feeling cold and weak.

The dog, having paced around the room and come across to sniff her over, now stood very close to the fire.

"Won't he scorch his fur," Lizzie asked, "if he gets so close to the flames?"

The man chuckled heartily. "He's got it down to a fine art. You'll see him backing away in a minute when he finds that he's burning his nose. The silly beast. I'm always telling him." He smiled lovingly down at the dog. "Move over, Duke, I want to cook."

The dog moved to one side. He stood, fixedly watching his master, who crouched on the hearth beside the fire, balancing a pot on a trivet.

"Duke loves tomato soup," the man smiled apologetically, finally serving out three portions: two into mugs, one into a bowl. Then he cut thick chunks of bread and placed them on an enamel plate.

Having tugged Lizzie up into a comfortable sitting position, he bolstered her up with several pillows, handed her the warm mug and propped the plate of bread by her side. The dog advanced towards her slowly, looking hopefully at the plate.

"No Duke. That's not for you," the man said firmly to the dog. "I'm ashamed of you, scrounging like that."

The terrifying 'wolf' looked sheepish. He turned from Lizzie and stared at his master.

"Duke is especially fond of this soup. It's home-made by Hester Rowe. I think you're staying with her, aren't you. I'd heard that she had let her cabin."

"Home-made by Mrs Rowe?" Lizzie queried.

"Yes, and full of her special herbs."

"So I see," Lizzie said doubtfully, staring suspiciously into the mug and poking the mass of herbs with her spoon. "You know that she dabbles in magic, don't you? She uses these herbs in her secret potions. I've seen her brewing them on her range in a big, black, smelly cauldron. Goodness knows what effect they'll have."

The man's loud laughter filled the room. "Drink it all up and we'll see what happens," he teased. "I hope it won't turn you into a mouse. Duke is rather partial to mice and he's looking very hungry."

The dog was pacing excitedly now.

"Yes. OK. I know what you want. I'll find you some of your special biscuits. You deserve them. You did a great job. You rescued a very special person." The man smiled warmly towards the girl.

"Yes. Thank you Duke," Lizzie said. "I don't know what I'd have done without you. The sea looked calm, but the currents are wicked. I was being towed away. The water was colder than I'd expected. Another few minutes and I'd have drowned."

The tomato soup was fabulous: the mug so warming for her hands; the hot soup itself delicious. And the chunks of bread were good. She was hungrier than she'd thought. Her doubts about herbs were soon forgotten.

She sat contentedly, watching the dog: pushing his empty bowl around; licking up every last trace of soup; then crunching noisily on his biscuits. Then he went to lie on the mat by the fire, stretching his limbs and sighing loudly. Steam was rising from his body. She could smell that hot, damp, dog-fur smell.

After a while Lizzie said, "I've never seen a German Shepherd with such funny, curling ears." The dog stood up and stared at her.

"Goodness!" she exclaimed in amazement. "Does he know that I'm talking about him?"

"Oh yes," her father laughed. "He does. He's such a clever dog. Aren't you, Duke?"

As if in reply, the dog sneezed loudly. Then he stood watching his master carefully, his tail swinging gently behind him.

"He is a very beautiful dog," Lizzie said smiling at Duke. "But I'm not so keen on his voice. Does he have to howl like that?"

"That's Duke's special party trick. Isn't it boy?" the man beamed. "It doesn't take much to get him going. I only have to start him off. Shall I show you …?"

"No. Please don't," Lizzie begged. "I've heard more than enough," she added, shivering at the horrible memory of that ghostly howl on the wind, echoing across the water. The howling that had haunted her dreams.

"Are you warmer now?" the man asked.

As he bent down to tuck in the blanket and take away the mug and the plate, Lizzie could tell that he'd noticed something.

"Do you mind my asking you?" he said quietly. "What are you wearing around your neck?"

Lizzie stared fixedly back, her mind spinning in disarray. There was no avoiding it now. She'd have to tell him the full story.

She lifted the ribbon from around her neck and handed it across to him.

"That's a key to a crucial box," Lizzie told him, watching his face. "And those are Mum's rings," she added gently. "I treasure them. They go everywhere with me."

No matter what happened in Lizzie's life later, she would never, ever forget her father's gasp and the look on his face: the heartbreak written in his eyes, as she began her tragic story … and as the whole truth gradually dawned.

58

Heartbreak

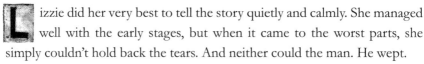

L izzie did her very best to tell the story quietly and calmly. She managed well with the early stages, but when it came to the worst parts, she simply couldn't hold back the tears. And neither could the man. He wept.

"I loved your mother so much," he sobbed. "I've always dreamt we'd get back together … I didn't know how … I didn't know when, but it was the one thing that kept me going. I always had to believe it would happen.

"To think that we came so close to it … before she was cruelly snatched away."

They sat together hugging and weeping: the first time Lizzie had wept for her mother. In the early days she had been too stunned. And even as the months went by, she had simply never allowed herself to open the floodgates and let it all out, terrified lest she lose control. She'd known that, above all, she must keep strong—though there had been many dodgy moments when she'd had to grit her teeth.

Now held close in the man's strong arms and with her head pressed into his chest, she howled and shook like a little child, finding it very hard to stop.

Duke was very upset as well. He knew from all the horrible noises that something must be badly wrong. He almost clambered onto the sofa, trying to prise the couple apart, shoving his nose in his master's chest and pushing his head up under Bob's arm.

And then he paced around the room, circling behind the sofa, loping along with his curious gait, his head held low, his tail tucked under. When all the sobbing had finally died, he returned to the rug in front of the fire and sat there wide-awake and watchful, whimpering from time to time.

"Now," at last the man said firmly, handing the girl a box of tissues, "did you say your name was Lizzie? To think that I didn't know you existed … didn't know I had a daughter." He stepped away and stood staring at her.

Lizzie, mopping her eyes, stared back, taking in his strange appearance. The man was tall and strongly built. His bearing was upright, almost military, and yet his movements were swift and fluid: a man of action, in his late forties, or maybe even, as Lizzie guessed, maybe very close to fifty.

Having been soaked from carrying her, he'd changed from his soiled and sodden clothes. Now, he wore jeans and an old blue shirt. The clothing appeared to be freshly laundered. Lizzie observed the long, sharp creases down the arms of the faded shirt: evidence of careful ironing. So someone was taking good care of him.

None of this was remarkable, but his head and his face were amazingly hairy, producing the very strange appearance. The full moustache and the long, black beard looked wavy and silky and out of control. His shoulder-length hair curled down his neck, just exactly the way Tom's did. But it seemed to be growing into the beard, providing a thick and shaggy mask, revealing only his nose and his eyes—presumably a great disguise.

No wonder Lizzie had thought him the Wolfman. She shuddered at the horrible thought. Yet this was her father … her long-lost father … whose warm, brown, smiling eyes now only made her think of Tom. She was completely lost for words.

"Is there something wrong?" he asked.

"No … not exactly," she answered slowly. She pursed her mouth and looked at him sideways.

"I'm sorry. I hope you'll forgive me," she said. "I'm just not used to saying Dad."

"Of course you're not," the man said lightly. "Why don't you use my Christian name? Everybody calls me Bob. I think that would be easier, don't you?"

"Yes," said Lizzie, smiling shyly. "I think perhaps it would … for now. Thank you … Bob," she experimented.

Then "Oh!" she gasped. "I've just remembered."

In all the excitement and the upset, Lizzie had completely forgotten an all-important piece of news—perhaps the most important of all.

"Do you remember Johnny Finn?" she asked.

"I've not heard that name for a brave few years," her father answered, looking surprised. "How do you come to know about Johnny?" He was watching her very closely. "I've always wondered what happened to him."

"Ah!" said Lizzie mysteriously, her face creasing into a grin. "Just you wait and I shall tell you."

"Where did you put my wet clothing," she asked, "and most importantly that bag—the one I was wearing around my waist? I have a special surprise for you." She dangled the words temptingly.

Lizzie was soon enjoying herself. Delving into the soggy bag, she lifted out an envelope. The photocopy was still intact and, after she'd managed to tease it out flat, the text was clear enough to read. She sat back quietly, watching and waiting: studying the man's expression as he read down through the letter.

When Bob had finished reading the letter, his eyes returned to the top of the page. He worked his way back down again, only eventually looking up and staring at Lizzie in disbelief.

59

If Only ...

"What do you think of that?" she asked, delighted by his stunned reaction.

"I don't know what to say," he said. And then a sudden thought struck him. "This isn't the original letter, is it?"

"No, of course not," Lizzie replied. It was very pleasing to think that she and Betty had been so efficient. "The original letter and the map are safely stowed away in the bank—together with your Victoria Cross."

The man breathed a sigh of relief. "This will take time to sink in," he said.

Lizzie was fingering the key, which was back again round her neck, hanging on the ribbon with the rings.

"The letter was in the box," she said, "together with a big, fat scrapbook—jam-packed with newspaper cuttings—all about your VC and the theft. Finding all that was quite a shock. Tom and I had always been told that our Dad had been a travelling salesman."

Bob snorted in delight, bringing the watchful Duke to his feet.

"That's a wonderful joke," he roared. "Your Mum always had a creative streak.

"If only I had been a travelling salesman," he added wistfully. "We wouldn't be in this awful mess. And your Mum would still be here."

Bob sat quietly, wrapped in grief, staring sadly into the fire. Duke sat close beside his master, his velvet muzzle propped on Bob's knee.

"Yes," Lizzie said miserably. "The whole of my life is like that now. If only this, if only that. There are so many things that might have been. So many things that I regret."

Lizzie's father looked up sharply. "We mustn't go down that road," he said briskly.

"Very few people could have done what you've done. You've been a brave girl. I'm proud of you."

"Ever Courageous and Persevering." Lizzie smiled back at Bob. "Isn't that the family motto?

"But I couldn't have done it without Tom," she continued. "I couldn't have managed without his help and his constant company."

"No," her father said thoughtfully. "I can see that he's played a vital role."

"And now," he continued even more briskly, "what we need is a cup of tea. But first I ought to take Duke outside."

"I need to make a visit too," Lizzie said, looking embarrassed.

Then her eyes were filling with tears again, as she suddenly remembered. "How shall I manage without my chair? I can't live without my wheels."

"Hush now," her father said, putting a comforting arm round her shoulder. "I'm sure the lads will find it tomorrow."

"And there's something else," Lizzie sobbed. How could she possibly have forgotten!

"Whatever is it?" Bob asked, seeing the look of fear in her eyes.

"The henchmen," she wailed. "I'd forgotten the henchmen. They're hunting for you. I know they are. They even tried to kidnap me." She trembled at the memory.

"Perhaps they're on the island now." Lizzie looked towards the door. "They might arrive at any minute."

60

Driven by Loyalty

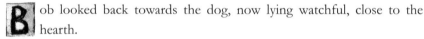ob looked back towards the dog, now lying watchful, close to the hearth.

"If anyone puts a foot on this island, our early warning system will tell us." He nodded with a grin towards Duke.

"I'm not sure who you mean by henchmen," he continued, "but if you're referring to Smarmy Sam and his sidekick Sid the Stinker—then I have some excellent news for you."

Lizzie couldn't control her giggles. "Sid the Stinker! I like that. And, oh yes, he did smell dreadful." She wrinkled her nose at the memory.

"He is a horrible hulk," she continued. "But isn't it strange, as time went by and the more I thought about them both, I found it was the smarmy man who was the really frightening one. That sickly kindness, those horrible eyes—colourless, reptilian eyes. Pure evil, veiled by smiles.

"I can't seem to get him out of my mind. I'm so afraid of seeing him." Lizzie hung her head in shame.

"Wes tells me that they're well-known villains," her father said. "And I know you are right about Sam. He is a totally wicked man—the brains of an evil partnership.

"But," he continued hastily, seeing the terror in her eyes, "you needn't be afraid any more. I think you'll find that my friends have been busy—guiding those nice men onto the moor—sometime early yesterday evening—to visit that interesting old mine? To meet the hermit in the cottage? Perhaps you know the one I mean?"

Lizzie grimaced, remembering.

"I believe you had a narrow escape. I can't tell you how sorry I am—about the way the lads treated you. I heard about it afterwards. Of course, I didn't know it was you," Bob added hastily.

"And I don't condone their behaviour," he continued. "Although, I know that it's driven by loyalty and by their constant fear for my safety. But this time I think they've done us a favour."

"Do you mean Wesley played the same trick?"

"Yes, I think he did," Bob said.

"But I was naive and easily hoodwinked," Lizzie said, remembering. "Those villains are quite another matter. How did he get them up to the mine?"

"Knowing Wes and his sense of humour," her father suggested with a grin, "he probably stage-managed it all, so that the postmaster in the shop—who happens to be his cousin, Walter—might just make some passing mention of somebody living up on the moor. 'A man of mystery', he would say. Perhaps the man they were hoping to meet? Perhaps they would like to pay him a visit?

"Wes would probably be on hand, doing his local yokel act. And being a very kind local yokel, he might even offer to be their guide, assuring them that the mystery man liked to have people dropping in." Bob gave a hearty chuckle.

"And as it was dark by the time they arrived, drop in is what they will have done. We won't be seeing them again."

"But are you sure?" Lizzie asked doubtfully. "The stinker said they were indestructible. Are you certain that they're dead? Perhaps they'll find a way of escape."

"There is no way of escape," he answered.

"Ugh! Horrible!" she grimaced. Despite her relief, she couldn't forget the terror of that gaping chasm. How close she had come to a lingering death. Even the thought of it made her feel shaky.

"And now we're all going to pay a visit," Bob said briskly, changing the subject. "I have some very smart mod cons—invented, needless to say, by the lads."

He got up and called to Duke. "Come on my handsome. Shift your rump. Then we'll have tea and I'll butter some buns.

"How about that?" her father asked. "It's nearly three o'clock in the morning. But I'm feeling peckish again. Hester makes great saffron buns. The lads brought some over this morning. Mind you," he grinned wickedly, "goodness knows what she put in the mixture. Some kind of magic charm, I expect. One bite of one of those buns ... "

"You shouldn't joke," Lizzie said sternly. "I think she does have special powers."

"She does make a magical Stargazy Pie," Bob laughed. "It's one of my favourites. Quite delicious."

As he lifted her up from the sofa, Lizzie clung tightly around his neck. It didn't seem so bad this time ... carried along in Bob's strong arms.

"I haven't forgotten my Royal Marine days," he joked. "We learnt how to deal with all eventualities. Though I have to admit that carrying maids was not a part of the basic training."

Her forehead pressed dark, curling hair, scented with the smell of the ocean mixed with a perfume of fresh shampoo.

'How extraordinary! My father ...'

Lizzie closed her eyes tight, savouring the magical moment.

61

The Swan Returns

When they were all safely back again, Duke lay down beside the fire and watched the preparations for tea, closely observing the dish of buns as it was ferried across the room. Yet he didn't move from his place on the mat. He licked his lips just once, then lowered his chin back down on the rug. But Lizzie could see that his eyes were watchful.

"You mustn't worry about your wheelchair," Lizzie's father said to her, as she was happily munching a bun—lavishly spread with fresh-churned butter, which oozed from a slit across its belly.

"I'm sure the lads will be able to find it," he continued, pouring the tea. "We'll get it all cleaned up tomorrow. Wesley's good at that sort of thing. He's a first class engineer."

"Wesley?" Lizzie said in disgust. "Not that beastly little man—with his horrifying stories?"

She told him all about the chanting. Bob tried to keep a straight face. He'd never seen the lads in action, but he'd heard some colourful tales—of terrified visitors driven away.

"Oh yes," he said. "The Wolfman story. I believe they may have got the idea from some old film they all liked to watch. And you must admit—it worked."

"Worked!" snapped Lizzie. "It was horrible."

"Well, I think they deserve an Oscar … or at least some kind of award. When we've sorted out this mess, I'll have to see what I can do… perhaps a statue of a wolf? What do you think we should call it, Lizzie? We wouldn't want to call it an Oscar."

Bob eyed her stony face. "I think we'll have to call it a Duke." He smiled broadly at the thought. A tail thumped on the mat by the hearth.

"But do you realise," Lizzie continued, ignoring the man's obvious intention to turn the whole thing into a joke, "Wesley tried to bump me off? I shouldn't want him touching my chair. He'd probably booby trap it or something."

Her father couldn't control his laughter. And even Lizzie had to smile.

"Wes is one of my oldest friends," he said. "We went to the local school together, up on the hill behind the village. If it hadn't been for him and, of course, the other lads, I'd have been captured long ago. I'd have ended up locked away, or worse. Then I should never have had the chance—the chance I have now to clear my name.

"I'd rescued Wes on the battlefield. He always said that he owed me his life. Whether that's the case or not, he has worked tirelessly for years—saving my life and protecting me here—despite the pain of his crippling wounds. He's a true and loyal friend. You don't get many friends like that."

"How long have you been here?" Lizzie asked. "And how have you managed to keep it a secret?"

"I know it seems incredible, but I've been here now for more than ten years. The lads have always believed in me. They've taken such good care of me. Visiting almost every day to make quite sure I have all I need. Trying to give me a reasonable life. Keeping any snoopers away. Taking me across to the pub, properly disguised of course." He laughed when he thought about the disguises.

"They've kitted this place out very well. Wesley had all sorts of ideas."

"I can imagine," Lizzie scowled. "He seems to have a fertile brain."

Bob laughed. "Yes, you're right. He certainly does. He was even determined in the beginning to provide me with electricity—with solar panels or a windmill. But in the end he shelved the idea. We couldn't stick any kind of structure on to the outside of the castle, which would give the game away— anything that could be spotted—from the land, the sea or air.

"Besides, I don't need electricity. I've always managed well without it. Did you see my gramophone?" He indicated a strange shaped object, standing on a small cabinet in a corner of the room.

"It's a real antique," he said proudly, crossing the room with a torch in his hand so that Lizzie could see it better.

"What a weird contraption," she said.

"You don't see the old wind-up players much now. This gramophone's been my great salvation. The cabinet is well stocked. Some of the oldest records are priceless. One of my earliest favourites is 'Come into the Garden, Maud'. I suppose you're too young to know that one.

"Come into the garden, Maud, For the black bat, night has flown." Bob obviously had a good tenor voice.

"Come into the garden, Maud, I am here at the gate alone …"

Lizzie was enjoying the performance until she noticed Duke's response. He'd risen slowly to his feet. Standing rigid, he raised his muzzle, clearly intending to add his own voice.

"No! Please!" Lizzie shouted. The man stopped singing. The dog froze.

"Duke, I'm sorry," Lizzie said quickly. "I know you have a beautiful voice. But I'd rather not hear it … not now. Come on, boy," she called with a smile, doing her best to entice him over. The dog, aloof, stood staring at her.

"What other records have you got?" Lizzie asked, changing the subject. The dog's reaction was disappointing. She wished she hadn't shouted at him.

"By some strange trick of fate," Bob answered, "your mother's favourite music is here—a piece by Sibelius that she loved."

He opened the doors at the front of the cabinet, sliding out an old-fashioned record, sheathed in a faded brown cardboard sleeve.

"I must have played it hundreds of times. It's nearly worn out," he said with regret, slipping the record out of its cover, winding up the gramophone and carefully setting the needle.

Bob sat quietly in his chair. Lizzie could see there were tears in his eyes. The big dog lay back down by the fire: his muzzle resting on the mat; his eyes alert; his ears a-wiggle.

A stream of music filled the room—somewhat crackly, it was true, but nevertheless a glorious sound: swelling strings, an echoing cello and, soaring high above all else, the haunting, reedy voice of a horn.

Lizzie froze on the sofa. Her mouth was slowly dropping open. Goose bumps formed on her skin as she floated: across the wide and misty lake; as she recognised the swan … the arch of his pure white, sinuous neck, the golden beak, the emerald eyes, turning as ever, watching her.

"Ah!" she gasped in recognition, as her memory flooded back.

How many times had she and Tom sat together with their mother, listening to this piece of music? Warm and cosy beside the fire, on a bitter winter's night, gazing into the glowing embers? Or sitting in the dusky gloaming on a balmy summer's eve, seeing their Mum's contented face, whilst they'd feasted on the music?

Lizzie was struck by a sudden thought: that as she'd battled for her life and as she'd struggled every day, it was as if her Mum had been with her, filling her heart and her brain with the music … bringing her daughter the simple beauty, which would strengthen her for the battle … which would give her the will to live.

Lizzie could even remember the name now … the oh so beautiful Swan of Tuonela. Ever mysterious. Ever inspiring.

"Thank you Swan," Lizzie whispered, as the music died away.

"Please don't think I forgot you, Mum … I simply couldn't bear to remember …"

62

The Priest Hole

Bob and Lizzie were mopping their eyes. Even Duke looked miserable: his ears pinned back, his brown eyes staring. He came to the sofa and nuzzled Lizzie. She put out her hand and stroked his head: soft and silky and comforting.

"Come on now," Bob said finally. "We must pull ourselves together." He turned briskly, asking Lizzie, "What else would you like to know?"

"I still don't understand," she began, doing her best to find her voice, "how have you managed all these years? It must have been incredibly boring. What on earth did you do all the time?"

"I feel as if I've been quite busy," Bob said thoughtfully. "I haven't just stayed here in this room. I often go across to the mainland. They pick me up in one of the boats from the seaward side of the island.

"I've spent many happy hours in The Smugglers. I've even watched the World Cup –both the football and the rugby—on the TV in Wesley's Dad's house. Did you meet Wesley's Dad? He's a remarkable old buzzard—into his mid eighties now—a very wise and wily old bird."

"Yes I did meet Wesley's Dad." Lizzie pursed her mouth and grimaced. "And I thought he was horrible too. He has a face like a wrinkled walnut."

"I'll tell him that." Bob laughed aloud. "The lads and I all call him The General. He does so like to take control. He's always played a vital role in helping to hide me away from the world.

"Of course this place has been a godsend. It was built in the early thirteenth century—an important castle in its day."

"Really! As long ago as that?" Lizzie was amazed by the date.

"It's always been home to the Tregarrows. Tomorrow morning I'll show you the chough."

"Surely they're extinct," said Lizzie.

"Ah! Well that's where you're wrong," Bob grinned. "The choughs have never left Tregarrow.

"There are three pairs breeding here this year. It's been a very well kept secret. Though I think it's given the lads some worries. Afraid lest someone spills the beans, which would bring in hoards of birdwatchers."

"Oh yes. I remember," Lizzie said. "Wesley calls them the twitching band—emmets, causing nothing but trouble."

They both enjoyed a good laugh.

"The castle is now little more than a ruin," Bob continued regretfully, "but the dungeons are still intact."

"Dungeons?" Lizzie asked with a shudder.

"Yes. That's where we are now," he answered. "We're in a secret part of the dungeon. It was closed off hundreds of years ago to provide a place of safety for Catholics."

"For Catholics?" Lizzie asked. "But why?"

"When England became a Protestant country, the Catholic faith was forbidden, you see. Priests who wouldn't toe the line were especially vulnerable. That's why this sort of secret chamber is often referred to as a priest hole.

"The official Protestant Church sent out search parties after the Catholics —rooting them out wherever they could. It must have been a grizzly business. People literally fled for their lives. If they were caught they were killed—or worse.

"Some poor folk were hidden away, often in small hidey-holes, for weeks or even months on end," he continued, "or, quite possibly, even for years."

"For years?" Lizzie exclaimed, astounded.

"There were, so it seems, quite a lot of Catholics in this northern part of Cornwall," Bob explained.

"But were the Tregarrows a Catholic family?" Lizzie asked in some surprise.

"No they weren't … not as far as I know … but they'll have had many friends who were. My family will have taken great risks in harbouring such folk in the castle—walled up here in secrecy."

"What a dreadful thought," said Lizzie. "It's horrifying to think of people living cooped up in this room, terrified to show their faces."

"Like me, do you mean?" Bob asked gently. "Being shut away like this is no fun. Though I know it's been made easy for me. And, of course, as priest holes go, this is a luxury apartment—what with the fireplace and all. Did you notice the family motto?" They looked across to the ancient stone lintel.

"Prest colonnek ha dywysyk." Lizzie recognised it immediately, but she struggled with the words.

"That's not bad," Bob said, surprised. He repeated the motto fluently and then more slowly, word by word, encouraging Lizzie to follow him. She laughed with delight when she finally got it.

"Ever Courageous and Persevering. It's been my motto too," she smiled, "since we found the coat of arms and managed to get a proper translation."

"It's beautifully carved," her father said, "presumably by some frightened inmate, trying to while away the hours and to keep his spirits up. It's certainly helped me over the years."

Getting up, he crossed to the fireplace.

"When I run my hand along the words," he said, as his fingers traced each letter, "I feel a presence standing beside me. But don't be afraid," he turned quickly, aware of Lizzie's sudden gasp, "it is a very friendly presence. I don't know what his name is, of course, but I've always called him Petrok. And he doesn't seem to mind. Duke always treats him like a friend. We often sit and chat to him."

After a hasty look round the room, Lizzie changed the subject quickly. "But what about the smoke from the fire?

"Surely that would be seen on the mainland and by sailors on passing ships and, in modern times, by aircraft?" Lizzie asked, intrigued by the story and by the problems of living entombed.

"It certainly would have been seen," Bob said, "if it hadn't been for some crafty planning. The hearth has a cunningly vented chimney, designed hundreds of years ago, in order that anyone hiding down here and wanting a fire to cook or keep warm could light one up without risking detection. The smoke is vented into the caves on the seaward side of the island. It filters out through clefts in the rock."

"How fantastic!" Lizzie exclaimed.

"Yes. It's amazing," her father responded. "You can sometimes smell the smoke in the cave, but you wouldn't notice it from outside. The system must have been carefully planned and created by highly skilled, clever people—people determined to keep their secret."

"But if this was such a secret place, how did you come to know of it?" Lizzie still didn't understand.

"When Wes and the lads and I were boys, we used to take a rowing boat and sneak across to visit the island," her father said. "It was out of bounds, of course. But that didn't make any difference to us. Some of us may have felt a bit guilty, but it certainly didn't stop us. It only made it more exciting—doing something that we shouldn't."

"Boys!" Lizzie tutted, nodding wisely.

"During the long school holidays, we had some fabulous times here," Bob continued with a smile. "We called ourselves The Island Gang. And we set up wonderful camps, always on the seaward side, where we couldn't be seen from the shore.

"It gave us endless hours of fun. Catching crabs and roasting them. Prizing limpets off the rocks. They can be very tasty, you know."

"How lucky you were!" Lizzie exclaimed. "Tom and I would have loved to do that. We used to make our camps in the shrubbery that ran along the garden fence. Sometimes we managed to smuggle in snacks. But nothing as thrilling as limpets or crabs.

"Tom always loved cheese sandwiches," she continued, "made from doorsteps and chunks of cheese, smothered in Mum's tomato chutney. I wanted her strawberry jam—in the sandwiches, I mean. Mum told us her Dad had liked cheese and jam."

"But do go on," Lizzie insisted. "I want to hear how you found this place."

"Ah yes," Bob said thoughtfully. "That was quite a shock, I can tell you … because of what we found in here."

63

A Nasty Shock

"What do you mean—what you found in here?" Lizzie looked anxiously round the room. "And how did you come to find it at all?"

"There's a very big cave," her father answered, "on the seaward side of the island. It's only accessible at low tide. Our favourite camp was in that cave. We always knew that we had to be careful. We knew that if we were caught by the tide we would be cut off in the cave."

"But surely you could swim?" said Lizzie.

"Yes, we were reasonable swimmers," he told her, "but lots of people have died on this coast. No one would want to swim out of that cave. The incoming breakers are much too powerful. And the currents are treacherous. Even the most powerful swimmer would end up battered against the rocks and then sucked helpless out to sea. So we always took care to watch the tide.

"But one day we were having such fun that we simply forgot about it. We were cooking some succulent sausages over a fire well back in the cave. Wes had nicked them from his Mum's larder. 'Only borrowed them,' so he said." Bob chuckled at the memory. "I remember how much we laughed at that … until we suddenly noticed the tide.

"By then the cave was filling up. Breakers were smashing against the entrance. And so we were driven far into the cave, further than we'd been before, hoping to find a place of safety. And that was how we found the tunnel."

"The tunnel!" Lizzie exclaimed. "What tunnel?"

"The Secret Tunnel," he said in a whisper, doing his best to add some drama. "It stretches from the cave to the castle. It opens from the back of the cave, just above the high water mark. The entrance is hidden behind a huge boulder.

"Goodness knows how they made the tunnel. It's cut right through the solid rock. The entrance this end is through that door." He pointed to a wooden door, iron bound and strongly bolted.

"I don't think I like the thought of that." Lizzie stared at the door in dismay. "You didn't bring me that way, did you?"

"No," Bob answered her. "I didn't. Although, when it comes to taking you out, we're going to have to take you that way. We won't want anyone to see us. We'll put you on the trolley, I think. Wesley made it years ago. It's used to carry my stores from the boat. The lads come most days—just before dawn.

"Because of the tunnel's irregular walls, it takes two people to manage the trolley—one to pull and the other to push. But," he added with obvious pleasure, "it's never been used for carrying females. Goodness knows what Wes will say." Bob was enjoying the joke now. "I only hope he won't go on strike."

Lizzie was finding it hard to smile. She didn't feel like trusting Wesley, despite her father's glowing accounts. Yet she wanted to hear the rest of the story, so she kept her mouth firmly shut.

" There are two entrances to this room," Bob continued. "The other one leads in from the dungeon, through a hidden door in the wall. It's just a matter of pressing a stone and that gives access to that door," he pointed to the back of the room, where Lizzie could see another doorway.

"It's easy when you know how," he said, "but, in those days, we didn't know—not until we found this place, then worked it out from the other side."

"But people must have known about it—in the distant past," Lizzie argued. "The members of the Tregarrow family…"

"Yes, of course. They must have known. But, as people sometimes say—the secret went with them to the grave."

Lizzie shivered at the thought. "Lots of secrets must go that way."

"Yes. I'm sure you're right," he said. "After our discovery here, the members of The Island Gang made a very solemn pact—never to tell a soul about it. That pact has been kept to this very day, although one or two wives have had to be told—in total confidence, of course—because of their men taking care of my needs."

"You mentioned some kind of shock," Lizzie said.

"Yes. That's right—a horrible shock. We almost frightened ourselves to death."

64

A Sleeping Figure

"**D**o tell me what happened," Lizzie begged.

"I hope you're feeling strong," Bob laughed, "because it's a bit of a spooky story."

"I love spooky stories," said Lizzie. "Please go on. Go on …" she begged.

"The tunnel is about five feet high and around two feet wide," Bob told her. "It's a bit cramped, you'll understand. But it's only about a hundred yards long and so it's not too difficult. When the tide is right, Duke and I go out that way. We have a lovely time on the beach, running about and exercising. Sometimes we even go for a swim.

"The water's deep on that side of the island, but there's a natural outcrop of rock which runs out from the mouth of the cave and which acts as a simple jetty. As long as the sea's not too rough, a skilful boatman can tie up there. The lads bring all my stores that way, carting everything through the tunnel. And that's how they smuggle me out to the mainland.

"Shortly after I disappeared," Bob continued, "the Special Branch appeared on the scene. That was when the press arrived and some of the lads were interviewed. Later, after my return and when I'd been installed down here, the Special Branch raided the island twice. Wes had been afraid it might happen. So he and the lads had rehearsed the rescue. ORT is what they called it." He laughed. "Operation Rescue Tregarrow.

"The first time it went as smoothly as clockwork. Local intelligence gave us good warning. I used the tunnel as my bolt-hole. They slipped me quickly out to sea, before anyone noticed the boat. The gang and I were jubilant. "

"It sounds like a close run thing to me," Lizzie said disapprovingly. "And what did you mean by local intelligence?"

"It was probably led by your friend, Hester. All those 'special powers', don't you know?" Her father laughed heartily.

Lizzie scowled in response. "And what about the second time. Are you saying her powers failed?"

"The second time nearly led to disaster," he admitted. "Wes didn't get any wind of the raid until it was almost too late. We'd barely left the jetty behind and were making out to sea, when a big powerboat drew alongside and two officers boarded the boat. I'd been pushed down into the hold and covered with a layer of fish."

"Ha! I like it," Lizzie laughed. "Except I feel sorry for the fish."

"Did you know how slimy they are? Fresh fish?" he asked with a shudder, seeing Lizzie's grinning face. "It was a horrible experience. Most of them were still flapping. I had herring and haddock over my head and an octopus around my neck."

"Pooh! How disgusting!" Lizzie exclaimed. "You must have smelt terrible afterwards."

"Yes, I'm afraid I did smell bad," Bob answered, grinning broadly.

"Probably worse than Sid the Stinker, " she giggled merrily at the thought.

"Well, nearly as bad, but not quite," he laughed. "The lads have never let me forget it. Even now they hold their noses and jeer when I go into The Smugglers."

"But what about the Special Branch? They didn't

find the priest hole then?" Lizzie wanted to know all the details.

"No. We think they searched the dungeon, but they didn't find this place."

"Oh my days! How fortunate. But what about the rest of the story? What about the nasty shock?"

"Oh yes," her father said. "I haven't told you the best bit, have I?"

"No you haven't." Lizzie waited.

"When we found the mouth of the tunnel, behind the boulder in the cave, all the gang were so excited. Wesley was the smallest boy and the only one with a torch, so we pushed him in ahead of us and followed along as best we could. I was the tallest. I hated it—trapped by the boys who were coming behind, bumping my head on the roof of the tunnel and desperately trying not to freak out at the thought of the thousands of tons of rock that seemed to be pressing down on me. But I did my best to pretend it was fun.

"When we finally came to that door—the one you see across the room —Wes had a struggle opening it. It didn't seem to be locked or bolted. The hinges must have been jammed with rust. When he finally got it to open, with me pushing from behind, it made a horrible groaning sound—like they produce in those scary films. I have to admit it—it frightened us all."

"Ooh! Horrible," Lizzie muttered. "I'm glad I wasn't there," she said.

"You'll be even more glad in a minute, when I tell you what we found. Even now I remember that feeling— the hair rising on the back of my neck."

"But what was it?" Lizzie begged.

"As we pressed forward through the doorway, Wesley's torch was running low. But as he swung it around the room, the beam lit up a sleeping figure."

65

Such Loyalty is Very Rare

"Oh no!" Lizzie gasped. "You mean there was someone in the room?"

"We could see a peculiar shape stretched out—on a bench along the wall."

"Somebody was lying there?" Lizzie's voice had dropped to a whisper.

"Well, not much of a body, exactly. It was more like a skeleton. We could see the outlines of bones and the shadows they cast on the wall behind. And the large round bony skull."

There was a sharp intake of breath, as Lizzie's mouth dropped wide open. "Ahhhh! How beastly ... " she whispered hoarsely.

"I can't pretend," Bob said, "we were all quite terrified. We'd all been jostling in the tunnel and some of them were even giggling. Now we stood shaking in our shoes, our mouths gaping wide in horror."

"I'm not surprised," Lizzie murmured, suitably impressed by the story.

"Then something truly horrible happened." Her father shuddered, remembering.

"Wesley's torch finally died ... leaving us standing in the dark."

"But what on earth did you do?" Lizzie asked, glancing quickly around the room, as if she feared she might see the corpse now.

"Nobody spoke. Nobody moved. And then, as if by unspoken agreement, the gang started creeping back through the doorway.

"I had problems. I couldn't move. My legs were giving out on me. I felt as if I was stuck to the floor. Wes was the one who rescued me. He ended up almost carrying me—which was impressive when you think, because I was much bigger than him."

"And then?" Lizzie asked impatiently.

"After a hurried and whispered check—to make quite sure that we were all there—one of the gang closed the door behind us. We fumbled our way back down the tunnel—loudly mumbling our prayers and only hoping that nothing unpleasant was following along behind. Well, we were only kids, of course."

"Well, I'm not a kid, but I know I'd be scared. And then what happened?" Lizzie pressed.

"Oh boy! Were we in trouble—when we all got back so late that night. The only fortunate thing was that each of the parents had assumed that their son was staying with one of the others. And so they hadn't raised the alarm."

"What about the borrowed bangers?" Lizzie asked with a grin. "Wesley's Mum must have noticed they'd gone."

"Yes. I think she was furious. She's never, ever let Wes forget. Even more than thirty years later, she's still bemoaning the loss of those sausages.

"Soon after that I was sent away—to a boarding school up-country. When we finally all grew up, several of us joined the forces. Wes and I ended up in the Falklands.

"The funny thing is that when he was wounded and when I was carrying him away to safety, I remembered that very day in this room—how he had almost carried me, when we'd fled from the skeleton and when my legs had let me down."

"Perhaps he's nicer than I thought," Lizzie said begrudgingly.

"No one could ask for better friends. Such loyalty is very rare. I've been a very lucky man."

"But surely you must have been lonely here?" Lizzie asked.

"Yes. Of course, I have been lonely, mostly because I've missed your mother. I've worried a lot about her and Tom. But Wes came to my rescue again. I'll never forget the day he arrived, carrying what looked like a ball of fur."

The man smiled at the big dog, sleeping soundly on the mat.

"It's hard to believe when you look at Duke now, that he was that little, woolly ball. He's proved to be a wonderful dog. He's been my ever-constant companion.

Lizzie had thought that the dog was sleeping. But he must, she supposed, have heard his name. For, although his eyes didn't open, his ears swivelled on his head. His tail thumped gently on the floor.

"Come on now," Bob said, checking his watch. "It's very late. We must get some sleep."

"There's something I'd like to ask," Lizzie said.

"Then ask away," he encouraged her.

"I remember reading the citation—about your Victoria Cross—that you'd saved the lives of two men. I wondered … who was the other man?"

Lizzie's father's expression hardened. It took him a moment or two to answer and, when he did, it made Lizzie gasp.

"The other man …" he paused reluctant. "The other man was Johnny Finn."

66

Water Under the Bridge …

"Oh no! Not Johnny Finn … how could he?" Lizzie gasped in amazement. "After all you'd done for him … saving his life on the battlefield?"

"Yes. I'm afraid so," Bob answered. "He wasn't as badly wounded as Wes. He soon got back into active service. Although I doubt if he would have survived … if I hadn't happened to be there," he added, sighing heavily.

"I chose him as part of my team for the Africa trip, because I knew I could always trust him."

Lizzie was shaking her head in disgust.

"But that's all water under the bridge," Bob continued. "His letter tells us about his problems. And I guess he was easily led."

"And," said Lizzie thoughtfully, " … he did the right thing in the end. I will always be grateful for that."

"Yes. We must all be grateful for that. Now come on," he said more briskly, "I think we ought to get some sleep."

"I suppose so," Lizzie said, looking nervously round the room. "Only I don't think I want to sleep."

"Why ever not?" he asked, surprised. "I would have thought that you'd be exhausted."

"Well I am," she said doubtfully.

"Aren't you comfortable on the sofa? You could have my bed, if you like."

"No thank you," Lizzie said hastily.

"Something must be wrong?" he questioned.

"I can't stop thinking … about … that skeleton," Lizzie said haltingly. "It isn't still somewhere in here … is it?"

Seeing Lizzie's frightened eyes, Bob knew that he mustn't laugh.

"No. It certainly isn't," he said, keeping a very straight, serious face. "When the lads were preparing this place for me, the remains of the body were carefully removed and buried with all due ceremony in a grave at the end of the island."

"Do you think that it might have been Petrok?" Lizzie asked, uncertainly.

"No. I don't," her father said. "I think Petrok carved the motto, during what's called The Reformation. That was during the sixteenth century. The worst times were the 1580s when Catholics were hunted countrywide. The poor soul that we found in here probably perished later on—maybe during the Civil Wars."

"I can't bear to think of him," said Lizzie, "or … had you thought … it might have been her … lying … dying … waiting here for the help that never came.

"It's too horrible," she moaned. "I'll never be able to sleep in here."

67

A Bedtime Story

"I tell you what," Bob said, seeing Lizzie's anguished face, "suppose I tell you a bedtime story—all about my mad adventures. Do you think you might like that?"

"Yes please," Lizzie whispered sheepishly. "Mum always used to read us stories…" Her voice trailed off.

"Shall I tell you about my African trip?" her father offered temptingly.

"Oh yes," Lizzie said more firmly. "I read all those cuttings from the papers, over and over and over again. I've always wondered what happened in Africa. The theft of the jewels and all that stuff. And how on earth did you get back here?"

"I warn you … it's a very long story." Bob jumped up and crossed the room. A lighted oil lamp stood on a desk: one of those antiquated things with the wooden top rolled back and the surface cluttered with stuff. The back of the desk and the table beside it were stacked high with mounds of paper.

Bob indicated the stacks of paper. "I suppose it's a bit like organised chaos," he laughed apologetically, "but I've been keeping a daily diary. And I'm writing a book as well. It's kept me busy, I can tell you."

He pointed to an old-fashioned typewriter, nestling amongst the clutter. "Goodness knows where the lads found this. None of your fancy modern technology, but it's certainly done me proud. It's gone on working year after year, though

Wes has problems now finding new ribbons."

"Before you tell me the African story," Lizzie wheedled hopefully, "I'd like to know more about your VC. And how could Wesley have been involved? The how and the why have been puzzling me."

"Then I'll need to go briefly back to my childhood," Bob said. He drew the old armchair towards Lizzie and settled himself just a few feet away.

Lizzie waited expectantly.

Duke, who had crept up close to his master, slumped down comfortably at his feet and propped his head against Bob's leg. He gave a very heavy sigh then closed his eyes in readiness for what he must have somehow sensed was going to be a lengthy session.

How could he possibly know, Lizzie wondered? He was the most extraordinary dog.

"Wes and I are exactly the same age," Bob began. "We share a birthday early in May. I was the only child in our family and he was the only boy in his. I suppose we were more like brothers than friends. When I was sent away to school, he had to stay at the local school. Yet we always managed to keep in contact. And then there were the holidays. We spent every possible minute together."

"Ah yes," Lizzie murmured, grinning, "The Island Gang. I do remember."

"We made a pact when we were children that when we grew up we'd be Royal Marines. We used to imagine ourselves in battles, always fighting side by side. We knew we could beat the rest of the gang, if we ever wanted to fight them. And, of course, we sometimes did," Bob added with a chuckle.

"Hmm!" Lizzie chose to ignore this comment, frowning and pursing up her mouth. Her life with Tom had taught her a lot. No matter how much she loved her brother, she had never ceased to wonder at the strange behaviour of males—especially when it came to fighting. And she was often struck by the thought that men were simply large, small boys. But perhaps this wasn't the moment to say so.

"I suppose you went to college, did you?" she tried. "Sandhurst? Or somewhere posh like that?"

"No, as a matter of fact I didn't. They don't do that for the Royal Marines. I joined up straight from school, after I'd completed my A-levels—Physics, Chemistry and Maths."

"How extraordinary," Lizzie gasped. "Those were Tom's A-level subjects."

"That's my boy," Bob muttered quietly.

Their eyes met as Lizzie continued, determined to pursue the story.

"What happened next?" she asked firmly.

"I'd applied for a Potential Officers Course. There were several hurdles to jump, of course, but when I eventually passed out , I went to join Four Five Commando. They're based at Arbroath, up in Scotland. That was where I first met your mother."

"But Mum wasn't Scottish, was she?" asked Lizzie. "I don't remember her having an accent."

"No, she didn't," her father smiled, "but she had a beautiful voice. And did you know, she could sing quite well?" His voice trailed away, remembering …

"Her parents originally came from Scotland. That's why she's Allison with two Ls," Bob continued finally, finding it hard to use the past tense. "Your mother was their only child. They were living in London when she was born, but when she was grown up they left the south and moved back up to Scotland again. For all I know, they'll still be there."

"I've never met them, of course," said Lizzie, "although I'm sure Mum had some help from them—in our early years at least."

Lizzie sat thoughtful for a moment. "I'm beginning to understand now, why they always kept their distance. Why they kept well out of sight … to hide her new identity and to shield her from the press.

"But how does Wesley fit into all this? He's such a weedy little man," Lizzie said in a scathing voice. "I can't see him as a Royal Marine. Surely they're big, hunky guys?"

"Huh!" Bob laughed a wry laugh. "Don't ever underestimate Wes. What he may have lacked in size was more than made up for in guts and resilience. He was a very determined child and he was much tougher than me. When we grew up he was just as strong or maybe even stronger than me. He was so wiry and quick on his feet.

"There was a long military tradition in our family on both sides," Bob told Lizzie. "My Dad had followed on after his father. They were both in the Royal Marines.

"There was soldiering too on my mother's side," he continued. "Her father and his father before him had both joined up in their youth—The Duke of Cornwall's Light Infantry. Her grandfather fell in 1915, at Ypres during the First World War. Her father died in the Second World War—in 1940 at Dunkirk."

"It sounds to me," Lizzie said sadly, "as if you didn't stand a chance. It looks like you had to go into the forces."

"No, it wasn't like that," he assured her. "I was perfectly happy to join. The only real regret I have is that Mum and Dad didn't get to the Palace—to see me receiving my VC. They'd died in a big motorway pile-up, a couple of months before the event." Bob shook his head sadly.

"They would have been so proud," he sighed. "And Mum would have worn a fabulous hat—bigger and better than anyone else."

Bob laughed heartily at the thought of his mother wearing some flowery creation.

"Mum always did love large hats—and the more flamboyant the better. After she died and I cleared her wardrobes, I counted over eighty hats. Can you imagine … eighty hats!"

Lizzie joined in with the laughter. Duke, adjusting his position, thumped his tail a couple of times, before drifting back to sleep.

"I wanted to be a Royal Marine," Bob continued. "Although, I can tell you, it wasn't easy. One of these days I'll take you to Lympstone. I'll show you how and where they train. I'll show you those awful assault courses. Just the thought of them fills me with trepidation. They would be more than a challenge now.

"But in those days we were young and strong. We thought of ourselves as invincible. And as we always used to say, 'Train hard, fight easy'.

"When we were under fire near Port Stanley, in those bleak and rocky hills,

I can assure you I blessed that training, every exhausting moment of it …
especially," he added ruefully, "the techniques that we'd all been taught for
carrying bodies of fallen soldiers."

68

One of Those Rare Coincidences

"And Wesley?" Lizzie prompted impatiently. "Where does he come into all this?"

"Wes had a problem with his Dad, who wanted the boy to follow him … to work the land as he'd done himself," Bob explained. "Hester married a fisherman, but the rest of the family had always been farmers. There was no military tradition. Nor was there ever going to be one, if Wesley's Dad had got his way."

"I'm starting to feel sorry for Wesley, having to deal with Old Walnut Face." Lizzie shuddered at the thought.

"Oh yes," Bob laughed. "He's a tough old nut. But in the end he had to give in. He'd reckoned without his determined son. And he couldn't have known about our pact, nor could he ever have guessed upfront the lengths to which poor Wes would go in order to honour that childhood pact—which we'd signed in blood, I seem to remember."

"Gross!" groaned Lizzie. "Just like boys."

"By the time I was struggling with my O-levels," her father continued with a grin, "Wes had left home and gone away to become a Royal Marine recruit, despite his father and his mother, both of whom made an awful fuss … although in the end they gave their consent. I was amazed when I heard the news. I was only sorry because it meant that over the next few years or so we hardly ever saw each other."

"So how did you end up fighting together?" Lizzie asked, urging him on.

"That was the most extraordinary thing," Bob answered. "I'm still amazed when I think of it now. It was one of those rare coincidences that happen only once in your life, but end up changing its course forever.

"When the Task Force sailed to the Falklands ... in the April of '82 ... I was thrilled to be given command of a troop of thirty men. I'd long since lost track of Wes. I hadn't had time to think about him.

"As my troop was leaving San Carlos, two of my men were seriously injured in an unexpected air strike. I needed to replace them quickly. You can imagine my surprise when I was given the names of men being brought in as BCRs—as Battle Casualty Reserves.

"And yes ... you've guessed it, I can see," Bob added with a laugh. "One of those turned out to be Wes. We were astounded—both of us—and so pleased to see each other. The rest is history, as they say."

"Oh go on," Lizzie begged. "Tell me more. Tell me exactly what happened to Wesley."

"I certainly won't do that," said Bob. "All I will say is that the poor old lad ended up severely injured, stranded out on the open hillside. I could see one of my men had fallen, though I didn't know who it was at the time. I simply went out under fire, scooped him up as best I could and carted him away to safety."

"I've read your citation," Lizzie said. "I know there was much more to it than that. I know that you were also wounded but that you carried on regardless. I know you must have been very brave."

"I didn't think I was being brave. I just got on and did the job. It's what you do in those circumstances. And as far as Wes was concerned, he was the brave one to survive—never to give up fighting for life. Most men would have died of those wounds. Now he's horribly shrunk and twisted. And I'm afraid he's in constant pain, although he would never let on that he is."

Bob's face was lined with sorrow. "He's done so much to help me here. If and when I get out of this mess, I mean to do what I can for him. One of my old school friends is a surgeon—a very successful one, I believe. I wouldn't mind betting he'll know what to do, to try to make life better for Wes.

"Yes, I shall take Wes to Jiffy Rogers," Bob continued thoughtfully.

"Jiffy?" Lizzie asked with a giggle. "That's a very funny name."

"It was the nickname we gave him at school. If anyone asked him to do anything, he always answered 'In a jiffy', whilst carrying on with something else. I remember he said it once to the Head 'In a jiffy … Sir!'," Bob laughed. "Goodness knows how he got away with it. It wasn't a laughing matter then. It should have been a caning matter."

"I should just think so," Lizzie agreed.

"But Jiffy was what you would call a high flier. He was one of those irritating people who never seemed to spend time working. And yet he always came out top. I used to swat away at my studies, but when it came to exam results, he was always way in front. Nobody could ever beat him."

"I've had friends like that," said Lizzie.

69

Chapter Two of a Bedtime Story

"And now I think it's time to sleep," Bob said firmly, preparing to rise and jolting Duke awake at his feet.

"Oh no, please," Lizzie begged. "That was only Chapter One. Now I'd like to hear Chapter Two."

She glanced at the old bench along the wall. "I don't think I could sleep … quite yet. I'd like to hear about Africa … pleeese."

"It's a complicated story," Bob said. "I can only give you a potted version. But I'll do the best I can," he added, seeing Lizzie's anxious face. "Although I hardly know where to begin."

"Begin with Her Majesty's jewels," she said. "Whatever happened to them … and to you? And even if they did disappear, I don't understand why you were blamed.

"You can settle back down again, Duke," she whispered.

The dog gave her a long, hard stare then retreated to the mat by the fire, where he curled up close to the dying embers.

"I've had plenty of time to wonder about it," Bob said, "and yet I'm still not certain myself … how it was planned and carried through with such speed and efficiency … and, as I would find out in due course, with my carrying all the blame. I knew it must be an inside job. Though I have to tell you," he shook his head slowly, "I never suspected Johnny Finn.

"Having read his letter now, I think I can see what must have happened. Or at least I can see what part he played. Though there must have been others who turned a blind eye."

"But how did it happen?" Lizzie insisted.

"It all happened long ago … on that fateful royal visit … well, very nearly fatal for me."

Her father began the story slowly, doing his best to pack in the drama, relieved to see from Lizzie's expression that the gruesome corpse was forgotten.

"Although it was only early evening, the sun was on the brink of setting as I crossed the empty compound—towards Her Majesty's private quarters."

"Her Majesty's quarters?" Lizzie queried.

"Yes. We all lived in huts or tents ranged around the edge of the compound. A large and almost palatial hut had been built for the royal visitors.

"I was ferrying Her Majesty's jewels and her favourite State Tiara in their special carrying case. The Queen was planning to wear them that evening at a reception for local dignitaries. She always liked them delivered early—to give her lady-in-waiting time to help with her hair and to settle the tiara."

"I can understand that," Lizzie said with a frown. "If I had to wear a tiara, probably heavy and dripping with diamonds, I wouldn't want it slopping about. I'd need to know that it was secure. Just think how awful it would be—if it slipped off and fell into the soup." She giggled merrily at the thought.

"Precisely," Bob said, keeping a straight face.

"And so we had started out early. Johnny Finn was my support that night. He was following close behind. The normal procedure would have been to deliver the case to Her Majesty's hut and then for him to stand guard outside. But we never got that far.

"The very last thing that I remember was glancing back over my shoulder, just to check that Johnny was there. Seeing the final glow of the sun, the last rim of the huge, red orb slipping down below the horizon. Then that was it."

"How do you mean … that was it?" Lizzie pressed.

"I don't remember anything else until I woke up the following day, lying in a stinking hut with an enormous bump on my head and the biggest headache ever."

"How dreadful," Lizzie said in horror. "It's a wonder that you weren't killed."

"Yes. I know," her father said. "It was pure chance that I turned my head, so that when the blow fell, it hit the thickest part of my skull rather than the side of my head.

"It was sheer luck," he said, "like so many things in life." He smiled tenderly at his daughter. "Sometimes good luck. Sometimes bad."

"Yes, that's true …" Lizzie murmured. "But you can't just leave the story there."

She smiled at the early warning system, lying sound asleep on the mat.

"I don't feel sleepy yet," she said.

"My captors were a funny crowd—local tribesmen, I supposed, brandishing huge knives and spears. But they didn't treat me too badly. And at least I was fed and watered, although at a pretty basic level.

"After they'd completed their deal, passing on the precious case with the tiara and jewels, they didn't seem inclined to kill me. But nor, so it seemed, could they let me go. I guess they'd made some kind of pact—to whisk me into obscurity—so that I'd carry the can, as they say, and everyone else would get off scot-free.

"And then … the most extraordinary thing. My captors came to realise that I was valuable merchandise. And, to cut a long story short—they sold me on as a high-class slave."

70

A High Class Slave

A slave!" gasped Lizzie in amazement. "Surely not in modern times."

"Many cultures kept slaves," Bob said, "and still keep them, to this day. You'd be amazed by how many there are"

"But you … a slave? It must have been horrible." Lizzie grimaced in disgust.

"It wasn't too bad," her father assured her. "I was trekked across the bush … the journey took us several days … to meet my new owner, a powerful Chief. He had good reason to value me. And so I was always treated well.

"His mother had been the old Chief's favourite. But she'd died soon after his birth. His father, who'd been sent to England—to Eton and Oxford, so I believe—had great plans for his firstborn son.

"And so he'd employed an English nanny—properly trained, with a uniform. I know because I saw the photos. She even had one of those big, posh prams, like you'd see in Kensington Gardens."

"How bizarre," Lizzie murmured, "in the middle of Africa."

"Yes, deep in the African bush. Goodness knows how Nanny managed, in such extraordinary circumstances. But manage she clearly did. She educated the child well. She taught him English and excellent manners.

"He even used to correct my grammar." Bob laughed at the memory.

"And … ?" asked Lizzie, sensing drama.

"A terrible accident befell Nanny. She was bitten by a black mamba—a highly dangerous, venomous snake. Despite the witch doctor's very best efforts, she died soon after … a horrible death.

"The child, aged ten, was heartbroken, though I don't think he was allowed to show it. Then, to make matters even worse, his father died soon after that. The boy was thrust at an early age into the role of Chief of the tribe, thus destroying his father's plans to send him off to school in England. To Eton, no less, but it all fell through."

"Poor child," Lizzie murmured.

"During her lifetime, beloved Nanny had, as part of his education, filled his head with all kinds of stories—many about our Queen and Prince Philip. She had, so it seemed, been presented at court. Her stories included first-hand accounts of members of the royal family."

"But if Nanny had come from such a good background, what was she doing working in Africa?" Lizzie couldn't work it out.

"Nanny," Bob said "had a very sad life. It had indeed been a very good background, until her family fell on hard times, when her father and her brother gambled away their estates and their money. Her mother died of a broken heart. The poor young woman found herself not just homeless but penniless too.

"Her suitors and friends all drifted away. Sadly forsaken and needing a job, she decided to train as a nanny. Africa sounded just the thing—as far away as possible from her mean fair-weather friends. And well away from the love of her life, who'd abandoned her for another girl—somebody with money and status."

"Hateful people," Lizzie said. "But do go on about the boy."

"Nanny may well have been shocked—to find herself in such a place—in such primitive surroundings," Bob continued with the story. "But she grew very fond of the boy and she showered her love on him.

"Holding on to Nanny's memory and to all the fabulous stories, meant that the boy became fixated … almost mad about our Queen. Even later, as a grown-up, with wives and children of his own, he still hung on to those stories for comfort. He still longed to meet the Queen.

"He even thought that if he met her, they would be able to talk about Nanny. After all, they'd met at the palace, when dear Nanny had been presented. He felt sure that the Queen would remember her."

"That's such a sad story," Lizzie said. "But how did all of that affect you?"

"The Chief, so it seems, had been very upset when he learnt that he'd missed the Queen, on her recent trip to Africa. But when he heard that I was available and that I had worked for the Queen—or at least that was the way that he saw it—I suppose it seemed like an opportunity, the next best thing to meeting the Queen. And so he decided to purchase me."

Lizzie laughed out loud with amazement. "I wonder how much he paid?" she mused, grinning cheekily at her father. "I suppose you were worth a pound or two. I hope he thought he'd got a good bargain?"

"The Chief treated me like a slave," her father said, ignoring the comments, "but as a very special slave … a slave who would tell him wonderful stories about our Queen and about Prince Philip and about their children too … Charles, Anne, Andrew and Edward.

"I kept him happy for endless hours … creating ever more colourful stories, mostly total fantasies, all about our royal family. One day I'll have to go down on my knees and apologise to the Queen for some of those more way-out stories, which I invented especially for him—just in order to save my skin and to stay alive for another day … and for yet another story.

"Now I come to think of it, it was like The Arabian Nights—although of course this was Africa. Do you remember that story, Lizzie? The one about Scheherazade? She told the cruel Sultan such good stories, he simply couldn't bear to kill her. So he kept her on, day after day, in order to hear yet another great story."

"Yes I do, Bob. But please go on. How long did you have to stay? And how did you manage to escape?"

"I lived with that tribe for more than two years. I had some adventures, I can tell you. Our conversations were always lively. But I made a big mistake, telling the chief how I'd first met the Queen when I'd received my Victoria Cross. The Chief just loved to hear that story. He asked for it on a regular basis … over and over and over again.

"When I'd finished telling the story, he would sit quietly, thinking about it, doing his best to imagine the scene. And then he would have the list of questions—always the same and always important:

"Where was the reception held? Was it a very big room? Was there a carpet on the floor? And what about the windows and curtains? Everything had to be described in the most minute detail."

"Good grief," Lizzie murmured.

"And then there were questions about the Queen. This was the most important part. What colour and manner of dress was she wearing? Was it long or was it short? What style of shoes and what colour? What colour stockings? What jewellery? Did I think she was wearing hairspray? What about lipstick and nail varnish? Was it bright or was it pale?

"If I altered so much as one word, when I was repeating the details, he would remind me very sternly of what I'd said the time before. And then I'd have to prevaricate—to embroider the story even more and hope I'd remember it next time around.

"Oh dear, oh dear, oh dear, oh dear!" Bob laughed almost until he cried, remembering his outlandish descriptions.

"No matter how fanciful my stories, the Queen's dignity was preserved." Bob was trying to be serious now. "It was an unwritten rule. But I admit that I had some fun in dreaming up preposterous stories. I even remember describing in detail Prince Philip's favourite pyjamas."

"What were they like?" Lizzie beamed. "Do tell."

"I can't," her father hooted with laughter. "I'd never had the chance to see them. But I was able to dream some up—just for the purpose of my stories. They were red, white and blue, of course, and based on the union flag.

"They were very smart," he added thoughtfully. "I might design some for him later. He's such a great character, you know. I'm inclined to think that he'd like my ideas."

"And did the Queen have a nightie to match?" Lizzie couldn't resist the question.

"How did you guess? Of course she did." The man could barely control his laughter.

"The Chief just loved the thought of it all. I think he could see them, in his mind, standing side by side in their bedroom, wearing their fabulous night attire. I gave Prince Philip a matching nightcap.

"And I created pillowcases with embroidered coats of arms—but using two rather different designs. The Chief knew that they'd have to have His and Hers."

71

Chanel No. 5

hen Lizzie recovered from her giggles, she begged her father for more stories.

"The Chief always had one other question about my visit to the Palace. Had the Queen been wearing perfume? Might it have been Chanel No. 5?"

"Aahh!" Lizzie gasped at the name of the perfume. "Whatever made him ask you that?"

"The Chief had kept all Nanny's possessions. When he got to know me better, he showed me the hut where she used to live. A cut glass dressing table set sat on an embroidered cloth that was stretched along a bench to one side. All the usual items were laid out, just as they had been in her time, including an elegant, silver backed hairbrush together with matching comb and hand mirror.

"I remember a large round cardboard tub, still full of talcum powder—Old English Lavender, with the original powder puff. Sometimes the Chief would lift the lid and let me have a sniff at the powder. But that wasn't always encouraged, because, as he pointed out at the time, too much sniffing might wear it out.

"The hut was tended every day by the Chief's own favourite wife.

Everything was immaculate. It was all faded and looking tired, but much too precious to throw away."

"Yes, but what about the perfume?" Lizzie was determined to know.

"Yes, I'm coming to that," he said. "Amongst Nanny's treasured possessions, there was an empty perfume bottle. The label was almost worn away. But you could just read 'Chanel No. 5'. The Chief would lift the stopper with care and hand the bottle across to me.

"There was only the faintest whiff. And when I'd satisfied my senses, I would tell him, yet again, that this had been my wife's favourite perfume. We'd stand together side by side, staring tearfully at the bottle."

Lizzie could feel the tears starting too. She remembered her mother's dressing table. How she had gathered her personal items, including a similar bottle of perfume. How she still had that very bottle, tucked in the top of the chest of drawers.

"Go on, please," she begged her father. "Tell me more about the Chief and the stories that you told him. I don't think I could sleep quite yet."

Seeing Lizzie's expectant face, her father did his best to continue.

"As time went by, it became more tricky repeating the stories for the Chief over and over and over again and trying to make them interesting.

"The Chief always wanted to know what the Queen's exact wording had been, when she had pinned on my VC. That was fine, except for the fact that I had very foolishly told him how she had commended my bravery. Whenever I repeated the story, I did my best to miss that bit out. But he seldom let it pass without insisting on hearing it.

"'Ah yes. Bravery,' he would say. He had a deep and rich-brown voice, if you know what I mean by that. And he had a very loud laugh.

"'I think we shall have to set you a test,' he would say in his booming voice. 'I'll think up something for tomorrow—something creative and interesting— to test out that famous bravery. If you succeed, we shall keep you around. But if not … we'll dispose of you.'

"His thunderous laughter suggested he would."

72

All's Fair in Love and War

How horrible!" Lizzie exclaimed with a grimace.

"Yes. Some of it was horrible. But it wasn't all so bad, you know, especially when I thought up the wheeze of setting up a kind of wager, which was, so I claimed, the right thing to do—what an English gentleman would do. It meant that each of my achievements had to be later matched by him—with a similar achievement. It also meant that every so often, I was allowed to propose the wager."

Lizzie's Dad laughed at the thought of those wagers.

"Some of them were completely mad. But in the end we became great friends. In the end he agreed with the idea that there would be one final wager. That if I survived, I would have my freedom.

"It was I who set up the final challenge—the catching of a poisonous snake. I'd read about the trick as a boy, in one those books about survival. And, most importantly, I knew that the Chief was scared stiff of snakes. I knew that he'd never be able to do it.

"It says a lot about the man that when I won the final wager, although he knew the odds were against him, because my wager had played on his fears, he repeated one of Nanny's old sayings: 'All's fair in love and war'. He gave me my freedom and sent me away, together with three men and six camels.

"When I left, we hugged like brothers. I'd grown attached to the old boy. I found it difficult to leave … if that doesn't sound too silly?"

"No. It doesn't sound silly at all," Lizzie insisted fervently, watching him walk across the room and lift down something from a shelf.

"When we parted he gave me three gifts. And this," he said, "was one of them." He handed Lizzie a handsome dagger in a decorated scabbard.

73

The Three Gifts

"Three gifts?" Lizzie questioned. "Wouldn't one have been enough?"

"No. Apparently not," Bob said. "Each gift had a special purpose to ensure my safe passage. He spoke of them accordingly—Protection, Wisdom and Knowledge.

"I've never forgotten his words to this day.

" 'My first gift to you is this dagger. Watch your back and keep it handy.'

"That's his dagger you're holding now. It's one of my most treasured possessions."

Lizzie cradled it in her hands, turning it over carefully. The curving blade and its fancy scabbard had a used and well-worn look. She handed it tenderly back to her father.

"So what was the second gift?" she asked.

"The Chief was very proud of that. 'The second is my ruby ring,' he told me. 'See the colour of the stone. Feast on its brilliance whilst you may. Enjoy the lustrous glow of the gold. Let its splendour feed your mind.'

"He went on to tell me of Nanny's theory—that focusing on simple beauty, whether made by man or nature, could feed and strengthen hearts and minds.

"He told me that even as a small child, he would go out walking with her, seeking out some thing of beauty, which they could enjoy together—the amazing colours of a flower or the texture of its petals, or a painted tile on a wall, maybe a butterfly or a beetle, with its iridescent wing case. Nanny pointed out these things and they feasted on their splendour. She used to quote a poem to him.

"In the tragic event, when he lost her, he discovered she was right—that if he could find a thing of beauty, on which to focus and feed his mind, it helped him through his darkest days.

" 'So I'm passing Nanny's wisdom on,' the Chief told me with a sad smile. 'Feast on the splendour of this ruby and let that feasting feed your mind. Let it strengthen your resolve. There will, I know, be dark days ahead'."

As Lizzie listened to this story, her eyes widened, her mouth dropped open. She could hardly believe her ears. She shivered convulsively. It was uncanny …

"Is there something wrong?" Bob asked.

"Not exactly. But tell me more—more about Nanny and her poem," Lizzie begged excitedly.

"The Chief claimed Nanny had been a poet—in her youth and before she'd left London. But he had always felt frustrated. For, although she often quoted verses, she would never write them down. And he was discouraged from doing so.

"It was a long time after she died before he could bear to go through her belongings, hoping to find a book of her poetry. But there was nothing to be found—only her clothing and her toiletries. We must suppose that before she'd left England, in a bid to break all ties and clearly with a broken heart, Nanny had destroyed her work along with other personal possessions."

"Oh my days!" Lizzie exclaimed. "Can it be such a very small world? Because I'm sure I know her poem.

"But please go on," she begged her father, seeing his surprised expression. "I will explain to you later, I promise. What was gift number three?"

"The Chief's third gift, he told me, was Knowledge—knowledge which would enable me to decide on the safest and best way forward. Laughing at my look of surprise, he handed me an envelope. It was full of old newspaper cuttings. He said that his father's old friend in Oxford had often sent The Times on to him.

"'Read every word of these cuttings,' he told me. 'And read in between the lines. Then let this knowledge guide your steps. This is my warning. You must beware. Because I can see you've been branded a traitor.'

"He told me he hadn't believed the stories. Somebody must have set me up. But he said that it obvious to him that I would be in serious trouble—unless or until I could clear my name, which of course I knew I couldn't.

" 'If you're going back to England,' he told me, 'you *must* travel incognito … or you'll end up spending your life behind bars … perhaps a worse fate than being my slave.'

"He slapped my back and roared with laughter. We hugged and then we said goodbye. That was the very last time that I saw him," Bob added with a sigh.

"But what about the ring?" Lizzie asked. "I really like the sound of that."

"Yes," her father grimaced sadly, "it was such a beautiful ring. It was heavy gold with a massive ruby that must have been worth a king's ransom. I never ever dared to wear it. I hung it round my neck on a thong and managed to keep it out of sight."

"So where is it now," Lizzie demanded. "Surely you didn't lose it … did you?"

"No. But I had read the cuttings and I knew the Chief was right. I needed a new name and false papers. Things like that cost a lot of money. So I had to trade the ring for a passport. It was made for me by an expert in Cairo, in a room in a tiny back street.

"The passport was a work of art. I couldn't have crossed to Europe without it. But I was sad to give up the ring. It was such a thing of beauty. I hope the Chief would have understood …

"He was such a good old boy," Lizzie's father said with a smile. "If it hadn't been for him and for his ring and his wise warning, I certainly wouldn't be here today. I would have walked straight back into trouble, completely unable to clear my name and locked away somewhere very secure.

"If I ever get the chance, I'll recommend him for an honour," Bob mused. "Wouldn't that be wonderful? Then he could meet The Queen himself—just as long as he didn't get chatting. Reminding her of some of the stories. That could be disastrous." Lizzie's father's face was a study. "Oh dear. I'd never thought of that."

"I bet he'd ask about the pyjamas," she teased. "That would have made a big impression. And, of course, the matching nightie." Lizzie couldn't control her giggles.

"That's almost certainly treason," she gasped, "giving away the Queen's personal secrets. You'll probably end up in The Tower. But I'll come and visit. I love those ravens."

74

Camels

"So what happened next?" Lizzie pressed her father, keen to keep the story going.

"It was to prove a difficult journey, which would take us many months … camping under the stars each night … coping with sandstorms, snakes and scorpions. But the Chief's men became great friends and they took good care of me. When they turned back, I was sorry to lose them."

"So then you were safe and well on your way?" Lizzie asked anxiously, sensing that there was more to come and that it might not all be good.

"I'd thought I was safe. But I found that I wasn't. I'd been handed over with one of the camels into the care of another tribe, who, it was promised, would care for me and see me safely onto the next leg of my journey. But that simply wasn't to be.

"It turned out that the men were rogues. All they wanted was my camel and my labour from dawn to dusk. They belonged to a tribe that kept many slaves.

"I often worked with a slave named Hassan. After long months of planning, we managed to escape together. It was a daft thing to try to do. And yet it worked out well in the end.

"It was like so many problems in life—the ones that seem insurmountable. *The* most difficult thing of all is to recognise and accept the challenge. Once you decide what you're going to do, if you work hard and long enough, you'll probably find that you can do it."

He smiled warmly at his daughter. "It looks as if you've learnt that already."

"Go on," said Lizzie. "I want to hear more. Judging by that heap of paper," she looked across the room to the desk, "it must be a long and exciting story."

"Hassan had always worked with the camels. He was little more than a boy, I guess. But with a lot of planning and care, he managed to find me some suitable clothing—a long robe and a tatty old scarf, which I could wrap round my head like a turban.

"With some charcoal sticks from the fire, so that I could black out my face, once on a camel and out on the trail, we thought that I would pass as a local. Hassan had taught me some of their language.

"We slipped away at dead of night taking two of his favourite camels— animals that he'd handled from birth, who would follow him anywhere. We padded off silently into the night. It was a risky thing to do. But we got away with it.

"Of course we did have some hairy moments. We'll have to keep those for another time," Bob insisted firmly, seeing Lizzie's crestfallen face.

"All I have time to tell you now is that it was a gruelling journey. We almost died along the way. In fact we certainly would have done, if we hadn't been rescued again—but this time rescued by good men—a nomadic tribe of Bedouin who welcomed us as needy travellers. We lived with them for several months, in comfort in their big, black tents, before they sent us on our way,

stronger and better prepared than before.

"I've often wondered where Hassan is," Lizzie's father said thoughtfully. "He was such a steadfast friend. We had to part along the way, before I made my crossing to Europe.

"It took me many months from that point to make my way slowly back here, using my bit by bit policy and working my way along as I went. I posed as a variety of characters: a travel writer, a scholar, a tramp. Once I pretended to be a clown and almost ended up in a circus."

The man sat smiling at his memories. "Crossing the channel wasn't so easy. My fake passport was pretty good, but I didn't dare to risk it back here. I finally managed to hitch a lift on a dodgy fishing boat. Goodness knows what they were running. Some kind of contraband, I should think. They dropped me on the south Cornish coast.

"It was heaven. I could hardly believe it. I lay on the sand, beneath the stars, thanking God for my deliverance—and for my beloved Cornwall.

"I knew they wouldn't know who I was, when I finally got back here—I was so thin and brown and hairy. I'll never forget sloping down the street, slipping quietly into The Smugglers and seeing all those suspicious faces."

Lizzie's Dad laughed with glee. "They simply didn't recognise me.

"I had a good joke at their expense. Greeting each of them by name, but using a very strange, foreign voice. It was The General who finally guessed. I told you he was a clever old buzzard."

"A clever old buzzard." Lizzie yawned.

"Right. That's all for now," he said firmly, "we must get a few hours sleep. Wes and the lads will be here at first light.

"We need to get you back to the village. There's going to be a hue and cry as soon as it's discovered you're missing. The police might be called and we don't want that. That could mess up everything."

75

The Mills of God

The delicious aroma of frying bacon woke Lizzie early next morning. There was no sign of Duke in the room. Bob was crouched beside the fire, cooking.

For the first time Lizzie noticed the scarring: the damaged and disfigured fingers of her father's left hand. She'd read the citation so many times. Now it all came back to her.

"There's so much to do today," he said, as they chomped their eggs and bacon and munched thick chunks of crusty, brown bread, thickly spread with golden butter. "Wes came over earlier, hence Hester's fabulous, freshly baked bread."

"You ought to get your facts right, Bob," Lizzie admonished with a grin. "This bread isn't simply bread—it's prize-winning bread," she corrected him. "I've seen the silver cups. I know."

"And there are prize-winning scones for afters," Bob added with a chuckle.

"Together with the prize-winning honey?" Lizzie asked hopefully.

"Absolutely right," said Bob.

"Wes was stunned to hear about you," he continued, "and, I think, quite mortified to realise what he'd nearly done—trying to polish you off at the mine. I promised him that you would forgive him."

"Huh!" said Lizzie. "Well … I might."

"He's hurried immediately back to the mainland to calm any fears regarding your safety. He'll come back soon to pick you up. You'll find the trip through the tunnel interesting," Bob added with a grin. "We think we can squash you into the trolley."

Lizzie did her best to glare, whilst licking honey from her lips and mopping butter from her chin.

"Someone's already spotted your wheelchair," Bob continued. "Wes has promised to sort it out. Then later we'll all meet up in the village."

"Good," said Lizzie, "that sounds great."

"But I have something else to tell you, which I know is going to upset you," Bob said slowly, reluctantly.

"Upset me? What do you mean?" asked Lizzie. She didn't like the sound of that.

 Bob looked anxiously at his daughter.

"Wesley brought some uncomfortable news. I think I ought to tell you now. But don't let it frighten you. You're safe. And everything is under control."

"That sounds serious," Lizzie said. "Please tell me. What has happened now?"

"Hedley's daughter is a nurse," Bob started to explain. "She works in Intensive Care in Truro. Two men were brought in late last night, rescued, it seems, from up on the moor."

"Two men?" Lizzie gasped, her eyes staring and frightened now.

"I'm sorry to have to tell you this," Bob was watching Lizzie's face. "They fit the descriptions of Sam and Sid."

"Oh no!" Lizzie cried. "No! No! No! *No!* Please don't tell me they're still alive. Still out there somewhere planning to get me." She couldn't help bursting into tears.

"Steady now. Steady," Bob said, putting a comforting arm round her shoulders. "They won't be planning anything. Both of them are severely injured.

"A walker on the moor located them, after his dog had heard faint cries coming from one of the disused shafts. It was a complicated rescue involving the Culdrose helicopter.

"But maybe it's better this way, Lizzie," Bob said unexpectedly.

"How could it be better?" she sobbed, unable to control her tears.

"If they survive they will have to face justice. And the lads won't face a murder charge—which they could have done, you know."

"I hadn't thought of that," Lizzie sniffled, taking the handkerchief he offered.

"Goodness knows how they survived, after falling into that chasm. They must be indestructible," Bob said.

"But that's what the Stinker said," Lizzie wailed. "I'll never forget his horrible words. 'You're already broken,' he said. 'We are indestructible.'

"I can't be mended—I know I can't." Lizzie tried to control her tears. "But maybe they can and they will be mended and then they'll come after us both again."

A sudden scratching at the door which led to the tunnel and thus to the beach, made Lizzie nearly jump out of her skin. "Oh no! Oh no!" she moaned in despair, clutching hold of Bob's arm.

"Hush!" he said sternly, then quietly "Duke?"

A gruff bark answered his voice. He went across and opened the door. Duke came bounding in from the tunnel; he'd been out running on the beach.

"I'd quite forgotten him," Lizzie said, in a small and shaky voice. "Oh Duke! Thank heavens it was you." The dog came across and licked her hand, allowing her to stroke his head. Then he retreated to sit by the fire.

"For one terrifying moment, I thought it must be Sid and Sam. That was silly. I'm sorry, Bob."

"No it wasn't silly," Bob said. "But I can promise, they won't be coming." He paused as if deliberating. "They're both in a very bad way," he said. "Sid is in intensive care and Sam has serious spinal injuries. He'll probably never walk again."

"Uhhh!" Lizzie caught her breath. "I'm tempted to say that it serves him right … and yet I know … that would be … wicked."

"I think it's all down to the mills of God," Bob said, sighing heavily.

"What do you mean by the mills of God?" Lizzie asked, mystified.

"Perhaps you don't know that old quotation—about the mill and God being the miller?" Bob asked gently, watching Lizzie. "It dates right back to the seventeenth century. It was one of my father's favourite sayings. I must have heard it hundreds of times.

"Though the mills of God grind slowly, yet they grind
exceeding small;
Though with patience He stands waiting, with
exactness grinds He all."

"It simply means that all human actions are thought of as corn or grist for God's mill. We may have to wait a long time for justice, because His mill grinds very slowly. But because it grinds so small, evil people seldom escape. Eventually they will be caught ... and punished."

76

Plans

"Now whilst we're waiting for the boat, there's something I want to discuss with you," Bob said in a serious voice.

"It's going to take time to sort out my affairs. I'm in a very tricky position. It may take weeks, or even months to get all the charges against me dropped ... and, hopefully, to recover 'the loot'. Meanwhile you must go back to your flat."

"That's alright," Lizzie smiled. "I've sent a couple of cards to Betty. But knowing her, she will be worried. And I have to admit that I have quite missed her."

"Hester's nephew, Denzil, will help," Bob said. "He's been our eyes and ears in London. And he knows some useful people. He'll probably make some approaches for me. But it will have to be handled with care. I can't just turn up out of the blue. I'd almost certainly end up in jail before I could put my case across.

"There'll be some very tough talk in the Smugglers. The lads and I will work out a plan. But once we've sorted out this muddle, I'd want to take proper care of my family. Would you like to live down here?"

"I might like it," she answered cautiously, "if the local people were friendly."

"I think you'll find they'll be very friendly—when they discover who you are and the crucial part you've played. I think they'll all be mortified at having treated you so badly—even though their intentions were good. There are going to be a lot of red faces. Of course, it may be that Hester guessed—although she wasn't sure what she'd guessed.

"She and your mother became good friends on one of our extended visits. It was when we were planning a second child, but it didn't seem to be happening. Most of all we wanted a daughter," Bob said, smiling warmly at Lizzie. "Allison hinted that Hester was helping—some sort of magic charm I'd supposed.

"I remember how cross I was at the time. She'd cut off a chunk of your mother's hair. And she had such beautiful hair."

Bob sat staring into the fire. Duke nuzzled his hand and whimpered.

But Lizzie sat staring into space, her eyes wide, her mouth gaping.

"Oh my days!" she finally gasped. "Hester's magic charms work. The lock of hair … of course," she murmured, "and the wish I made myself…"

"I don't believe in that sort of thing," her father reprimanded firmly. "I told your mother I thought it was bunkum."

"Oh Bob!" she cried excitedly, "but don't you see? Mum did believe. And here I am, the living proof—all down to Hester and the … pit." She only just stopped herself saying Swan pit.

"I see," said Bob, not seeing at all. "But what has it got to do with a pit?"

"I can't tell you," Lizzie said firmly, with a smug grin on her face. "It's a secret and only for women. The menfolk aren't allowed to know. And I bet you wouldn't say bunkum to Hester."

224

"Probably not," Bob agreed wryly. "But now I'll ask you the question again. Would you like to live down here?"

"But where would we live?" Lizzie asked, looking quickly around the room.

"Certainly not in here," Bob laughed. "I've always planned to restore the castle. It would be a mammoth task, probably taking several years. Meanwhile we could live in the cottage. It has three bedrooms. There's plenty of room."

"The cottage?" Lizzie asked. "What cottage?"

"The cottage at the end of the causeway. You must have seen it—set back from the road. It's always belonged to our family. It's where we lived when I was a child."

"Oh yes … " Lizzie said uncertainly. "I know exactly where you mean. It does look like a beautiful cottage. But Hester told me a nasty story," she paused, looking uncomfortable now, "How nobody would enter the place. How it was best to keep away."

Her father let out a roar of laughter, which even raised Duke's head from the mat.

"You can laugh," Lizzie said. "Hester told me that it's haunted—and by Knockers—lots of them. She made them sound so horribly real."

"Haunted by happy memories," Bob said, grinning broadly at Lizzie. "It's where your Mum and I spent our honeymoon."

"Ah! That explains it," Lizzie exclaimed. "I always though there was something about it—something that I recognised. There's a photo in the box—of you and Mum in the cottage porch."

"Well. There you are then." He smiled at Lizzie. "It's a lovely sunny cottage. Hedley's kept it well maintained. Hester has kept it spick and span and, it would seem, somewhat overprotected."

"It wouldn't take much rearranging and a bit of adding on to make a comfortable home for us," Lizzie's father said thoughtfully. "Who knows, eventually, we might all end up in the castle.

"Meanwhile the cottage can be our base. We'll have all sorts of adventures together. Perhaps we'll go to Africa and see if we can find the Chief.

"And then …" her father stopped abruptly. "I'm sorry. I'm running on too fast. I'm sure you've got some plans of your own. What do you think you'd like to do?"

Lizzie hardly knew what to say.

"I always wanted to be an athlete. Running was my special joy." Lizzie's voice began to crumble. "Tom and I were training hard. I was aiming for the Olympics," Lizzie was trying not to cry, "but all of that's impossible now."

"It's not impossible," Bob answered, adding as he saw her face, "and even if it seems impossible … "

"Yes, I know what you're going to say." Lizzie tried to control her tears. "Difficult things take a while. The impossible takes a little bit longer."

"Well, there you are then," her father said. "That's what my Dad used to say to me. And it looks as if we've proved him right.

"There are inspirational people," Bob continued enthusiastically, "men and women racing in wheelchairs. Serious paralympic champions, at the very top of their sport. Some of them have several gold medals."

"Yes. I suppose you're right," she mumbled.

"You've come such a very long way, Lizzie. I bet you could make it to the Olympics in your wheelchair like the others. And upholding the family motto." He glanced at the lettering over the hearth.

Duke sprang suddenly to his feet. Someone was coming along the tunnel. The dog stood staring across at the door, his tail swinging happily.

"Wesley's here. It's time to go. We don't have time to talk any more now," Lizzie's father said with regret.

"But you've proved your courage, your perseverance." He smiled proudly at his daughter.

"As far as the Olympics go … ou can do it. I know you can."

Epilogue

t was several weeks later. Lizzie sat patiently in her kitchen watching out for the postman's van. She was expecting a card from her Dad.

His fabulous birthday gift to her was standing outside on the drive. Lizzie was stunned by the little car: bright red and very shiny. After it had been delivered, Betty, grinning and looking knowing, had arrived, as if on cue. She then proceeded to announce—smugly, Lizzie thought, but firmly—that driving lessons had been arranged and would start the following week.

When at last the postman arrived, Lizzie was surprised to see that he carried not only an envelope—which was bound to be her card—but also a large and mysterious package. She hadn't expected any more gifts.

The package was wrapped in strong brown paper and tied together with thick blue string, what Lizzie suspected was baler twine—the stuff that modern farmers use to tie up bales of hay or straw.

She didn't recognise the writing. Taking the package from the postman, she placed it carefully on her bed, whilst she concentrated on the envelope. And, yes, it was a card from her Dad, and a beautiful card at that: a picture of herself and Duke, posed on the beach along by the causeway; the waves breaking on the sand; the island visible in the background. She was almost sure she could see the chough, whirling high above the castle.

Lizzie grinned happily at the picture. Duke was such a beautiful dog. His feathered coat was thick and lustrous: a rich golden tan and black. He was sitting close beside her wheelchair, his body leaning, just touching her knees. His warm brown eyes smiled back at the camera.

The handwritten message inside the card made her smile even more:

Happy Birthday and love to Lizzie
from Bob, your Dad—and your good friend Duke.
ps
The Special Branch has recovered the jewels. Rumour has it Her Majesty's 'thrilled'.
And documentation has finally come, confirming that all the charges are dropped and

acknowledging my innocence.

pps

The cottage is nearly ready now. Another few weeks and we'll all be together. A certain young man named Digory is spending all his spare time there, working on your ground floor suite, which, he assures me, will be a palace ... and fit for even the fairest of maids! It will, he says, be ready d'reckly, which, as you probably know is Cornish for the day after mañana!

Sorry I can't be with you today. Look forward to seeing you tomorrow when we shall all make the visit together. B

Having read the message over and over, Lizzie took the card across and stood it in a place of honour on the middle shelf of the bookcase, together with three other cards. Then she turned her attention to the package: cutting the baler twine carefully; easing off the brown paper and exposing a cardboard box.

"Whatever can it be?" she wondered, peeling back layers of tissue paper.

"Ah! Awesome!" she finally gasped, revealing a stunning patchwork of colour: blues, greens, yellows and reds—all the colours of the rainbow and in the centre a purple panel on which there swam the silk-white swan.

As she lifted the stunning garment, a card fell out and onto the bed.

Lizzie read the message aloud, her eyes slowly filling with tears:

"Here is your Coat of Many Colours

Feed on the Harmony

Wear it with Love

Let its Magic Guide your Wheels

With love to Lizzie—from your friend Hester x"

In one corner of the box, carefully wrapped in layers of plastic, there was a jar of the prize-winning honey.

At eleven o'clock on the following morning, wearing the colourful jacket with pride, Lizzie was paying the promised visit to the churchyard near her old home. She'd been too ill to attend the funeral. And yet she had always known that, with time, she'd have to make this pilgrimage: that she'd sit at the foot of her mother's grave, her eyes and her mind awash with pain at the thought of all that might have been.

So far Lizzie was doing well: her eyes dry, her face determined. Directed by the churchwarden, the three visitors made their way down the narrow tarmac path that wove its way between the graves. Crocker's head stuck out of the rucksack slung across the back of her chair. His battered body had been re-stuffed and his wounded snout healed by Betty, whose clever needle had done a great job.

The winding path led them on towards the yew tree in the corner and then along beside high walls that enclosed and sheltered the sleeping dead. Finally Lizzie stopped her wheelchair in front of a simple, sparkling-white headstone.

In Loving Memory of Allison Tregarrow

Much beloved wife of Bob and mother of Tom and Lizzie

Died in a tragic motor accident

1963 — 2010

Lizzie was holding a small posy—freesias, her Mum's favourite flowers. Leaning forward as far as she could, she dropped it at her mother's feet.

Her eyes were rapidly filling with tears, as she tried to focus on the stone.

"Thank you Mum. I'll always love you."

But soon her eyes were sliding away … as she turned to look for another grave.

As she edged her wheelchair closer, Lizzie could feel her body shaking.

Another similar, simple, white headstone glistened in the morning sunshine. With eyes already awash with tears, she struggled to read the words on the stone, gritting her teeth and murmuring quietly "Come on Shrimp. You can do it … "

In Loving Memory of Tom Tregarrow

Much beloved brother of Lizzie and son of Bob and Allison

Died in a motor accident together with his mother

1991 – 2010

Lizzie fumbled for the second posy and lowered it carefully it at Tom's feet. Then she sat beside the graves, clasping Crocker tight and weeping.

A wet nose pushed her hand. It snuffled the edge of the colourful jacket, recognising familiar smells. A long, feathered tail swung gently.

She bent to smile through her tears at the dog. "Don't worry Duke. I'll be alright." She put out her hand to stroke his head.

She felt her father's hand on her shoulder.

"I could never have managed … without Tom," Lizzie said in a faltering voice. "I used to feel his hand on my shoulder. I used to hear his words in my head: 'Come on Shrimp. You can do it.' " She sniffled loudly, mopping her eyes.

"I could always see his smiling eyes—in my mind's eye, as it were. I could always feel his loving presence.

"I knew what he would expect of me," Lizzie whispered with a sigh. "That I must accept The Challenge … that if I didn't … I'd be letting him down.

"But I couldn't do it without his help. I simply couldn't let him go. And so I clung on tightly to him. He became my constant companion. He became my inspiration."

"Tom became your guardian angel," her father offered thoughtfully.

"Yes. He became my guardian angel. His spirit seemed to fill my heart."

Lizzie sat very still, remembering. Tears ran silently down her cheeks. A robin sang somewhere in the churchyard. A light wind rustled the ancient yew.

"Does everyone have a spirit … Dad?" Lizzie asked her father at length.

"Yes. I'm sure they do," he answered, "and those spirits never die … as long as we keep them alive in our hearts."

"Then I think we're very lucky," Lizzie was smiling through her tears, looking from one grave to the other, "because we have two guardian angels."

Duke was standing beside her wheelchair. His chin was resting on her lap. His warm brown eyes were watching her. She smoothed the silky dome of his head.

"And we have a furry guardian," Lizzie announced in a stronger voice, beaming down at the faithful dog, admiring as she always did the adorably curling tips of his ears.

And then a sudden afterthought, "Do animals have spirits too?"

"Oh yes," Lizzie's father answered. "Animals have spirits too."

Acknowledgements

I have always been blessed with wonderful friends … and with kind, supportive colleagues. As with my previous works, this delightful state of affairs has continued throughout the writing and the research for *Howl on the Wind*, leaving me with so many people to thank—not only for taking the story so seriously, but also for their great generosity in giving me of their valuable time and expertise in order to help me to 'get it right'.

Steve Braund, my publisher at Atlantic Press, who is always supportive and inspirational, deserves a very special 'thank you', as do his team, including: Roger Combe, for his expert assistance in production; Mark Woodhams, who has designed *Howl on the Wind* and without whose tireless input and patience there would be no book; and Rose Forshall, whom I thank warmly for her all her beautiful illustrations. It has been a great pleasure and a privilege to work with a group of such special people who, because of the charitable nature of the project, have given their time so generously. A special thanks therefore to University College Falmouth in supporting this work.

Acknowledging properly all those who have helped me, over the four years' gestation period for *Howl on the Wind*—including wonderful help that was given to me by staff and patients at Stoke Mandeville—would provide enough copy for another book. So all that I can do here is to list them in alphabetical order and thank them for their much valued help:

Jackie Bailey (National Spinal Injuries Centre); Nick Bentham-Green; Frances Bratchley; Sylvia Braund; Mark Broad-Kemp; Eddie Clampin; Juliet Cleave; Beth Cowan; Diarmid Cross; Jean Cross; Chris Crump; Pat Crump; Joyce Froome; Allison Graham (National Spinal Injuries Centre); Didy Grahame (Victoria Cross and George Cross Association); Ian Hosking (Spinal Injuries Association); David Ivall; Graham King (Museum of Witchcraft); Rachel MacEachern (Royal Marines, Lympstone); Joanna Mattingly; Rose Mullins; Annie Ovenden; Oliver Padel; Simon Parker; Katie Roscorla; Duncan Semmens (Hancocks); Nigel Steel (Imperial War Museum); Jo Welch (Deco Living Media); Si Welch (Royal Marines, Lympstone); Hugo White (Duke of Cornwall's Light Infantry Museum); Michael Williams.

I should also like to thank the many friends and family members—especially my son Nick Steele and my husband, John Hussey—all of whom have given me their long term, kind, continuous support and encouragement, throughout a most difficult period of my life—enabling me to complete this book.

Charmian Hussey, Cornwall, September 2011

Select Bibliography

Anderson, William. *Green Man: the Archetype of our Oneness with the Earth*. Compass Books, San Francisco, 2002

Collins, Andrew. *The Cygnus Mystery: Unlocking the Ancient Secrets of Life's Origins in the Cosmos*. Watkins, London, 2007

Culpeper, Nicholas. *The Complete Herbal*. London, 1653

Culpeper, Nicholas. *Culpeper's Complete Herbal*. W. Foulsham and Co Ltd., London, 1994

Duckers, Peter. *The Victoria Cross*. Shire Publications, Princes Risborough, 2006

Froome, Joyce. *Wicked Enchantments: a History of the Pendle Witches and their Magic*. Palatine Books, Lancaster, 2010

Glanfield, John. *Bravest of the Brave: the Story of the Victoria Cross*. Sutton Publishing, Stroud, 2005

King, Graham. *The British Book of Spells and Charms*. Awaiting publication

Ladd, James D. *By Sea, By Land: The Authorised History of the Royal Marines Commandos 1919 – 1997*. Harper Collins, 1998

Mattingly, Joanna. *Looking at Cornish Churches*. Tor Mark, Redruth, 2005

Mazzeo, Tilar J. *The Secret of Chanel No. 5: the Intimate History of the World's Most Famous Perfume*. Harper Collins, 2010

Mullins, Rose. *White Witches: a Study of Charmers*. PR Publishing (Cornwall), Launceston, undated

Paston-Bedingfeld, Henry and Gwynne-Jones, Peter. *Heraldry*. PRC Publishing Ltd, London, 1993

Preston, Claire. *Bee*. Reaktion Books, London, 2006

Ryde, Joanna. *Self-Sufficiency Beekeeping*. New Holland Publishers (UK) Ltd., 2009

Semmens, Jason. *The Witch of the West*. Jason Semmens, Plymouth, 2004

Sinclair, W. *Life of the Honey Bee. A Ladybird Natural History Book*. Wills and Hepworth Ltd., Loughborough, 1969

Southby-Tailyour, Ewen, Gen. Edit. *Nothing Impossible: A Portrait of the Royal Marines*. Third Millennium Publishing, London, 2010

Thomas, Charles, and Mattingly, Joanna. *A History of Christianity in Cornwall AD 500 - 2000*. Royal Institution of Cornwall, Truro, 2000

White, Hugo. *One and All: a History of the Duke of Cornwall's Light Infantry 1702 – 1959*. Tabb House, Padstow, 2006

Wilkins, Verna. *Boots for a Bridesmaid*. Tamarind Books, London, 2003

Williams, Michael. *Ghosts around Bodmin Moor*. Bossiney Books, Launceston, 2005

Relevant Organisations

The Back-Up Trust
Jessica House
Red Lion Square
191 Wandsworth High Street
London SW18 4L
www.backuptrust.org.uk

British Wheelpower
Stoke Mandeville Stadium
Guttmann Road
Stoke Mandeville
Buckinghamshire HP21 9PP
www.wheelpower.org.uk

The College of Arms
130 Queen Street
London EC4V 4BT
www.college-of-arms.gov.uk

Duke of Cornwall's Light Infantry Museum
The Keep
The Barracks
Bodmin
Cornwall PL31 1EG
www.cornwalls-regimentalmuseum.org

Hancocks
52-53 Burlington Arcade
London W1J 0HH
www.hancocks-london.com

Imperial War Museum
Lambeth Road
London SE1 6HZ
www.iwm.org.uk

The Museum of Witchcraft
Boscastle
Cornwall PL35 0DH
www.museumofwitchcraft.com

National Spinal Injuries Centre
Stoke Mandeville Hospital
Aylesbury
Buckinghamshire HP21 8AL
www.buckshealthcare.nhs.uk/
NSIC%20Home/spinal

The Poppa Guttmann Trust
Hill Farm Cottage
Thame Road
Piddington
Bicester
Oxfordshire OX25 1QB
www.poppaguttmanncelebration.org

The Royal Marines
Commando Training Centre
Lympstone
Devon EX8 5AR
www.royal-navy.mod.uk/royalmarines

Spinal Injuries Association
SIA House
2 Trueman Place
Oldbrook
Milton Keynes MK6 2HH
www.spinal.co.uk

The Victoria Cross and
George Cross Association
Horse Guards
Whitehall
London SW1A 2AX
Although not connected to the Association,
one very good and informative website on the
Victoria Cross is:
www.victoriacross.org